pure sky life

# pure sky life

book 3
in the story of

## Lin of Luratia

a novel by
Melanie Pahlmann

ISBN-13: 978-0692023655

Printed in the USA

Albereo Press
www.albereo.com
press@albereo.com

*To you who are*

*a mystery unraveling.*

I am Lin di Ana

of the planet Luratia,

and this is my story.

# 1  FALLING

We laughed and screamed as the sub-orbital airbus touched the black of space and fell toward the clouds at terminal velocity. I was one of the screamers, screaming some from fun, some from fear, and some from the sickening sensation of weightlessness. This was the day I learned I wasn't cut out for space travel.

The laughers were happy and proud, shouting triumphant words in the Culti language I didn't understand. I strained to make sense of the nearest voices, but the concentration made me queasy. I closed my eyes, breathed deep, and tried my best to ignore them.

I shouldn't have been jealous, I shouldn't have been angry, not today, but I was. Jealous that they were born where they were born, in places of privilege and progress and culture. Angry that I was born in Bree — ignorant, backward Bree, the laughing stock of all Wershonia.

A boy came near and whispered garbled words in my ear. The warm breath of his voice tickled in the itchy kind of way. I opened my eyes to see him smiling at me, his seat hovering in front of mine.

"How can you sleep?" he said in that slow Culti cadence of the people of Algalon.

"I wasn't sleeping," I said.

"Your eyes were closed."

"I was concentrating."

"What's there to concentrate on?"

"Why do you care?"

He shrugged. "Just curious, I guess."

"Well, take your curiousness to one of fren," I said.

"Fren?"

"Yes, go bother one of fren."

"What's a fren?" he asked.

I pointed at our schoolmates. "Fren! Fren!"

"Oh, to one of *them*," he corrected me.

"That's what I said."

"You said it 'fren'. It's *them*, not fren. *Them.*"

"Thanks for the Culti lesson I didn't ask for."

He gave a smug smile and shrugged again. "I can't help being helpful," he said, "especially where the need is greatest."

My face burned with rage. Fortunately, I remembered father's technique for warding off an angry explosive. I bit the inside of my cheek, not hard enough to cause a hurting pain, just enough to steal my attention. As hard as I bit, I was still angry.

The boy's smile stretched wider the longer I said nothing. He grinned like a victor in a fight we hadn't fought. And even though there was no fight, I didn't like losing. I had nothing to say that wouldn't make matters worse, so I turned away to the window.

When I saw what I saw, all the anger left me. The clouds had thinned in places and pieces of pink sky were coming into view. Soon we would see the ocean, the eastern coastline of the Continent, and the violet sands of the island of Vona.

I pressed my forehead against the clarkon window and waited for the other side of the world. I had waited so long for today, for my future to begin. My glorious future. Today. Today!

Nin spun her seat in my direction and floated it next to mine. "Nervous?" she asked in Welbi.

"Yes," I said. "And happy."

"Me, too," she nodded with an easy laugh. "Nervous happy. That's the best kind of happiness, when I'm shaking a little all over. It makes the happiness bigger, don't you think?"

"No," I said. "I'd rather have the happiness all by itself."

"You're talking Welbi," said the boy from Algalon, who had ignored my disinterest in him and floated to my right.

"Are you *trying* to ruin my day?" I asked him in Welbi. "Because if you are, you don't deserve Vona."

Though he didn't understand a word I said, he smiled knowingly.

"Welbi," he said, "the ancient language of the kings. It makes you sound ... hmm ... makes you sound..." He bent his head to one side and squinted.

My anger rose as he searched for an insult.

"Like a what?" I heard Nin say.

"Like a scholar," he smiled.

I looked at Nin and rolled my eyes.

"He likes you," she said in Welbi.

"I doubt it, and I hope not," I told her.

"Hey, look," said the boy from Algalon, pointing out the window, "there's Vona."

I gave him an elbow punch. "You made me miss it."

"You didn't miss it," he said. "It's right there."

"No, I mean ... forget it," I said. "And will you please not say anything for a while?"

"You need to concentrate again?"

"Stop annoying me or I'll—"

"I'm not trying to annoy you," he said. "Really, I'm not."

"Birgard," a boy interrupted. That was his name, the boy from Algalon, Birgard.

"Well, got to go," Birgard said. "See you around, scholar of Bree."

He tipped his head and turned his seat and drifted off into the crowd.

"I told you," Nin said.

"Told me what?"

"He likes you."

"He likes annoying people, and he thought I'd be a good target. But he's wrong about that. Very, very wrong."

Nin giggled. "I can't believe we're here."

"I know, I can't believe that's Vona."

I had flown over Vona on my holophone countless times before, but it had never looked this beautiful. It hadn't look this *real*. It hadn't *been* real. Not until today, this day I worked so hard for, the day my life begins.

\*\*\*

One step off the sub-orbital airbus — one stinking step — and my life was ruined. A transport drone was flying overhead, and knowing nothing about transport drones, I took it for a falling object.

"Look out!" I shouted to everyone near who might be in its path. "Duck!"

I ducked fast, fell hard, and slid off the disembarkment ramp onto the ground below. My arm throbbed with a pain so great I couldn't keep from whimpering, the meager result of my best attempt not to cry.

Above me, I heard laughter and unkind repetitions of "look out!" and "duck!". I didn't dare look up. I didn't have to. Their faces were reflected on a mirror-like wall that encircled the sub-orbital landing pad. I sat, frozen, waiting for this horrific moment to end, wishing it were just another nightmare I would soon wake up from.

I looked up at the sky and saw a steady stream of transport drones flying in a tidy line, nearly silent. I wondered how often they broke and fell from the sky. I wondered why I had never seen them all the times I had flown over Vona. I wondered what else I hadn't seen.

On my left, a dim whir grew louder as it moved in my direction. A sliver-white oval creature appeared and turned to face me. It was a MAB, a Medical Assistance Bot, the small kind that can fly anywhere and save the life of a dying person, if they could be saved.

The MAB whirred and tweeped, its odd semblance of a face staring at me half-smiling but expressionless. It shone two red lights into my eyes.

"Lin di Ana," its voice said, a voice that was not a man's or a woman's or any person of any age. It was the voice of a machine. I had seen MABs in the Holographic Library on my holophone, but I had never heard them talk. "Are you experiencing pain?" it asked me. And I had never talked to one.

"My arm hurts," I said through my tears. "My right arm."

The MAB twirled and hovered to my right then lifted a silvery hand from inside its body and passed it over my arm.

"Breakage detected," it said.

"I broke it?"

"Yes," it said with no compassion, "breakage detected."

"No! That's a *disaster!*"

"I will stabilize your arm and prepare you for transport."

I buried my face in my hands and cried. *This can't be happening. This cannot be happening. This cannot be happening,* was all I could think.

"Oh, dear, you took quite a fall," I heard a woman say. "Are you all right?" She put her hand on my back and moved it in small circles. Her kindness only made me cry more.

The MAB spoke to her in its thin, cold voice — words that were meaningless to me, words about my condition, I figured.

"We're going to stop the pain," she said to me, "and then we'll walk together to the Medical Unit. It's not far from here."

"I really broke my arm?" I asked her as the MAB passed its machine hand over my arm. It emanated a soft heat that tickled and took the pain away.

"Yes," she said. "A double fracture, a minor one. You'll be using your arm normally within the week."

"A week?"

"Yes. Thank you," she said to the MAB, "you can go."

The MAB folded up its hand and sailed away, humming, as if happy.

"A week's not so bad," I told the woman.

"Now let's get you to standing," she said.

She held out her hand and helped me to my feet. I kept my back to the disembarkment ramp, where a slow-moving stream of my privileged schoolmates laughed and whispered as they stepped off the sub-orbital and into their certain glorious futures.

## 2  FIELDS OF GROILE

The Medical Unit sat on a hill that overlooked one side of the island of Vona. Through my tear-bleary eyes, it blended into the hill, its domed roof forming what looked like a perfectly round hilltop.

The woman led me to a mesh-covered pathway that moved beneath our feet and did all our walking for us. She spoke words to the air, and the speed of the pathway increased until we were moving faster than a runner's pace.

"Did you just talk to the pathway?" I asked her.

"I did," she said.

"You told it to go fast."

"That's right."

"How can it hear you? How can it understand?"

"Embedded intelligence," she said.

"What does embedded mean?"

She told me, in four different ways, but still it made no sense, even after I put on my holophone to translate her Culti into Welbi. There is no Welbi word for embedded.

The woman took me to a room with a window that faced one side of the Residences — a ring of domed houses that circled the campus. From where I sat, each residence looked like a perfectly round stone stuck halfway in the ground. I wondered which one I would live in, and if it could be seen from where I sat.

"Now this will make some noise, but it won't hurt at all," a young nurse said in well-pronounced Culti. She positioned my arm in a long white tube. She spoke to the tube, it made its noise, and she was right, it didn't hurt at all.

"What's happening?" I asked.

"We're optimizing bone regeneration."

"Optimizing?"

"It's enhancing the growth of bone in your arm," she smiled. "A MAB will check on you every morning before school for the next five or six days. You have such excellent bone structure, I think five will be enough."

"I have to come back here every day?" I asked.

"No, she will travel to your residence. Your host parents will be informed and will know when to expect her."

"You said her," I said. "Is the MAB a girl?"

"Not in the sense that you and I are. When speaking of MAB's, we sometimes call them she, though they have no gender."

"How long will I be here?" I asked.

"We're very nearly done. Now, we need to contact your parents about—"

"Do you have to?"

She looked at me wide-eyed. "Yes, are you concerned about that?"

"I don't want father to know," I said. "My first day here, if this is the first news he gets, it wouldn't be good. He practically didn't let me—" I stopped myself. "Will you call my aunt? She's the primary contact person."

"Of course," she said.

The noise of the machine softened and was silent.

"Now we'll give you a casing," she said, "and we'll be done."

When I told her I didn't know where to go, the nurse called for a Teacher's Assistant. Elda was her name. She was a Continental, as beautiful as my mother, and she was as smart as she was cheery.

"The students just assembled for orientation," she said as we walked down a pathway that curved through a large field of groile.

"Look," I said, "it's groile."

"It is."

"Can I walk on it?"

"On the groile?" she said.

"Yes, just for a minute. I've never seen groile before. Well, I have, but not for real."

"Well then," she smiled. "I'll go with you. And be careful. It's wet."

The groile felt good under my feet — slimy, slippery, and soggy in places where bits of water had pooled. I jumped small harmless jumps and felt the squish of groile beneath my feet.

I laughed, happy. "I can't believe this is groile! I'm standing in groile!" I was the happiest I'd been since the boy from Algalon destroyed the joy of my first-ever sub-orbital airbus landing.

"We should be going," Elda said.

"I can't wait to go groile sliding."

"Then you're in for a treat. Some of the best groile sliding is on the hills on the north edge of campus. The water has eroded the beach there, so you slide off the edge of the hill and into the ocean."

"In Bree we have some old mudslides like that," I said. "You slide down them and land in the sea."

"So *you're* the girl from Bree."

"Backward Bree, I call it."

"Your Culti is quite good," she said, "given the short time you've been studying it."

"How do you know that?"

"I've been assigned to work with students from Southern Wershonia. I've read all your histories and essays. Of all of them, yours stood out as most unusual."

"Oh, because of my father, the one-legged Fisherman of Bree."

"No, because of your petition for satellite reception and the club you started. You instigated a lot of change in a short time."

"Instigated?"

"To bring about. Put into action. You're a doer, not a follower or a complainer. You're brave and daring, ambitious, enthusiastic. Excellent qualities of character."

I liked Elda. "Thanks," I said. "Now that I look back, it *was* pretty daring to start the Evolutionaries Club. It made me lots of enemies. Grown men, naysayers all of them. My aunt told me they're naysayers because they're afraid of change."

Elda smiled at me. "There is comfort and ease in keeping things the way they are."

"I suppose you're right." I tapped the casing on my arm. It was hard as stone but completely invisible. "There's clarkon in this."

"Yes," she said. "Clarkon and some other materials."

"I can't believe I broke my arm. My first day here. I hope it's not bad luck."

"Good luck, bad luck. It could be either. We can't know such things."

"How could it be good luck?" I asked her. "It was a complete and total embarrassment."

"Yes, but the embarrassments we go through are eventually forgotten. What's not forgotten, what endures for your entire lifetime, is who you are as a person and what you do with your circumstances — embarrassing and otherwise. Something might come out of this that you'll think of as good. Maybe soon, maybe later."

"You think so?"

"It's possible. Be willing to be surprised."

As much as I wanted to believe Elda, I knew she was just trying to make me feel better. I knew it the moment I walked into the Central Assembly Hall. The speaker stopped speaking, looked in my direction, and then all eyes followed and landed on me. There they were, the Vona entry class of 2296 — 31 students from the continent of Wershonia and 32 host students from the continent of Artunne, which everyone called the Continent, even though it was one big country.

In the quiet I heard the excruciating sound of muffled laughter. A boy said in the silence for everyone to hear, "It's the Broken Arm Girl!"

"Broken Arm Girl!" others said.

And that was the name that stuck. From that day, I was known as the Broken Arm Girl, which was seriously worse than being known as the daughter of the Fisherman of Bree. Elda was wrong. My glorious future was off to a very bad start.

I sat immediately on the floor on the outermost edge of what was an enormous, lop-sided clump of thirteen-year-olds. My face burned as I tried not to hate them all.

"I'm really sorry for what happened to you," the girl sitting next to me whispered.

"Thanks," I said. "Did I miss much?"

"Not really. The School Director's introducing the teachers and counselors."

The School Director was a woman, once a teacher herself. For a reason I couldn't explain, she reminded me of mother.

I watched her in soft-focus and imagined she *was* mother. *My* mother, Continental-born. Which would have made *me* Continental-born. And father, he wouldn't be a fisherman, he'd be a scientist or a diplomat or an astronaut. I'd have a glorious future and a glorious past, not neither, as felt true to me as I sat and listened to the School Director, who spoke Culti too fast and who I knew wasn't mother.

## 3   THE BOY FROM CLUD

I snapped out of my daydream disoriented.

I wasn't in Bree anymore. I was on the island of Vona, sitting in the Assembly Hall with a broken arm and bad nerves, where the School Director had finished telling us whatever she had been telling us. I gazed up at the ceiling, which looked nothing like a ceiling, not any I'd ever seen. It was tall and graceful, nearly invisible, a wide crystal tunnel that stretched to the sky and disappeared into a single point, infinitely distant. The thrill of its unusual beauty and of being here at all was smaller than it should have been, probably because daydreams usually ended badly these days.

Daydreams hardly comforted me at all anymore now that I was older, and if they did, the comfort was quick to burn in the brazen light of truth. I couldn't enjoy impossible daydreams anymore, knowing the impossibility of their impossibility. Aunt Tala had told me that this was good, a sign of my maturity. But as much as I loved maturity, I'd been learning that there was usually some price to pay for it, like the warm comfort of impossible daydreams.

Someone tapped my shoulder. It was Elda, who had come to escort me to the place I should have been sitting, but wasn't due to my lateness.

"Keep your holophones powered off and put away!" the School Director shouted as Elda led me around the outer edge of a restless crowd of schoolmates.

With nothing else to look at, some stared at me from where they sat, whispering, snickering. I ignored them all and asked Elda about the stiff piece of silver paper she had just rolled up and held like a twig.

She unrolled it, tugged on two corners to make it stiff, and held it close for me to see. It was a thin, invisible screen. On it I saw a circle with a thick cluster of dots inside.

"What is that?" I asked Elda.

"It's a locator map. This is how I found you. All I have to do is say your name. Watch the screen when I say it ... locate Lin di Ana." The device tweeped twice and one of the dots blinked green. "See," she pointed, "that's you."

"That blinking light is me."

"Yes, see how it's moving?"

"You can find anyone that way."

"Anyone who has a locator chip."

I rubbed my ear where the chip had been embedded during our pre-flight check-in earlier that morning.

"A boy told me that parents in Waturi put punishment chips in their kids' ears," I said. "Is that true?"

"Yes, that's still practiced in some parts of the world."

"Even Wershonia?"

"Not so much there. Waturi, Gostin, and some in Deloria."

I felt a pinch in my ear that was entirely unreal, and I shuddered. "That doesn't seem right," I said. "Parents shouldn't be able to punish their kids from far away. How can they even be sure if they really—?"

"Here's your Circle," Elda interrupted. It was all the students from the country of Strellin, the land of the ancient Welbi kings.

I was relieved to see Nin, my only other Welbi-speaking schoolmate. Like me, she lived in the far southeast corner of Strellin, which was in the far southeast corner of the Wershonian continent, the furthest possible distance from the modern cities of the North. I sat next to Nin and answered her questions about the arm-breaking incident. I talked in Welbi, partly out of laziness, partly out of spite. Welbi seemed to irritate those who only spoke Culti, and I was in an irritating mood.

The green-glow floor flashed blue — once, twice, three times — and the entire room fell silent.

"There's a good way to get someone's attention," I whispered to Nin.

Nin giggled and the floor flashed blue again, but only where we sat.

"Amazing," I couldn't help but say out loud. The floor flashed once again.

I tried to concentrate on the Head Counselor who was telling us what we would be doing next, but something else had my attention. I stared at the green-glow floor and wondered how it could hear us, and if it was listening to everyone all the time, and if *all* the floors everywhere were listening or just the floors that glowed. I wondered, if the floors could hear us, could the adults hear us too? Every word we said? Were we being listened to all the time?

"Lin," a girl behind me said with a nudge.

"What?"

"It's your turn."

"My turn to what?"

Nin answered in Welbi, "You have to nominate someone from our group to be the Strellin representative."

"Strellin representative?"

"Our Strellin Circle leader," Nin said.

I would have liked to be the leader. I had the experience, as much as anyone else from Strellin and maybe the most. But would it be right to nominate myself? I thought probably not.

"I nominate Nin," I said.

Four more students gave their nominations, none of them me.

"Good," Elda said as she studied her student-finding device, a data sheet, she called it. She said something to her data sheet in the Continental language and then read from it three names. Finalists, she called them. We voted on the finalists, and the winner was declared.

The lucky winner was a loud-talking boy from Clud, the capital city of Strellin. No surprise. I was beginning to learn that it was the loud ones who got all the breaks in life.

He acted surprised and said he was humbly honored, but I didn't buy any of it. He was boastful by nature. When he first introduced himself at student orientation eight months earlier, he went on and on about all the famous people his family knew since his father was the publisher of Strellin's biggest newspaper, the *Strellin National Recorder*, the very newspaper that put Bree on the map, as my best friend Mira liked to say. Although Mira was the only 10-year-old in the history of his family's newspaper to have ever published a story in it, the boy from Clud wasn't impressed.

I thought with a smile about Mira's article and the story it told of our petition drive to install a satellite broadcast tower so the people of Bree could have holophones. The article made Bree famous, not just in Strellin, but in all parts of Wershonia. The fame brought more tourists to Bree, the tourists brought more business to our merchants, the merchants got more rich and happy, and my father started a successful boat rental and storytelling business, which allowed him to retire from fishing four months out of the year and made him as famous as Bree for his gripping adventure tales of the life of a rugged man of the sea. The stories he told were true though greatly embellished. Father said the embellishments were for the tourists, not for him. "Give them more than what they paid for," he said, "and they'll come back again and again."

All these thoughts of father and Bree made me miss them both with a sadness that surprised me. I wondered what father was doing that very moment and if he missed me too.

The floor flashed yellow, which meant we could get up and leave. It was time for a tour of the Residences, where we would meet up with our host families and be shown the house where we would live.

"Stay in your groups and keep your holophones powered-off!" we were told.

After the tour we were given half an hour before dinner to do whatever we wanted. I found an empty field of groile, slipped on my holophone, then called Mira and projected her to my location. Though there was an ocean between us, she stood before me, as real as real.

"Look," I told her, "I'm standing in groile."

"Is it as slimy as they say?" she asked.

"No, not slimy like a gelfish. It's slippery. Slippery like seaweed."

"And blue."

"I know." Nothing blue grew in Bree.

"I heard you broke your arm," Mira said. "What happened?"

"Who told you that?"

"I saw your aunt."

"Was she mad?"

"No, I don't think so. She's worried, though. She said so."

"I wonder if she's told father."

"I don't know about that."

"Do me a favor and don't tell anyone," I said. "It's too embarrassing."

"Does it hurt?"

"No. It did at first. It hurt fiercely. But then a Medical Assistant Bot came and did something to make the pain go away. It hasn't hurt since."

"Amazing," she said.

"I know."

"Bree could use a medical bot."

"Among a krillion other modern things."

Our laughs were laced with sadness.

"I miss you already," she said. "It's only been a day."

"I miss you, too, Mira. I wish you could be here. You'd like it. You'd like it a lot."

Mira smiled and brushed a tear from her cheek. I had to look away. I was on the edge of crying myself.

"You should see the painted tails and ears," I said. "Almost all the girls have them. Some have tail trinkets. They call them trinks, and they're beautiful. One girl has a long row of golden trinks. Twelve, maybe twenty. They sparkle, even from a distance. I feel so plain."

"Then maybe you should get some color or trinks for yourself."

"I'm going to find out about it."

"What's it like there?" Mira asked. "The people and the place."

"The adults are nice, but the Wershonia kids are mean."

"Mean?"

"They laughed at me when I fell."

"When you broke your arm?"

"Yes."

"That's cruel."

"They're still laughing about it."

"It'll pass, though," Mira said. "It just happened."

"I don't know if it will ever pass. They're calling me Broken Arm Girl."

Mira giggled.

"It's not funny," I said. "It's completely painful. I may never live this down."

"Then you need another nickname. A better one. A positive one."

"You're right, Mira. That's a great idea."

"You could be Evolutionary Girl," she smiled.

"Evolutionary's good. But I don't know if I want to be 'Girl' anything."

"You're right," she said. "You're getting too old for that."

"Oh," I remembered to say, "here's something you should know. When you fly over a place on your holophone, you don't see everything that's there."

"You don't?"

"No, look." I turned on my holophone's video eye and aimed it at the sky.

"Are those airtrams?" Mira asked. She was the only other girl in Bree who had been on an airtram, having once gone with me to the Continental Embassy Island, where only a few ever flew overhead.

"Yes," I said, "airtrams and transport drones and all kinds of bots."

"There's so many."

"Too many, if you ask me. And you think there are a lot here? There's even more near the sub-orbital pad. And there they fly low." I shivered. "They make me nervous, Mira. What if one breaks and falls on you?"

"That'd be bad."

"Seriously bad," I said. "I'm going to ask and find out if that's ever happened."

Just then, for the first time, my ear tweeped.

"Did you hear that?" I asked Mira.

"Hear what?"

"The tweep."

"What tweep?"

"In my ear."

"What are you talking about?"

"My ear just tweeped."

"What's a tweep?"

"It's a sound my locator chip makes."

"Oh," Mira nodded.

"They make certain sounds for certain reasons," I said. "Louder than I thought."

"Did it hurt when they put the chip in?"

"No," I said, "it was just a pinch. Now I don't feel it at all. Anyway, I have to go. We're having dinner now."

"Dinner. That's funny. It's late here. Past bedtime."

"Oh, right." A silence passed. "Tell everyone hello and that I already miss them."

"I will," Mira said. "Call me tomorrow."

We waved and smiled and said goodbye.

I looked at the thin-clouded sky, squinting at what I thought was a spot of cloudlessness. But I couldn't tell. There were transport drones flying all over the place in that part of the sky.

I kept my eyes on the strange and beautiful flowers that lined the dirtless, mudless walking path. As I made my way to the Residences, I had two thoughts on my mind: what would be a better nickname and how I would make it stick.

# 4  GENERATION EIGHT

I kept my holophone on as I walked and asked it to guide me to Residence 26. I was lost, adrift in a sea of blue and magenta groile with no sense of direction.

In Bree — being small and perched on a hill — you could see the sea from almost anywhere, and since the sea was to the South, even the dimmest wit could easily guess the directions of North and East and West.

Vona was a different story. You could fit ten Brees on the island of Vona, which had rolling hills and buildings taller than any in Bree. From most anywhere on Vona, standing on the ground, you couldn't see the ocean at all.

I said hello to everyone I passed on the walkway, to people I knew and people I didn't.

"What's that on her head?" a young girl asked.

"Shhh," said her friend.

They squinted at me as they walked past and tried to hide a smile. Then they whispered and laughed.

All the way to Residence 26, I was met with stares, squints, whispers, and giggles. I tried not to be hurt by it, but I was. What was wrong with this place? Why had I been the object of ridicule since the moment I got here? This meanness was behavior I would have expected from the brats of Bree, but not from students of the most advanced school in the world, dedicated to the growth of good character and personal excellence, which every applicant had to possess at least a little of before being accepted at all.

I soon found Residence 26, where I would live for the next three years of my life with a girl named Pella, four months younger than me to the day, and her parents and sister Pia. From the outside, the residences all looked the same, except for their color and landscaping. Inside they had large and small rooms separated by clean, shiny walls that appeared and disappeared with a simple voice command, although not just anyone's voice, only authorized voices, which were my host parents' and theirs alone.

Mrs. Tria was a scientist who had left her research to teach science at the Vona school. Like my mother, she was beautiful and bright. Mr. Tria was a linguist and translator and spoke nine languages, one of them the dying language of Welbi, which made him a perfect host father to me. Pella loved the stories of the ancient Welbi kings and chose to study their history when she was in grade school on the Continent. I was amazed that she could choose so many of her classes. In Bree, they taught us what they taught us, like it or not.

I arrived late for dinner. Pia made a point of announcing the fact when she greeted me at the door.

"You don't have to knock," she said. "This is your house too." She tipped her head to one side and stared curiously at my eyes and ears. "What are you wearing?" she asked.

"What?" I said. "My holophone?"

She scrunched her eyes to get a better look. "That's a holophone?"

Before I could answer, Mrs. Tria appeared. "Hello, Lin," she smiled, her voice as kind as I remembered. "It's so good to see you. Welcome home. Welcome," she said again, "to your new home."

"Thank you, Mrs. Tria."

"Look, mother," Pia said, pointing to my head, which wasn't necessary since her mother's eyes were already fixated there.

Mrs. Tria nodded a broadening smile. "That must be a first generation," she said as she gestured me indoors.

I stepped through the door, and a chill ran through me. I'd seen pictures of the insides of a residence, but I'd never been in one. It had sleek floors, smooth walls, no wood, no stone. And it was spotlessly clean.

"A first generation?" I asked, only half-paying attention.

"Yes," Mrs. Tria said. "My husband will be delighted to see it." She gave me a warm embrace, asked about my arm, and welcomed me again. Then, turning to the kitchen, she cried, "Trita, honey! Lin has a first generation holophone!"

During dinner we talked about holophones and all their generations, the first generation being the oldest, most outdated, most unused. They were indestructible and not good for much anymore, so Generation Ones were the holophones the Continentals gave for free to the more impoverished people of the world, like the technology-deprived people of Bree, who knew nothing of generations two through eight. Nothing at all.

"It all makes sense to me now," I said. "The naysayers in Bree—"

"Naysayers?" Pia asked.

"People who are against progress," I explained. "They couldn't understand why the Continentals would give us holophones for free. They thought there was a catch. And I was right, there wasn't a catch. They gave us their throw-away phones."

Pella giggled.

I called Mira early the next morning to tell her the news.

"That explains everything," she said.

"It does, right?"

"Right. It does."

"If holophones hadn't been banned from student orientation," I said, "I would have found out about this a long time ago. I could have told father and all his naysayer friends. It would have given them one less thing to distrust about the Continentals."

"Tell me about the newer holophones," Mira said.

"The newest is the Gen 8. There's no cap and no screen. Just a piece you put in your ears and a film that goes in the eyes."

"A film?"

"You know, a film for the eyes, like the eye color film the tourists wear to make their eyes pretty."

"And what does the film do?"

"Everything the screen does."

Mira's mouth dropped open. "Amazing," she said.

"So, you should tell everyone."

"I will."

"And tell them that you can talk to a Gen 8 with your thoughts."

"Like that man at the Embassy Island who was moving a transport trunk with his thoughts?"

"Exactly," I said.

"You know, as much as I miss you, you totally belong there."

"You would too, Mir. I wish you could have come with me."

"Well," was all she said.

Mira was the most progress-minded person in Bree, aside from me, which was why I thought she should take over as president of the Evolutionaries Club now that I was gone. But she wasn't interested — "I'm not the presidential type," she said — so Bissa became president, as undeserving as I thought she was. Bissa wasn't interested in progress or character or goodness projects, she was interested in being in charge. She was bossy like the boy from Clud.

The boy from Clud was the first person I saw when we gathered in the Assembly Hall later that morning. I had gone there early so I could take a video of it while still empty. I wanted to show it to Aunt Tala, who I thought I should call to assure her I was all right.

"Did you tell father?" I asked Aunt Tala. "You know, about my arm?"

"No, not yet," she said. "His mood wasn't good last night. He blamed it on the bad weather, but I think he misses you."

A sweet warmth filled every part of me. "You think he does?"

"Yes, he does, I'm sure of it."

"I miss him too. I miss everyone. More than I thought I would."

"That's good," she said. "It's healthy and natural. I'm sure all the students are missing their parents and friends from back home."

"Maybe. Probably."

The boy from Clud walked into the Assembly Hall.

"How's your arm?" Aunt Tala asked.

I told her in hushed tones all about the Medical Assistant Bot and the clarkon casing and the fact that my arm didn't hurt at all.

"The marvels of modern technology," she said, shaking her head in disbelief.

My mind filled with other marvels of technology I'd seen in just one day. I described as many as I had time to, starting with the Gen 8 holophones. "I want one," I told her.

"We'll see," she said.

The Assembly Hall was filling fast with people, so I went off to one far side so my holophone wouldn't be seen. I'd had enough ridicule already. Enough for a lifetime.

"Glad you could join us, Broken Arm Girl," the boy from Clud said when I was the last to sit down with the other students from Strellin.

I told him in Welbi he was an idiot. Nin laughed. He made a hand gesture, some big city cultural thing neither Nin or I understood.

"You're not children any longer," the Head Counselor was saying. "The transition years are a long and exhilarating passage from childhood to adulthood. I say 'long' because to all of you, six years seems a very long time. It represents half the years you've lived thus far. Think, for a moment, how much you have changed, how much you have grown, since you were a helpless infant."

She paused for us to think a moment, and from the silence rose whispers, giggles, and stifled laughter.

"Similarly," she went on, "the transition years are a time of enormous growth and change. The more intelligently we support this growth, the more wisely we guide this change, the more excellent you will be as adults, as parents, as leaders and decision-makers. As you set out on this educational adventure, ever keep this end goal in mind … personal excellence."

*Personal excellence.* The words echoed in my mind and stirred a sour soup of guilt and doubt and sadness. I wanted to be excellent — I knew I could be — but I also knew that I'd been acting quite unexcellently since the moment I boarded the sub-orbital. I hadn't been this unexcellent since Bree first got holophones and the naysayers retaliated by spreading insults and rumors, some about the Continentals, some about holophones, and some about me. Even now they were repeating lies long proven untrue. Just last week old Califer Crigs was roaming the marketplace telling anyone who would listen that the Continentals gave us free holophones so they could spy on us and that I was a wicked girl who had killed her mother.

"Quiet," the Head Teacher said, "quiet, everyone. We have your team assignments. Group Leaders, we're transmitting them to you now."

"Transmitting?" I asked the boy from Clud.

He unscrolled a data sheet and held it up for me to see.

"When did you get that?" I asked.

"This morning," he said with relish.

I was peeved that I hadn't fought for group leadership. "That's just like Elda's student-finding device," I said. I had wanted one when she showed it to me, and I wanted one now.

"Oh, his doesn't do that," said the smartest girl among us. "It only receives administrative transmissions. Nothing else."

The boy from Clud glared at her.

"And the rest of you," the Head Teacher said, "keep your holophones powered-off. We can instantly detect violations, so don't think you can get away with it in the din of the crowd."

After Nin explained to me what a din was, the boy from Clud read off our group assignments.

"Bag," he said, looking up at me, "Team Ten."

"Bag?" I asked him.

Smiling, he silently mouthed the words, "Broken Arm Girl."

When he had finished reading off our names and team numbers, I noticed that none of us had been assigned to the same team. Nin and I would be separated all year. I would be on my own with expert Culti-speakers and no method of translation — not with Nin and not with the instantaneous translator of my holophone, which I wouldn't use even if I could. I wasn't going to be caught dead wearing my Generation One.

I had to talk Aunt Tala into letting me get a Gen 8.

And I had to come up with a plan for getting a better nickname.

## 5 TEAM TEN

It was a short distance to Team 10, which was made apparent by a glistening number that floated mid-air above a large glow-color circle on the floor. I was the first to arrive, so I walked around the circle's edge and studied the number from every direction.

In the unmistakable accent of Algalon, someone behind me said, "It's the same, isn't it, from every place you stand?"

I turned and saw a boy.

"I'm Novi," he said. His eyes were golden, his smile was friendly, his voice was kind and slow.

"I'm Lin," I said.

"I know."

Ashamed, I hid my arm behind my back, though it made no difference. He already knew, everyone did, and the casing was invisible.

A boy emerged from the crowd and gave a wave. "Greetings, Team 10," he said.

"Greetings," said Novi and I.

"You're the girl from Bree?" the boy asked.

I nodded.

"She was voted one of the Leaders of the Future two years ago," Novi told him.

I turned to Novi. "How did you know that?"

"I was one too," he said.

More schoolmates arrived until we numbered seven: four Continentals, three Wershonians. Fast talkers, all of them. All but Novi, who spoke slow and well.

The eighth and last of our team bounded in, breezy and bubbly.

"Hello everyone. I'm — *you?*" she said, surprised and aggravated and looking at me.

*Great,* it was Saamta Sio, the privileged daughter of a famous diplomat. I knew from experience that she never perfected the art of whispering, which I thought was odd because whispering is a tool of tact and isn't tact what being a diplomat is all about? "How did *she* ever get accepted?" she unskillfully whispered about me sitting only one seat behind at a student orientation meeting. She made other unkind remarks about Bree and me and my father, unwhispered and punctuated with hushed laughter. After a while I turned and told her, "I can hear *everything* you're saying." That shut her up.

I decided to do my best to be my best. "Hi, Saamta," I kindly said.

"Sio," she said. "Saamta *Sio.* Both names." She smiled and looked around the circle. "Hello, everyone."

No sooner had everyone said hello than Elda appeared.

"It's nice to see all of you," she said. "I'm Elda. I'm your team supervisor this year." She told us a little about herself before explaining the first exercise of the day: "Tell us your life story. You have five minutes. Volunteers?"

The four Continental students were the first to volunteer, and each told stories of world travel, childhood achievements, ambitious life ambitions, and their parents' impressive vocations.

Novi was next to volunteer and told a fascinating story. Like me he was born in a town on the sea and was an only child. His mother was a customs official and his father was a flight craft engineer. For two years, Novi's family had lived at the Clarkon Flats Space Center at the North Pole, where the air was cool and parts of the sky were cloudless nearly every day. Novi was seven when he had taken his first trip up the space elevator to the Forton satellite. He said that that's when he decided he wanted to have a career in space exploration.

I decided to be the last to volunteer. Waiting would give me time to think about what to say and what not to say so as to produce the least amount of embarrassment, which was made difficult by the presence of Saamta Sio and her ability to make me feel more uncultured and inadequate than I already did.

While Saamta Sio told her story, I blurred my eyes and thought of mother and silently asked her, *What should I tell and what should I not?* I waited for words that didn't come, so I made words for her. I imagined she would have told me to tell the most interesting parts and be truthful and don't embellish as father so often did to make his simple stories grand and great.

"Lin," I heard Elda say. "Are you all right?"

Mother's face disappeared, Elda's took its place, and there I was, standing in the company of strangers in a tall, crystalline room, everything about it beautifully, eerily strange.

"I'm sorry," I said.

Elda smiled and told me, "We're ready to hear your story."

I cleared my throat and, best as I knew how, I cleared my head.

"I was born in a place not of my choosing," I said, "the small fishing village of Bree on the Strellin Sea. Bree is far from here, very far. Not just in distance, but in heritage and culture. After clarkon was first discovered, the elders in Bree formed the Committee of Technology. Their sole purpose was to protect Bree from the radishes of technology."

"Radishes?" Elda asked after everyone stopped laughing.

"Radishes," I said.

"Do you mean ravishes?" Novi asked.

"Oh, right ... to protect Bree from the ravishes of technology. I call them the Committee of No Technology since they're against modern things and all they do is vote to make every new technology illegal to own or buy or sell. They made progress against the law. That's how I see it. Although they did one good thing when my grandfather was young. They approved an energy relay dish so that Bree could get free electricity from the satellites like everyone else. But that was a money decision, not a progress decision. Since then, there's been no progress in Bree at all , not until two years ago when I started a petition to get a satellite broadcast receiving tower. My friends and I collected 1,000 signatures, and four months later, the first Continentals ever to visit Bree came with a tower and a trunk of free holophones. They were free," I said, "because they were Generation Ones."

Saamta Sio gasped, she and some others.

"Most everyone in Bree got one," I said, "except for most of the old people and the naysayers, who are against progress as much as the Committee of No Technology. One night some naysayers broke into the Mayor's office where extra holophones were stored. They dumped the holophones in the sea, hoping to drown them, but the next morning they had all washed up on the beach. What's amazing is that they still worked. The naysayers made me their sworn enemy and gave me and my father constant grief. My father was against holophones at first, but then he got one of his own. My father is a fisherman and not much interested in progress or culture, but he's incredibly brave. He once fought a grangefish underwater with his bare hands. He lost his tail and left leg, but he survived. My mother—" I suddenly wished I hadn't mentioned her. But I had, and what could I say about her but the truth? "My mother died two days before my tenth birthday. She was bit by a murtali waterspider when we were swimming. I tried to save her, but we were too far from father's boat. She was a school teacher, one of the favorites of everyone. Everyone loved her and everyone misses her. I hope I grow up to have her kindness and wisdom." And there I stopped, not having thought of anything else to say.

A long silence passed as I stared at the floor, using all my power not to cry.

"Unbelievable," one of the Continental girls said.

Others agreed with words and nods.

"A Generation One?" someone asked.

"I like that they tried to drown them," said a boy.

"Do you still have it?" asked another.

"I do," I said.

And just then an idea was born in my mind. An idea for a new and better nickname. I passed it by Mira when we talked later that day.

"Generation One Girl."

"Mmm," Mira smiled, "that has potential."

"Or what about Gen One Girl?" I asked. "That's more—"

Mira interrupted with a bothersome question. "How are you going to get everyone to call you this new nickname?"

"I'm not sure yet," I said. "I haven't had time to think that out.

They've got us doing stuff constantly. And everything's in Culti and Continental. My brain is swimming. And I can't believe it, they separated me from Nin. I haven't heard a word of Welbi since this morning."

"But you're having fun, right?"

I actually had to think about it.

"Not as much fun as everyone else," I said. "It's all so easy for them. Why is my life so hard, Mira? Why does everything have to be a fight and struggle, everywhere I go?"

"Because you were born in Bree."

"The daughter of my father."

Mira gave a sympathetic smile.

"At least they liked my life story," I said. I explained that we had to tell our life stories to seven total strangers. "Then we got into new groups with all new people and did it again. That story was much better."

"I wish you could have video-recorded it," Mira said.

"I wish I could use my holophone. Then I could understand everyone perfectly." I shook my head. "But this holophone thing, Mira. They *like* my Generation One. I tell you, it's a great angle."

"Angle? Angle of what?"

"My nickname. Gen One Girl."

"Oh, right. Good luck with that."

"If you have any ideas—"

"For how to get a bunch of strangers to call you a new and less interesting nickname?"

"Less interesting?"

"From their point of view, not mine," Mira said. "Personally, I like Gen One Girl. It's growing on me."

"How is Broken Arm Girl more interesting than that?"

"Because it's tragic and people like tragic things. Much more than ordinary things."

"How is Gen One Girl ordinary?"

"It's about a holophone."

"Yes, but—" Suddenly our conversation seemed completely stupid and meaningless. "I miss you, Mira."

"I miss you too, Lin. More miserably than I can say. I've lost my best friend."

"You didn't lose me," I said. "I'm right there, in front of you, almost like real."

"Until we disconnect. Then you're there. And I'm still here. Bissa wants to be my best friend, but she's so ... difficult."

"I wish I could live two lives," I said. "I would live one there and one here. The best of both worlds."

"Two lives," she laughed. "You think your brain's swimming now."

"You're right, Mir. Two lives would be too much."

At least the one life I was living was here and not there. It was what I wanted. As hard as it was, it was what I wanted.

# 6  PURE SKY

I couldn't stop looking at the sky. There were holes in the clouds, big holes, the most and biggest I had ever seen, which wasn't saying much. Bree was one of the cloudiest places in the world, due to its short distance to the equator. I knew I was going to be late to Morning Circles, but the sky, the sky!

I'd tried to look *and* walk, but I feared falling again. Even though my broken arm didn't hurt, the inconvenience and embarrassment of another injury was more trouble than I needed right now. And someone would start calling me Clumsy Girl or some awful thing and my plan to get Gen One Girl to stick would have been ruined.

So I stood and stared, in a patch of groile a short way off the path where schoolmates were shuffling in thin and thick bunches on their way to the Assembly Hall, which from here looked like a crystal funnel turned upside down and stretched tall. Behind it was a large hole in the white puffy clouds.

The sky was a soft pink, the color of young, unripe wistberries. I put on my holophone to video-record it for Mira and father and Aunt Tala.

"This is what pure sky looks like," I narrated. *"Real* pure sky, not some holographic picture." Although Mira told me later that on her holophone, and on father's and anyone else's, it was still a picture. "Yes, but a moving picture," I told her, "of something I was actually seeing." Mira smiled and said, "A moving picture is still a picture." She had a point, so I let her win that disagreement.

"The tall, clear, pointed building you see," my narration went on, "is the Assembly Hall where we meet every morning for school. It's made of clarkon nanotubes. A big difference from the Teaching Rock, don't you think? For an island on the ocean, there isn't much made of rock here. Yesterday a boy from the Continent said that the Assembly Hall is shaped with a pointed top because storms and fierce wind can't blow it down. There's nothing for the wind to catch. Bree could really use some point-top buildings."

"Hey!" someone shouted from the walking path. "You're going to be late!"

"Don't know if you heard that," I said. "But I'm going to be late. Isn't it beautiful, the pink sky? I miss you, and I love you!"

I sent the video to Mira and father and Aunt Tala, then powered off my holophone, tossed it in my satchel, and trotted at a good clip to the walking path. That's when I learned to never trot on groile, especially in the early morning when it's still damp from dew. I slipped and fell, landing hard on my behind. Sharp blasts of pain throbbed like a drumbeat and made it impossible to rise fast on my feet. I sat, paralyzed, feeling stupid, certain I'd be late, and wishing a Medical Assistant Bot would show up and do whatever it is they do to make pain go away.

No MABs showed up, but some schoolmates did — first a few, out of kindness, then more, out of curiosity, then even more after someone shouted to the students gawking from the walking path, "It's the girl from Bree! With the Generation One!"

I smiled. "That's why they call me Gen One Girl," I told the thickening crowd. "Gen One Girl," I said again.

I was helped to my feet and complimented on my unusual life and asked many questions, which I did my best to answer as I hobbled in their company to the Assembly Hall.

Nine of us showed up late, and due to my limp, which I slightly exaggerated, we were not reprimanded.

"What happened?" Nin whispered when I sat down in the Strellin Circle.

"I slipped on some wet groile," I said in Welbi, happy for the effortlessness of it.

The boy from Clud cleared his throat, loud and with meaning. Leaning close, he said, "Glad you could make it, Bag."

"It's not Bag," I whispered to him. "It's Gog. Gen One Girl. That's what they're calling me now, Gen One Girl."

He laughed. "Gog, eh?"

"Gog," I said.

I didn't care that in Culti gog meant slow, dull, and when used to describe a person, stupid. Bag meant road, which as Mira would have said was too ordinary an insult. My plan to be freed of Broken Arm Girl was coming along excellently, almost as if a genius had planned it, not that I was a genius, and not that it was planned. Neither was the case. Sometimes life just goes your way.

Since yesterday had been long and we were restless, the team supervisors made a joy-making announcement.

"We're off to the North Shore to clear the groile fields of stones and sticks," Elda said. "We're going to go groile sliding!"

Shouts erupted, filling the Assembly Hall with an electric happiness that made me shiver. I looked up at the ceiling. The curved, crystalline walls were more invisible today than yesterday, revealing pink patches of clear sky. I was doubly happy. Groile sliding under pure sky conditions. I couldn't wait to tell Mira.

We headed north on foot on a dirtless path that was soft as sponge beneath the feet but stayed bone dry even in a downpour.

"That's why it's called a slip-proof surface," Pella explained to me.

"And how does it stay dry in the rain?" I asked.

"Some kind of clarkon nano coating that repels water."

Clarkon. I smiled. "Is there anything clarkon *can't* do?" I said.

Nin saw us and joined us on the path with her housemate Kita, a Continental girl who loved blue. Her ears were trimmed with a shimmering blue paint, her tail was adorned with blue and silver trinkets, and painted on the tops of her shaved feet were flowery patterns of iridescent blues.

"Why are your feet shaved?" I asked her.

"It's a new fashion," she said.

"Kita's parents are really cool," Nin said in Welbi. "I'm going to love living with them."

"Are you talking in secret?" Kita asked us.

"No," said Nin. "It's habit. It's because we both speak Welbi."

"You should turn your instantaneous translators on so you can understand us," I said to Kita and Pella. "We're bound to slip into Welbi."

They liked my idea, and Nin and I talked in Welbi most of the rest of the day.

"I've never seen sky like this," I said. "Bree's constantly cloudy."

"You never have pure sky?" Pella asked.

"Not like this." I made a circle with my thumb and finger and held it to the sky. "We get little openings about this big, but only during the dry season. Wet season, you can forget it. The clouds are thick and cover the whole sky for months and months and months, without end."

"Hey, on Adri's we're allowed to go off-campus," Pella said. "Who wants to go with me?"

"I do," I said.

"Me too," said Kita.

"What's there to do off-campus?" Nin asked.

Pella knew. She and her family had moved to Vona two years earlier when Pia started her first year here.

"Go to the West Beach," Pella said. "The best sand is there. Soft and powdery. And we can shop at the international markets and eat at the World Café. They have food from everywhere in the world. I've been dreaming of fried Delorian sweetmoss."

"Do they have any food from Egli?" I asked.

"I'm not sure. What do they eat in Egli?"

"Fish mostly," I said. "I love fish."

"Look, it's Broken Arm Girl," a boy laughed nearby.

I turned to spot him in the crowd, which wasn't difficult. He was still looking at me, his face smeared with a spineless smirk.

"Cruel words are the weapons of cowards!" I shouted louder than needed so the greatest number of schoolmates would hear. Near and far, I heard them snort and giggle.

"And for your information," Pella shouted, "it's Gen One Girl!"

"Thanks," I told her. "That was really thoughtful."

Pella leaned close. "We're in it together," she said. "And you'll see, things are going to get better for you. You just had a bumpy start."

"Thanks, Pel," I said, wanting to believe her. Then I turned the topic of conversation. Egli was still on my mind. "I want go to the Embassy some time."

"The Embassy?" Kita asked.

"Right," I said. "The Vona Embassy has a Expatriation Center where escaped Egli slaves are taken."

Nin wasn't aware of the fact. "There are Egli slaves? Here, on Vona?"

"You say that like they're some kind of threat," I said.

"I—" Nin stopped herself. "I guess I did."

"They're not, you know."

"I admire them," Kita said. "A lot of them die trying to escape."

"The mine owners are completely heartless," I said. "If someone gets caught trying to escape or making trouble, they're horribly punished. Wedges are cut out of the edge of their ears. That way everyone knows just by looking at you how many times you've disobeyed."

"Oh," Nin moaned, "that's horrible!"

"Told you," I said.

Pella turned to me. "You know a lot about Egli slaves."

"I've studied them on my holophone," I said. "And I've seen some. Egli's close to Bree, you know. When a slave first escapes, they're taken by boat to the Embassy Island off Southern Wershonia. That's where I've seen them. They look so scared, so alone. Then they're brought here."

"I feel sad for them," Pella said.

"Me too," said Kita.

"Me too," said Nin.

In the distance we heard shouting.

"Uh, oh," Kita said.

"What?" I asked. "What's happening?"

"An ultra-speed transport drone, flying in the Mid Zone."

"Mid Zone?"

"The Mid-speed Zone," Kita said. "There are seven zones of air traffic. The higher in the sky, the faster you can go."

"So why was an ultra-speed in the wrong zone?" I asked her.

"A malfunction probably."

"A malfunction?"

"Probably."

"How often does that happen?"

"Almost never," Pella told me. "They hardly happen at all."

I believed Pella was telling the truth, but my fear of being struck by a massive object falling from the sky was only made bigger.

# 7 Non-Existent

"You haven't lived until you've gone groile sliding," I narrated to Mira and the people of Bree as I trained my holophone's video eye on a scene of total joy. The sliders now were mostly Continental students, who had politely let the Wershonians go first.

"Sure, mud is fun," I said, "but it's not squishy soft like groile. And there's no mess. I'm going to find out if groile can grow in Bree. Then Merchant Kam could get some, and you could plant it on that old mudslide trail where Califer Crigs' house used to be. The parents will like it because it would solve the mud problem they're always complaining about, and the kids will like it because it's so supremely superior to mud sliding. It's a win-win, all the way around."

I paused, exhilarated at the thought that the lives of the kids of Bree would be — *could* be — so vastly improved.

"Hello, scholar of Bree," I heard behind me. The accent was Algalon, the voice a boy's.

"Novi?" I said, turning to look, my holophone recording the jagged movement and the face that came into view.

"Birgard," he said.

"Oh, you." I disengaged the Video Record Mode and took off my holophone.

"How's your arm?" he asked.

"What do you care?"

"Just being friendly. I haven't seen you since the sub-orbital."

"Which you ruined for me."

"Ruined?" he asked.

"Yes, ruined. You wouldn't stop talking during the descent. That was the most special part of the entire day. And you ruined it."

"I'm really sorry," he said. "I didn't know. Honestly, I didn't know."

"Well, you do now."

"How can I make it up to you?"

"Leave me alone forever."

"I don't know why you don't like me."

I stared at him, wordless. I didn't know why either. Although it could have been because he reminded me of a naysayer boy back home who gave me grief me any occasion he could for bringing holophones to Bree. It wasn't that he was against holophones, he wanted one as much as the rest of us. His parents were against them and refused to let him have one. He was angry at his parents, but he took it out on me.

"Fame has followed you," Birgard said in the awkward silence, smiling an admiring grin.

"What do you mean?"

"You were famous in Wershonia, now you're famous here."

"My father was famous in Wershonia," I corrected him. "And here, I'd hardly say I'm famous."

"Well, think what you think," he shrugged. "But all the kids know you and talk about you."

"What do you hear them say?"

He thought before he spoke, his yellow-green eyes narrowing to a squint. "That you grew up in a primitive village that had no holophones and single-handedly turned that around. That your father is brave and you are too."

"What does single-hinty mean?"

"Single-*handedly.* It means by yourself."

"Oh. Well, I had lots of help."

"But you started it, right?"

"Yes," I said.

"And they say it's amazing that you're here at all."

"Why?"

"I guess because of where you come from. How different it is."

"Primitive."

"Right."

"Well," I said, with nothing to say.

He looked past my shoulder. "Then I'll leave you alone," he said. "I just wanted to say hi."

"All right."

"Bye, Lin."

"Bye, Birgard."

As soon as he was gone, Pella tugged on my arm.

"I was looking for you," she said like a parent — not a scolding parent like father, but a caring parent like mother. In that moment, I saw their faces in my mind and I missed them terribly. He as much as her.

"How long have you been here?" I asked Pella.

"I just walked up."

"Oh." I held up my Generation One. "I was recording the groile sliding for everyone back home."

"Who was that?" she asked as we turned and walked toward the cliff's edge, where a thinning number of schoolmates were running, sliding, and tumbling into the ocean.

"Birgard," I said. "He's from Algalon. Of all the kids from Wershonia, including Nin, I can understand his Culti the best."

"That's nice," she said, studying my face.

"What?" I asked.

"Nothing," she smiled.

"I need to find out if groile can grow in Bree."

"Oh, that's easy," she said as we walked. "I'll query the grid."

She powered on her Gen 8 and asked my question in Di'afani, the language of the Continent. After a silence passed, she hummed and spoke again. Then again and again she spoke, with pauses of listening nods in between, an entire conversation. A biting jealously rose up in me. You couldn't talk to a Generation One like that.

After more talking and listening, she shook her head. "There's not much of Bree on the grid at all," she said. "It's like it doesn't—" She stopped herself.

"Doesn't what?"

"Exist."

I wasn't surprised to hear that from her, and I knew it was no reflection on me, but still, my body filled with a familiar pain.

"Sorry," she said, "if that hurt your feelings."

"How did you know?"

"So I *did* hurt your feelings."

"Kind of, yes. It's just ... it hurt my feelings because it's true, not because you said it. I hate that I was born in Bree."

Pella took my hand and gave it a squeeze. "If I were born in Bree, I'd feel that way too. But look, you're *here* now."

"Where everything is impossibly difficult," I mumbled. "More for me than anyone else."

"When I was young," Pella said, "and I complained about how hard something was, my great-grandmother would say that ease breeds laziness and difficulty breeds strength. Then she would say, 'which do you want to be, lazy or strong?'"

"She sounds wise."

"She is."

We sat on a dry rock, and I gazed at the sky.

"Hungry?" she asked.

"Famished, actually."

"Want a tongi sandwich?"

"I'd love one," I said. Tongi seaweed sandwiches were my favorite new food. "I'd love two, actually."

Pella gave a series of commands to her Gen 8. "On its way," she said when she was done.

"What's on its way?"

"Three tongi sandwiches."

"How's that possible?"

"Food service drones."

"Are you joking?"

"No. Where do you think their food came from?" She pointed to a circle of girls eating and laughing.

"I envy your life," I said.

"This is your life, too, Lin."

"I guess you're right."

"And being from Bree, you can turn that into a positive. I'd say you already have."

"You think so?"

"Aren't you the one and only Gen One Girl?"

"Yes," I laughed. "Daughter of the world famous Fisherman of Bree."

"I can't wait to meet him," she said, "your father."

"I doubt he'll come here."

"Why?"

"He's not a curious type," I said. "He's not a traveler. To tell you the truth, I think he's afraid. All his courage and bravery, but he's afraid of the world outside of Bree."

"You never told me the grangefish story," Pella said.

As we sat and waited for a transport drone to arrive with our tongi sandwiches, I told in detail the story of father's daring underwater battle with the deadliest fish in the Strellin Sea. A small crowd gathered and sat around us, and I told other stories of father and his life and my life and Bree. Little Bree, a place so small and insignificant, it was practically non-existent.

# 8  TENEBRI ZERO

"Hi, Aunt Tala! Guess where I am?"

She looked side to side and up at my ceiling, which was curved, invisible, and showing a darkening sky. "I don't know," she smiled. "You tell me."

"It's my sleepingroom. Look!"

"You have no roof," was all she said.

"Not entirely," I said. "You'll see. Keep your eyes on the ceiling."

"There is no ceiling."

"I know, but ... just look up."

"At what?"

"At where the ceiling would be."

"All right," she said, impatient now, but through no fault of mine.

"Tenebri five," I spoke loud and clear, my eyes fixed on Aunt Tala's face as the ceiling went half-invisible.

Her eyes grew wide and her mouth fell open. "Did you do that?"

"I did," I giggled. "Now, watch this. Tenebri ten," I commanded.

The ceiling was instantly made a sweet shade of pink, a color I chose, the color of pure sky. The real sky outside could no longer be seen.

Aunt Tala laughed. "That's remarkable," she said.

"It's clarkon. It can do anything, turns out. I don't have voice clearance to change the walls, only adults can do that, but I can change my ceiling, anytime I want! Tenebri zero," I said. The ceiling was again invisible, revealing a mottled patchwork of sunset clouds. "We had pure sky today," I said. "I sent you a video. Want to see it with me?"

"Right now? No. It's late here, and I want time to talk to you."

"All right, look at it later by yourself. I narrated it, so you'll know what you need to know."

"How's your arm?" Aunt Tala asked.

"It's fine. The MAB comes every morning to treat it."

"MAB?"

"Medical Assistance Bot. A machine nurse, you could say. This morning she told me my casing can come off in three more days. She said I'm responding well to treatment."

"That's good. Your father's worried. You haven't called him yet."

"And he hasn't called me."

"You know how he is."

"Tell him I've been busy," I said. "They won't let us use our holophones during the day, except during breaks, although actually, they did today. We went groile sliding."

"Groile sliding?"

"That's in the video too. I have to find out from Merchant Kam if groile will grow in Bree."

"What's groile?"

"You'll see in the video. It's like a thick slippery grass. It grows everywhere here, but not in Bree. The kids would love it, and the parents too. You'll see."

"Halfway across the world, and you're still trying to bring change to Bree."

"To make it a better place," I said.

"Yes. And how are you getting along in school and with your classmates?"

"Aside from drowning in Culti every day, I'm liking it. We haven't done much learning yet though, not like we did last year in Lower School, where they cracked the books open on the first day of school."

"I know from the literature that the learning there is experienced-based," Aunt Tala said. "There will be much less book learning, which I'm sure is why this school appeals to so many youngsters."

"On Adri I'm going off-campus with some of the girls," I said.

"Is that safe?"

"Everything here is safe," I said while my mind flashed examples, real and imagined, of the certain untrueness of my statement. But I said nothing about that. "Everyone goes off-campus, it's completely safe and normal. But we can only go on Adri's, our day off."

"All right," Aunt Tala said. "I worry about you."

"I'm fine," I assured her. "Have you given any thought to the Gen 8?"

"The Gen what?"

"The Generation 8 holophones, remember?"

"Yes, I remember. And the answer is no."

"No you haven't thought about it, or no I can't have one?"

"I haven't thought about it," she said. "We'll see."

"We don't have to pay for it."

"I know."

"So why would you say no?"

"Because I haven't talked to your father about it."

"Oh, don't tell him, please? Can't this just be your decision?"

She tightened her lips and nearly frowned, which, coming from Aunt Tala's face, was a promising sign. That very expression had resulted in a positive change of mind many times before.

Just then, a lovely sound chimed.

"Did you hear that, Aunt Tala?"

"That moment of music?"

"Right. That means dinner is ready."

Aunt Tala laughed. "Much more pleasing that a shouting mother."

"I don't think Continental parents shout," I said. "Not at all."

"Are you getting along well with the Trias and their girls?"

"Supremely well. I like them all, even Pia, which is the closest I'll ever come to having a big sister. It's different. I like it."

"Good, I'm glad to hear that."

"Tell father I love him and I think about him every day. And tell him he's as famous here as he is in Wershonia. My schoolmates love hearing me tell stories about him."

"I'll tell him, he'll like that. And Lin?"

"What?"

"He misses you terribly. He loves you more than you'll ever know."

My eyes filled with tears for the sure truth of it. Aunt Tala was not a woman who said kind things to make a young girl feel better, not unless those things were true.

"I'll talk to you soon," I said. "Promise you'll watch the video?"

"I promise. I love you, Lin."

"I love you, Aunt Tala."

She disappeared from in front of me, and I made my way downstairs.

"How do the translient walls and windows work?" I asked at dinner.

"Translucent," Mr. Tria kindly corrected.

"What's the word in Welbi?" I asked him. "I want to tell my friends back home about it."

"There is no Welbi word for translucent," he said.

Pella asked him why not.

Certain I knew, I answered for him. "Because it's an ancient language invented long before sciencists learned how to make visible things invisible."

Mr. Tria smiled his agreement. "As for how translucency works," he said, "you'll have to ask my wife. She's the scientist in the family."

I looked at Mrs. Tria, who said without having to first think it out, "Clarkon has properties that allow us to manipulate the performance of matter from a distance. To manipulate means to change," she added.

"I know they mean the same thing," I said. "I've been accused of both."

Though the fact of it was painful, the Trias laughed.

"And how does clarkon do that exactly?" I asked.

"Perhaps first I should tell you what clarkon is," Mrs. Tria said.

"Oh, I know all about clarkon," I told her. "If you turn on your instaneous translators, I can tell you in Welbi."

Their translators were already on. I learned that translation is always on on a Gen 8.

"Clarkon is made of carbon atoms," I said. "Nothing more, nothing less. One unit of clarkon is a ring of six carbon atoms, which is the shape of a hexagon. A sheet of clarkon is made of a bunch of carbon hexagons connected to each other. And this sheet of clarkon is only one atom thick. Clarkon was the first two-dimensional material ever discovered."

Mrs. Tria beamed at me. "That's right, Lin," she said.

"Very impressive," Mr. Tria nodded. "You know more about clarkon than I do."

"I'm the Bree expert on clarkon. I've loved clarkon since I was a child. Probably because it was banned from Bree and—"

"Banned?" Pia asked.

"A hundred percent banned," I said, "by Bree's Committee of Technology, or *No* Technology, as they should be called. Thirteen old men meet once a month to decide what technology Bree should get and which it shouldn't. They say it's to prevent rapid progress, but it's obvious that they don't like progress at all. And they're appointed for life, so nothing will change until they're laid in the sea."

Pella asked, "What do you mean, laid in the sea?"

"It's an expression," I said. "We bury our dead in the sea."

"Oh," she winced.

"I guess it's convenient," I said. "All that water."

"I can't believe you have no technology in Bree because of thirteen old men," Pia said.

"The only place in the world," I told her, "I'm sure of it."

"But you got around them," Pella said.

"Me and a thousand people. That's how many signatures my friends and I collected."

"That's a lot of people for a small village," said Mr. Tria.

"A lot of people wanted holophones," I said. "They wanted to know about the world."

"I'm curious what kind of impact that had on Bree," Mrs. Tria said.

I remembered a newspaper headline — *Holophone Mayhem: Technology too Much for Little Town of Bree.*

"Mayhem describes it best," I said. "Progress isn't pretty, you know."

I told in detail the story of what Mira and I liked to call the Great Holophone Invasion of 2294. They laughed and laughed, and I laughed too. It was funny now, from a distance — the distance of time and the distance of place.

"I guess it's true what the wise ones say," I silently told mother as I fell asleep that night. "From a distance, the things that seemed big are really very small."

I saw her smiling at me, her face as real as it was when she was living, and I knew I'd never be without her.

# 9  THE COMPLEX

I slept until I naturally woke. It was Adri, our day of freedom.

Although I liked sleeping late into the morning, I missed hearing the woman's wake-up voice Pella helped me set up my first night here, which at half-past the Fourth Hour every morning but Adri, said gently and in a voice like mother's, "Good morning, Lin, it's time to get up." Until I said the words, "Thank you", she would repeat herself every minute. I always waited to say thank you so I could hear her more than once.

After a quick breakfast Pella and I met Nin and Kita at the nearest airtram station. It was on a hill that overlooked the ocean, which sparkled in places where thin streams of sunlight struck the water. I kept my eyes focused there so as not to see the air traffic above us, which was thick and still kind of terrifying.

"I say we go to the Embassy Complex first," Pella suggested, "then to the World Café for lunch. Then we can spend the rest of the day at the beach."

"And the shops," Nin said.

"Right," said Kita. "How about the beach first, then the shops? We might have rain in the late afternoon. I checked the forecast."

"What's a forecast?" I asked.

Kita spun around. "You don't know what a forecast is?"

"No, I've never seen one."

"It's a report about weather conditions," she said.

"Oh," I nodded, "a weather report."

"But in the future," said Pella.

"What future?"

"The future weather," Nin told me. Even she knew.

"A forecast tells you what the weather will be like later that day or the next day or next week," Pella explained.

"Next week?" I said. "That sounds impossible."

"It's not impossible," she said. "It's basic weather science. They're right most of the time."

"About next week's weather?"

Kita laughed. "When you said Bree was backward, I had no idea."

"Tell me about it," I said.

"I guess Gen Ones don't receive forecast reports," Kita said.

"Guess not," I muttered. "So don't forget to take me to see the Gen 8s at the shops today."

"You should more than see it," Pella said. "You should try one."

"They'll let me?"

"Absolutely."

"I want to try one too," Nin said.

"But you already have a Gen 7," I told her.

"The Gen 8 has more features," she said. "I want to see what they're like."

"You're going to love it, girls," Kita said. "Especially you, Lin."

My belly fluttered with the excitement of a birthday child sitting before a treasure of presents. This day, I was certain, was going to be one great present after another.

"Hey, look," Nin said, pointing to a speedboat streaking lightning-fast across the ocean not far from shore.

"Any chance we can ride one of those?" I asked.

"Sure," said Kita. "They're for the tourists."

Pella gave me a sympathetic glance and explained that parental permissions would be required. It was just yesterday I confided in her my father's habit of saying no to every little thing I wanted.

"Right, permissions," Kita said. "So we'll have to plan that in advance."

I watched the boat race out of view and wondered how many times faster it moved than father's fishing boat.

Our airtram docked at the boarding platform. It was an express tram to the Embassy Complex, and it was filled with small scatterings of passengers, some of them schoolmates, most of them adults or families.

The airtram ascended to the Mid-speed Zone, passing slower-moving airtrams, transport drones, and bots of every size, shape, and duty.

"This is just like the airtram I rode on the Continental Embassy Island," I said. "With the invisible floor and sides. You can see everything."

"Like we're birds flying," Nin said.

"Birds flying," I agreed. "Flying over *real* places, not holographic ones."

"There's the Assembly Hall," Kita said, pointing at its distant spire.

"We're *above* it," I said. "It's so beautiful from here."

"Get ready to look straight down," Pella told us. "We're going to pass right over a house."

We saw below our feet someone's dome-top home, which could only partially be seen. Two zones of air vehicles moved beneath us, cluttering the view. I looked up and saw more air vehicles above us, all moving at different speeds, but in one direction along a single, invisible path.

In less than ten minutes we were disembarking at the Embassy Complex docking platform.

"I brought a map," Kita said. She pulled a finger-sized scroll from her satchel, unrolled it, and tugged on the corners, which made the bendy material as stiff as a piece of wood.

"That's just like Elda's student-finding device," I said. "Can I see it?"

"Sure," she said, handing it over. "It's called a data sheet."

"Data sheet," I said, holding it up to the clouds to examine it from every side. "It's so thin! A piece of kipper-paper is thicker than this."

"You still use kipper-paper in Bree?" Nin asked.

"Sure," I said. "We learn how to make it in school. But most of it's made by a machine, if you could call it that. A machine of wood and mesh and cranks and a tray to catch the water." I turned to Nin. "Do you use kipper-paper in Mirapa?"

Nin laughed. "No, but I've seen it in a museum under a case of glass."

"Mirapa has a museum?" I asked.

"Two," she said. "Does Bree—?"

"No, we have no museums," I said, eager to talk about something other than Bree's total lack of culture. "What do you do with this data sheet?" I asked Kita after taking another long, close look and giving it back to her.

"You access the grid with it. Map," she said. "Present location."

Upon the invisibleness of her data sheet a map appeared, detailing the shape of nearby buildings from a bird's eye view.

"See that red flashing dot?" Kita asked. "That's where we are."

"I see," I said.

"Remind me, Lin, where you wanted to go."

"The Expatriation Center."

"And why are we going there?" Nin said.

"That's where they take escaped Egli slaves," I told her. "I'm hoping we can see some."

"See some why?" Kita asked.

"Because they're so interesting. Think about it, they've just escaped. They must be so happy. For the first time in their life, they're free. I want to see their faces. I guess I want to be inspired."

"I like that," Pella said. "I want to be inspired too."

And so did Kita and Nin.

But we weren't inspired, we were rattled and saddened, each in our own particular way.

"They don't look very happy to me," said Kita.

"No," I quietly agreed.

"I wonder why?" said Pella.

I felt sure I knew. They weren't happy for their new freedom, they were afraid of it, afraid of this big, new world that made no sense to them. Afraid like me, but not hiding it. I respected them for that — for being so real, so unembarrassed by their past and their predicament. If they were ashamed, if they cared like I did what others thought of them, I didn't see any sign of it.

I told this to my friends as we sat under a clarkon canopy on silken glass steps and watched the comings and goings of short-tailed, freshly-freed Eglians, none much older than my parents, most closer to our age, and some whose neck scars were so new they could be seen from a distance. We stayed a while and watched in silence. The few times we spoke, it was a wistful gratitude of the freedom we were born with and knew we would have all our life. I was the first to say we should go, and we left unhurried, each looking back once or more as we walked away.

We strolled pristine streets that looked like soft pink glass but were a crystalline material that had formed millions of years earlier beneath the ground and ocean floor. The people we passed by had eyes of every color.

Though it wasn't yet the lunch hour, the World Café was open. Like most buildings on Vona, it was round, not square, with smooth outer walls and a domed roof that were crystalline clear. Inside was a wonderland of trees and vines, trellised fruits and mosses, waterfalls and fish ponds, small and large fountains, and flowers of every color, which gave the impression of being outdoors in nature. I was breathtaken by the beauty of the place.

"I've never been in a building with trees and water inside of it," I said.

"Me neither," said Nin.

"I'm calling a flavor bot," Pella said. She tapped at her data sheet.

Kita got happy. She looked at Nin and me, grinning and holding a secret. "You're going to love this!" she said.

In less than a minute, a green oval-shaped bot dropped from the air and hovered in front of Pella. It was the size of two men's fists and made no sound.

Pella held her hand beneath it and said, "Delosi fruit."

After a whir and a hiss, a small, clear ball dropped into her palm.

"What's that?" I asked.

"It's a pellet." She popped it in her mouth, closed her eyes, and hummed a soft song of joy.

Kita took my hand and stretched it open under the bot. "What's your new favorite sweet flavor?" she asked me. "Something not from Bree."

"Tulimi syrup," I said.

A pellet dropped into my hand.

"Don't chew it," Kita said. "Just let it dissolve in your mouth."

I put the pellet in my mouth, which filled it with an explosion of big, fat delicious sweetness. I laughed and cried and hummed like Pella. The flavor was everywhere inside my mouth, everywhere at once.

Nin had a pellet, and she laughed too.

"It's a universal response," Kita said before having her own.

"What *is* this?" I asked after minutes had passed and the flavor was still exploding.

"Nanoparticles of natural flavors," Pella said. "Suspended in a gel that coats the mouth for a long time. People who want to lose weight like these."

"That makes sense," I said. "The fat people in Bree sure could use some flavor pellets."

"There's something you should know, Lin," Kita said. "You have to swish a *lot* of water to get the flavor out of your mouth, so you better choose a flavor you like. And never take a flavor pellet from a stranger."

"Or a friend," said Pella. "Giving someone an asper fruit pellet is a common prank."

"Asper fruit?"

"It's super sour."

"That's cruel," Nin said.

I shook my head in disbelief. "Continental kids actually do that?"

"Sure," said Kita.

"We're not perfect," Pella reminded me.

Kita laughed. "I know a boy who gave his brother five asper pellets all at once. They sent him to the hospital. He couldn't swallow."

I grimaced through the sweetness that still filled my mouth.

"This is my favorite place on the island," Pella said, who had seen everything on Vona there was to see, having lived here for two years already. "Come on, I'll show you around."

The ground level of the café was a shop of foods from around the world that could be purchased in small or large amounts and shipped to any destination in the world — even Bree, I was told. Pella led us through the maze of displays and rattled off names of foods that defied Welbi translation. When a word had no Welbi equivalent, my Gen One translator sounded a flat tone in place of the word.

"And this is tone tone-tone tone-tone," Pella said, pointing to a brownish mass. "It's a delicacy from Gostin. It's chewy and super salty."

"What's it made of?" I asked.

"Fronli intestines."

"That's disgusting!" said Nin.

"Fronli?" I said. "The little friendly forest animals?"

Kita nodded.

"But, they're so harmless."

"The intestines are grown from cells," Pella said. "They stopped killing fronli for food a long time ago."

I was curious how food could be grown from cells, but before I had time to ask, Pella was on to the next delicacy from Gostin.

We rode in a clear glass tube to the top floor of the World Café and found a table with a view of everything. Below us was the food shop and three circular floors of dining tables. Above us was the sky and distant zones of air traffic, which I didn't fear from here.

A full-function, multi-lingual food service bot arrived at our table and spoke to us in Culti, the language of our choice. Upon its chest was a screen that showed us vivid pictures of any food we asked about. From its belly was a span of tiny holes that produced the smell of that food upon request. The bot's patience was stellar. Had we put Aunt Tala through our asking and re-asking of questions, the interaction would not have gone well. But the Continentals never made interactive bots that weren't completely friendly, polite, and imperturbable.

By the time our food arrived, the café was filling fast with lunchers. Voices rose up in the central open space, voices from everywhere in the world. And though they drowned out the lively music that played in the background, I didn't mind. The symphony of languages was a different kind of music.

I dreamed of traveling the world someday, to places whose foods were spread across our table. We ate and laughed and voted on our favorites. Kita recorded on her data sheet the foods each of us wanted to eat again and the foods we would sometime like to send home to our families using the gift delivery service.

When it came time to pay, our eyes were scanned and each of our parents' accounts were charged according to our student status. Being a parent from an impoverished region, my father was charged nothing.

"I guess being from Bree isn't all that bad," Kita smiled. "Everything is free for you."

On that one point I agreed. "Even a Gen 8, if I get one," I said.

"*When* you get one," Pella said.

"They're actually not that expensive," Kita mentioned as we rose to leave.

Stuffed and sluggish and feeling no sense of urgency, we dawdled our way among the seated tables, eying as inconspicuously as possible the people we passed and the strange foods they were eating.

## 10 AN ADI EYE TO EYE

Thick clouds had formed, so we hurried to the beach.

We ran straight to the water's edge, on a fine powder of violet sand. The surf was high and wild, but that didn't stop Nin and Kita and Pella from going in for a swim.

I stayed behind on the beach with the excuse that someone needed to guard our satchels, and since I was the only one who had lived on a beach where I could swim however much I ever wanted, it should be me. They thanked me for my kindness and maturity and ran screaming into the water. I didn't tell them that I hadn't swum since the day my mother drowned and planned never to swim again.

I sat on the sand, stared out at the infinite ocean, and thought of mother. I thought of father and Aunt Tala and my grandparents and Mira. Mira! I put on my holophone and called her.

"How funny, I was going to call you," she said. "We just finished dinner."

"We just finished lunch," I told her, "and you'll never guess where."

"The World Café?" she said.

"How did you know?"

"You told me two days ago."

"Oh, right. Want to hear about it?"

"Sure," she said, "but don't go on and on, just the important parts."

I told Mira about the circular floors and the food store and the food service bot that lets you see and smell the food before you order it. I told her about the different foods and the flavor pellets. She too was happy that fronlies were no longer killed for their delicious intestines.

"You should send us some of those sweet pellets," she said.

"I will," I said. "Pella's going to help me decide which flavors."

"Nothing sour," Mira said.

"I'll only send sweet flavors. I think it will help everyone like the Continentals more."

"Maybe so."

"We saw some Egli slaves," I said, "and next we're going to the shops, where Nin and I are going to test drive the Gen 8 holophones."

"Test drive?"

"It's a phrase."

"And what do Gen 8s do that our holophones don't?" Mira asked.

"They store information, any information you give it. And they receive data streams, but I'm not sure what those are yet. Kind of complicated. And they remember every call you've ever had. If you talked to someone five years ago, you can go back and watch that call. It's preserved forever."

"That sounds convenient," Mira said. "In case you forgot something important."

"Right. And then there's the thought commands. You can change the shading of your ceiling or the temperature inside different rooms in your house with your thoughts, even if you're far from home."

Mira tapped her chin with her kipper-ink pen. "Amazing."

"What's most amazing is that you can talk to more than one person at a time. You can sit in a place with other people and have a conversation with them, all of them at once. They can be from different parts of the world, but they're in the same place at the same time. It's not a real place, but it seems real. It's called a grid space, and there are thousands of them. Most are actual places, like that famous café in the Arts District of Swef."

"Swef?"

"Swef, you know, the capital of Orilon."

"Oh, Swef," Mira nodded. "You said 'Swaf'".

"That's how it's pronounced. Everyone in Bree's been saying it wrong all this time."

"That's funny. And this grid place," she said, "it's real but it's not?"

"It's a real place that's been reproduced on the grid, and you can sit there with other real people and have a conversation, except that they're not really real, they just look real. They're projected. You're all projected into the same place at the same time. It's kind of complicated, now that I think about it."

Mira squinted and shook her head. "I don't know how that's possible," she said.

"Me neither, but if I find out, I'll tell you."

"And when you drive your Gen 8 today, you can go to this Swaf café?"

"I think so, maybe. Pella said something about waiting lists and invitations and limited space."

"That's a whole new world you're in."

"It is," I said. "Bree's such a complete and total relic, Mir. That reminds me, I think Bree's the only place in the world that still uses kipper-paper. Nin said they have it on display in one of their museums."

"Mirapa has museums?"

"Yes, and they don't write on kipper-paper. They use more modern stuff."

Mira shook her head. "I guess that's no surprise," she said. "Some days I really wish I could be there with you. Bree has gotten so dull since you left."

"Did the Evolutionaries meet this week?"

"Yes, we met, but it's not the same without you."

I was sad and happy to hear it. "How's it not the same?"

"Bissa, basically. She's not very interested in doing goodness projects, and it turns out not a lot of the other kids are either."

"I knew she'd be a rotten president."

"But on a brighter note," Mira said, "some of the teachers are petitioning the School Committee and Village Council. They want to lift the holophone ban in school — for themselves, not the students. They want to use holophones in their teaching."

"That'd be good."

"I know. It's up for a vote next week. Today the teachers were at the Pavillion talking to people about it, getting signatures. It reminded me of our petition drive. I miss those days."

"I kind of do too," I said.

"Everyone asks about you."

"Everyone?"

"You know, the ones you'd expect. They all say to tell you hello."

"Tell them hello back. And that I miss them too. I miss everyone."

Mira looked teary, so I changed the subject.

"I saw a woman today at the World Café," I said. "She pinched her arm and a sweet smell came out of her skin. Kita said it's a synthetic fragrance. Some women have ten different fragrances, each on a different part of their arm. Whenever you want to smell nice, you just pinch your arm."

"What's a synthetic?" Mira asked.

"I'm not sure, but they have a lot of it."

"You're right, it's pretty, violet sand."

I picked up a handful and held it up, letting it slowly sift through my fingers. "Look how fine it is."

"As fine as asi flour."

Tears blurred my view of the ocean. "I miss the sea," I said.

Mira laughed. "You live on an island."

"I know, but we're so far from shore."

"How far?"

"Over a hill and across a field. You can't even see it from our house or campus. I can't hear the waves at night. They used to help me fall asleep, you know."

"Are you having any nightmares?"

"Some nights, sort of. They're not drowning nightmares, though. They're different."

"Different how?"

"In one, I was standing in front of all my schoolmates, and I had to give a talk. It was an assignment. I started talking, but no sound came out. I talked louder and shouted even, but I couldn't hear me and they couldn't hear me. And I guess they couldn't see my mouth move. They couldn't see that I was trying to speak. They just laughed at me and called me a coward and a mute."

"And then what?"

"I woke up."

"Oh, that doesn't sound so bad, not compared to your old nightmares."

"I guess you're right."

"What's school like?"

"It's too soon to tell," I said. "We haven't really done that much, learning-wise."

"Well, that'll probably change. I saw your video. Groile looks great. My father said he doubts it would grow here, but we should at least try."

"I'm going to call Merchant Kam and set it up," I said. "But I need to call him early in the day, and that's when we have school. This time difference thing is so annoying."

"Lin!" I heard.

"Hold on, Mira." I lifted the eyescreen of my holophone and looked up. It was Pella, standing near and shivering, her arm outstretched.

"My satchel," she said.

I handed Pella her satchel and noticed Kita and Nin running in our direction. "Guess I better go," I said to Mira.

"All right," she said. "Have fun and be safe."

"I will. I miss you, Mira."

"I miss you too, Lin."

Mira's face faded and Kita and Nin fell upon the sand, laughing and breathing hard. Pella warmed herself with a hand-held drying device that was powered by electricity it captured from the air.

"It's warm," she said when I asked about it.

"Warm air?" I put my hand up to it and laughed from the sensation. "Where does the air come from?"

"From the air itself," Pella said. "It passes through here and is heated and then comes out this side."

After Kita and Nin dried off with the warm air, we left for the shops.

"We don't have that much time left," Kita said, studying her data sheet as we walked across the cooling sand. "I think we should take a land taxi. There's one about to come around that corner. I'll hail it."

Land taxis were like watertaxis except they ran on tracks and made no sound and had a clarkon top and windows with voice-activated translucency. I stopped changing the translucency of my window high and low and high again when I saw the young boy sitting in front of me doing the same.

In less than four minutes, we had arrived.

"You'd hardly know this was a marketplace," I said. "It looks like a garden."

"We landscape everything," Pella said. "More than anywhere else in the world."

We walked along a curved path that dipped into a sitting area that was populated with tourists and shoppers. Some sat on benches under low-hanging trees. Some sat in bowl-shaped chairs that lined a meandering stream. Some sat on thick patches of a type of groile made just for sitting upon.

The stream fed a small pond surrounded on one side by a flowerbed. And that's where I saw him, an adibadi, planting flowers. I stood frozen in my tracks, absorbing the moment, a moment I knew I would never forget.

"What?" Nin asked, sensing something was wrong.

"I've never seen an adibadi," I said. "Not in real life. Have you?"

"Sure," she said. "We have adibadis in Mirapa, a few."

Pella and Kita had turned back.

"What's happening?" Kita asked.

"Lin's never seen an adibadi," Nin told her.

"Can I—?" I wasn't sure what to ask. I wasn't sure what I wanted. Now that I had the chance to see one up close, I was strangely nervous. He was just an animal, but he looked so much like us.

"Come on," Kita said, taking me by the hand and marching in his direction. "We call them adis."

Kita was fearless when we stopped less than three paces from his backside. She touched his shoulder to get his attention, then spoke a word, a single word. I stepped back as he rose and stood before us, his face expressionless but for a slight smile.

*Unbelievable*, was all I could think as my fear, some of it, disappeared. Though his face was small like a child's, he stood almost as tall as a man. His shoulders were hunched and hulky and rose and fell with each breath. His eyes were a gray blue and shaped like ours in every detail.

"He's waiting for a command," Kita whispered.

She spoke again, a string of words, and gestured at a tree and then at me. The adi picked a fruit from the tree and held it out to me. He stood close, his eyes locked on mine for a long, breathless moment. I feared reaching out, I feared doing anything. *You don't want to startle an adibadi,* I once read.

"Take it," Kita said, "it's all right."

I took the fruit from his calloused hand and instinctively thanked him in the Continental language with a polite tip of my head. "Valou," I said.

The adi smiled at me and tipped his head. "Valou-ti," he said.

"Kita, he talked to me. He understood me!"

"He did," she said.

I felt like leaping and shouting, but I laughed instead. We all laughed, even the adi in his odd adi way.

"You're so adorable," I said to him. "Oddly adorable."

"He can't understand what you're saying," Kita said. "His vocabulary is pretty small, and it's all Continental."

"I don't care," I said. "I just like saying it."

"The girls are waiting," Kita said. "We should go."

I took in the adi's eyes and face before turning to leave, promising myself I'd see him again.

"I can't believe it," I said as we neared the shop entrance. "I can't believe I saw and talked to an adibadi." I turned to see him one last time, but he was out of view.

"That's nothing compared to what you're about to see," Pella said.

She was referring to my Gen 8 test drive, which never happened due to the fact that a child unaccompanied by an adult must have parental permission to access to the grid.

"But I'm not a child," I said to the store clerk. "I'm a young adult."

"Yes, but you're under 16," she said. "That's the rule."

"Can't you let me, just this once?"

She smiled sympathetically. "If I could, I would, but it's not up to me. Your eyes are scanned. Your age is known. It's all tracked in the system. But I'm happy to contact your mother or father right now."

"That wouldn't be good," I muttered. "It's very late there."

"I wish I could do something," the store clerk said. "But I can't override the system."

I wasn't sure what a system was, but I didn't like it. It had ruined my otherwise perfect day.

Nin tried to comfort me by saying she didn't have parental permission either, so that made two of us whose hopes were dashed to pieces.

Pella and Kita tried to comfort me too, Pella with a promise that we would come back next week and Kita with persistent repetitions of "of course he will" when I said it didn't matter anyway because my father probably wouldn't give permission in the first place.

In an act of sweet unselfishness in their efforts to cheer me up, my friends unanimously agreed to abandon our shopping plans.

"I think Lin needs some adibadi therapy," Pella had said.

After she and Kita explained what therapy was, we went in search of the adi, who was still planting flowers and who was glad to see us again and who made me forget all about Gen 8s and grid spaces and the joy-killing nuisance of parental permissions.

# 11  TALL AND STRONG

The next morning Elda shouted at us: "Stand tall and strong! There is greatness in you!"

I let her words stretch me tall and fill me with confidence.

"Feet to the ground! Head to the sky! Tall and strong!" she shouted.

Elda's words of encouragement were my favorite part of our Morning Strengths and Postures, which we did for twenty minutes at the start of every day. She didn't mind that we laughed and joked and made faces as we did them. And what did she expect? She put us in a circle, where we had no choice but to look at each other, and made us jump and kick and stretch and then balance on one foot for the longest time. "Like some kind of circus animal," Saamta Sio liked to complain.

When we finished our Strengths and Postures, Elda announced that we would each be setting a personal goal for the year.

"What you choose as your personal goal is entirely up to you," she said. "There are only a few rules to abide by. The first rule is: your goal must be attainable."

The second rule was that it had to pertain to us and no one else.

The third rule was that it had to be an improvement of some sort.

The fourth rule was that it had to be measureable.

We had one week to decide on our personal goal, and we had one day to choose someone from our team to be our personal goal partner. I wanted Pella to be my partner, but it had to be someone other than our host student. That being the case, my second choice was Novi, who I wanted to be friends with anyway because he spoke Culti so well and slow and because he was interested in space travel and seemed nice on top of it.

A week seemed hardly enough time to decide on a personal goal that I would have to stick with for a year, and I wasn't the only one who felt that way, though not for the same reason.

"I've narrowed my list of possible personal goals from eleven to six," I told Novi the next afternoon as we sat on a patch of groile that overlooked the ocean.

He was amused. "We have polar opposite predicaments, you and me," he said.

"What do you mean?"

"You've thought up too many choices, and me, not enough. But I've finally thought of two."

"*Two?* That's hardly any."

"At least I'm halfway to my goal of choosing just one," he said. "You, you're only one-sixth of the way."

"Up from one-eleventh," I said. "That's big progress, I'd say."

"Big progress," he smiled.

Though nothing funny had been said, Novi and I had a long laugh. Laughter came easily to us. I wanted to tell him how much I liked his voice, but I was struck by a type of bashfulness and distracted by the constant stares of Saamta Sio, who sat with Kita a conspicuously close distance away.

"Let's start with your goal choices," Novi said. "Tell me all of them."

"All right," I said. "This year I want to be a better Culti speaker."

"I think that's going to happen anyway," he said, "without you having to try very much."

"You think so?"

"Yes," he said. "What else?"

"This year I want to be more patient."

"That's promising. I guess you can measure patience."

"You can measure impatience," I said.

"Right. Good. Next?"

"I want to do better at adjusting to change."

"That sounds kind of vague," Novi said. "Tell me the next one."

"I want to be a better convincer."

"Convincer?"

"I want to be better at convincing people."

"Of what?"

"Of anything. A good idea. An opinion."

"I don't know about that one," Novi said.

"All right, I want to be more grown up with my father."

"Really? That's a goal?"

"For me it is."

"That might not qualify. Your goal is supposed to be about you, not anyone else."

"Oh, maybe you're right."

"Next?" he said.

"I want to decide on my vocational track."

"This year?"

"Yes."

"But we have two more years before we have to decide."

"I know," I said, "but Pella was telling me that it's good to know it early. You can choose the best courses to prepare you, and that way you'll be ahead."

"Ahead of what?"

"Of the others in your vocational track," I said.

Novi was silent, perhaps confused or uninformed.

I asked him, "You haven't heard about the parents who hire guidance counselors for their kids so they'll declare their vocation early and be ahead?"

"No," he said. "But it sounds like impatience to me."

"Well," I said.

"Let's come back to that one. You have one more?"

"I saved my favorite goal for last," I smiled. "I want to improve my ability to know what love would do."

Novi looked at me funny. "What love would do?"

"Yes, I think one of the best things we can do to be a good and wise person is to do what love would do, in small things and big things. I've been practicing it for a while, although, actually, not much lately. Not since I've been here."

"Do what love would do," he thoughtfully said.

"Do you like it?"

"It's kind of smarmy, but ... I sort of do. I don't know how you can measure it, though."

"Well...." I waited for a brilliant idea to flash up, but all that came to mind was a conversation I once had with Merchant Kam. "There's a man in Bree," I told Novi. "He's not *from* Bree, but he's lived there since before I was born. His name is Merchant Kam, and he's a merchant, obviously, but not an ordinary merchant. He's the wisest man in Bree, and he went to school here himself. He's probably sat on this very groile. I asked him once, 'When I ask what love would do, what am I listening for?' And he said that love is an inner presence that wants to be known like a friend. But unlike most friends, it doesn't speak in words. He said love is *felt,* not heard."

Novi nodded. "That makes sense," he said.

"So that's how my goal can be measured, by how much fear I feel. The less fear, the more love."

"Maybe."

"What do you mean, maybe?"

"Just because you're not afraid," he said, "doesn't mean you're doing what love would do. Some people are fearless and they do terrible things."

I looked over at Saamta Sio. "You're right," I said.

"I still like your goal, though. I think you should ask Elda about it."

"I *will* ask her. Thanks, Novi. And so, what are your two goal ideas?"

"I want to improve my math proficiencies."

"Wow, that's practical."

"And the other is, I want to be a better public speaker."

"That's practical, too."

"Call me Mr. Practicality."

"I think they're both good, Mr. Practicality. You could save one of them for next year."

"You're right, I could. I think I would start with the math."

"And do the harder one next year."

"Exactly," he grinned.

"Thanks for being honest about your opinion of my goals and for being kind about it."

"Sure," he said. "They're all good, you should keep them all ... privately, you know, for yourself."

"I probably will. I like having goals."

Elda showed up, and after I asked her about it, she said she seriously doubted the measurability of knowing what love would do.

"But you could ask someone about it, right?" I asked her.

"I'll ask," she said.

And the afternoon ended, Novi having effortlessly decided on his personal goals for this year and next, me having un-effortlessly decided on nothing.

## 12 Freedom and the Permissions

The moment the casing came off my arm, I felt free. Free and unburdened and more me again.

I was confident that the whole embarrassing incident would finally be forgotten by everyone. The number of Broken Arm Girl insults had already dropped to less than once a day, and more and more schoolmates knew me as Gen One Girl. Even the boy from Clud had taken to calling me Gog instead of Bag. It was an insignificant victory some argued (Mira), but I considered it big.

Mira was happy for me and glad not to talk about it anymore. She was more interested in hearing about everything else going on in my life.

"I talked to father yesterday," I said while we spoke in my sleepingroom one night before dinner.

"Oh," she said, "and how'd that go?"

"He was happy to see me. Really happy. It took me by surprise. He said he missed me. He said it more than once. It's funny, Mira, I think he loves me more me being here, being away from him."

"Maybe he's relieved that he doesn't have to take care of you."

"Maybe so. And he's not mad that I broke my arm."

"That's good," Mira said. "Did you ask him? About getting a Gen 8?"

I nodded. "I thought it'd take weeks to get my courage up, but he was in a good mood, so I straight out asked him. He didn't say yes, but he didn't say no. I would have pushed him on it if he hadn't gotten so confused about all the generations of holophones. And he didn't like hearing that Bree got the holophones that no one else wanted. So, I'm going to get Aunt Tala to talk him into it. At least he's giving me parental permission to test a Gen 8 at the shops. He said he didn't see any harm in that."

"Can't your aunt give permissions?"

"No, she's not my legal guardian. I wish she was, that'd make my life so much easier. I asked her if she would talk to the Parental Permissions Office with her video feed off and change her voice and pretend to be father, but she said that wouldn't work even if she was willing to do it. Holophones read voiceprints, even Generation Ones, and father's voiceprint is on file."

"I guess there's no way around that," Mira said.

I shook my head. "As much as I love technology, Mira, sometimes it really works against you. On a brighter note, we're going on a three-day excursion around the island next week."

"Three days?"

I nodded. "On foot."

"Where will you sleep?"

"In portable clarkon domes. Almost everyone brought their own. The school gave me one yesterday. They programmed it with my voice. I'm the only one who can change the translucency. You know, how clear or dark the dome wall is."

"I know," Mira said, "you told me already. I like that word, translucency. I like what it means."

"Another word that doesn't exist in Welbi, the dying language of the ancient kings."

Mira laughed, as if I'd said that for the first time. "I love your sense of drama, Lin."

"Drama?"

"Yes, you're a dramatic figure. Just like your father."

"I don't know what a dramatic figure is."

"It's a literary term," Mira said. "A figure is a character in a story. Dramatic figures are the characters who are the most emotional or the most troubled. Or both."

"I guess I'd be both."

"You'd be both," Mira agreed. "Did I tell you I've been studying literature on my holophone?"

"That's great, Mir. Elda would say you have excellent initiative, studying while school is out."

"Hali is too," she said. "He's taking some science classes. We're both already completely bored with the tourist scene here. Yesterday Hali told me he was jealous of you because you're in school all year long. 'Non-stop learning,' he said, 'what could be better than that?'"

"Non-stop learning on a beautiful, modern island," I said.

"I guess so. Anyway, we're counting the days until school starts ... 75 ... 75 days from today."

"I would count by months," I said. "Two and a half is a much smaller number. You might not feel so bad about it."

"I'll tell Hali you said that. It's his deal, really, the counting."

"Is my father getting big crowds at the Boat Rental?"

Mira smiled. "For so early in the tourist season, really big crowds. And there was a wedding on his boat two days ago."

"I know," I said. "He told me. I think he likes the wedding planner."

"Wedding planner?"

"She arranges the tourist marriages on father's boat. Every time he talks about her, he says how nice she is. And she's not married."

"That's interesting."

"Isn't it?"

"It is." Mira squinted and gave a nod. "It's really good that you left at the beginning of tourist season, when your father's so happy. I'm kind of surprised he didn't give permission for you to get your Gen 8, his mood being so good and all."

"He doesn't understand why I need a second holophone," I said. "That's his big reason, I think. That, and he doesn't feel like he's doing his fatherly duties if he doesn't say no to my fondest hopes and wishes."

"But he'll eventually say yes."

"After I pester him enough."

"I've been thinking lately that I might write your life story some day," Mira said.

"Mine? Why?"

"Because you have an unusual life, and I think you're going to be famous some day. More famous than you are now."

"Well," I shrugged, "time will tell about that."

"You should be the one to write it, though."

"I don't know, I'm not a writer like you."

"Well, think about it. It would be better coming from you. An autobiography. But if you don't write it, I will." She grinned her impish grin. "I will, really. And it will be a best seller, I'm sure of it."

"Because I'm a tragic figure?"

"Exactly," she said, "and tragedy sells, more than anything else. All the great writers write tragic stuff. Some just to pay their bills. There's a writer who wrote beautiful inspiring stories, but no one wanted to read them. So he wrote all these books about war and angst under a different name, and they sold like precious jewels. Now he's famous for both bodies of work."

"You learned all this on your holophone?"

"All that and a lot more. It's already making me a better writer."

My happiness for Mira rose only halfway, stifled by a pang of jealousy. "Thirteen," I said, "and you already know what you're going to do for the rest of your life. You're really good at that one thing, so of course you'll be a writer. I'm good at ... I don't know what. I don't know at all."

"Isn't that what you're going to figure out while you're at school there?" Mira asked.

"Oh, that reminds me," I said. "I decided on my personal goal."

"The love thing?"

"No, choosing my vocation. I'm going to figure out my life purpose."

"I thought you had two years to decide that."

"I do, but I want to know this year so I can be learning the right Culti and Continental words. All the vocations have special words."

"What if you decide on something and change your mind next year?"

"Then I can change my mind. Whatever I decide, I'm not locked in. Elda told me so."

The doorchime of my sleepingroom sounded. "Wait, Mira, I think it's dinner." I pulled up my eyescreen and spoke to the air, "Open." The door opened and there stood Pia, fresh back from an expedition to the International Space Center on the North Pole. In my ear Mira giggled. She hadn't seen the voice-activated door trick yet.

"It's time to eat," Pia said, peering at my scattered belongings that lay on the floor.

"Thanks, Pia, I'll be right there. I've got to go," I said to Mira.

"I know," she said. "I miss you, Lin. Life isn't the same without you here."

"I miss you too, Mira. I miss you a lot."

We promised we'd talk the next day, neither of us knowing that five days would pass before our next call.

After dinner, Pia told Pella and I about her expedition to the North Pole.

"In groups of ten we went up the space elevator and toured the entire Forton satellite. Now I know why they call it a city in the sky. It's massive inside."

"All of you went up?" I asked. "The whole Third Year class?"

"No," she said. "Some didn't want to go, and some *did* but their parents wouldn't let them."

My heart skipped some beats and my throat dried up. "You have to have parental permissions to go up the space elevator?"

"Yes," Pia said, "you have to have permissions for all the off-island expeditions. One girl didn't go just because her mother had a bad dream about something going wrong."

"Poor girl," I said. "So what did she do instead?"

"She went in the virtual."

"Oh, that's not so bad."

Pia raised an eye at me. "I think it is," she said. "If it's not real, it's not real. Virtual travel is overrated, if you ask me."

"Elsewhere's don't seem to mind," Pella said.

"Elsewheres?" I asked.

"People who spend too much time in the virtual," she explained, "they're called Elsewheres."

"It's a disease," Pia said.

"Why?"

"Think about it," she told me. "If you're somewhere else more than where you are, you're not really living your life."

"I guess you're right," I said, smiling at a funny memory. "When we first got holophones in Bree, all kids wanted to do was fly in Flight Mode. The parents hated it. They called us 'the standing dead' because, you know how it is in Flight Mode, you can't move or it shuts off, and it's more fun to stand than sit when you fly. So all over Bree you saw kids standing totally still, staring at space. They really did look like standing dead kids. It was kind of creepy, to tell you the truth. Father called them stone statues of stupidity. Anyway, we almost lost our holophones over it, but sitting saved it."

"Sitting?"

"We got all the kids to start sitting when they flew. The parents didn't mind so much then. I'm not sure why."

"Not so creepy," Pia said.

"Probably," I agreed. "No one ever complained about sitting dead kids."

We stayed up late, laughing and talking and indulging in some flavor pellets Pella stored in the kitchen. I wanted to hear more about their childhoods and their travels, real and virtual, but the more I heard, the more sad I felt that they were born where they were born and I was born in Bree. It was a sadness no flavor pellet could ever seem to sweeten.

## 13 THE WORD WAS GREATNESS

Early the next morning I called Merchant Kam, having made myself a promise. *No whining. No complaining. Keep it positive.* I let the words circle my thoughts until he answered.

"Lin," he smiled, "how wonderful to hear from you. How are you getting along, your first weeks of school?"

"Despite some bumps and disappointments and no instantaneous translation, pretty good, I'd say."

"Bumps and disappointments are to be expected," he told me, "but I hear from your Aunt that you're handling them well."

"Thanks, I hope so. I'm doing my best. It's not at all what I expected."

"Nor was it for me my first year there. I remember it being a time of tremendous discovery and adjustment."

"Discovery and adjustment," I said. "You know exactly what I'm going through."

"I have a sense of what you're going through."

"I love groile," I said. "And I was thinking, it would be great for the kids in Bree to have some groile for sliding. It could be planted on the mudslide where Califer Crigs' house used to be. Do you think you could get some?"

"Obtaining groile wouldn't pose a problem," he said. "As for how it would grow here in our soil, that's another matter. But since I personally know the joys of groile sliding, I would be glad to look into it."

"You will?"

"I promise."

"I'm surprised how mean some of the kids are," I said. "Not the Continental kids, they're all pretty nice. It's the Wershonians ... some of them act no better than the brats of Bree."

"You were expecting better behavior from them because they come from more modern societies than ours?"

"I suppose so."

"You'll learn, Lin, that technological achievement doesn't necessarily produce a more mature society. It *can,* but often it doesn't, and sometimes technology can make people less mature."

"Why?" I asked.

"Well, immaturity is our starting point," he said. "You see this in infants, who have the social skills of a wild animal. Yes, it's true, isn't it? And we will remain social animals, even into old age, unless we learn mature ways of living."

"Maturity isn't automatic."

"No," he said.

"Someone said that parents are our role models, whether they try to be or not, and that has a lot to do with how we turn out. I don't think father's been a very good role model."

"Most parents are imperfect role models."

"Not Continental parents."

"Continental parents are more mature than most, but perfect," he shook his head, "no. Perfection is a severe standard, Lin. Don't expect it from yourself and don't expect it from others."

"Or I'll be sorely disappointed."

"Yes. Perfection is an excellent goal post, but for most of us, it's unachievable. We do best to set *attainable* goals for ourselves, with perfection as a compass."

"Attainable," I said. "That's what Elda said about deciding on our personal goal. It had to be attainable."

"It will increase your likelihood of success," he smiled. "And what did you chose as a personal goal?"

I told him, in as few words as I could, about my eleven choices, the difficult decision, and what I chose in the end. He agreed that I chose wisely.

"Knowing what love would do isn't the most practical undertaking for a girl in your circumstances," he said. "Learning about vocations sounds much better. And I think you'll find it fascinating. You'll learn a lot about the world this way."

"Today I'm meeting with my goal partner, Novi, to make a plan of action. I like that, plan of action. It sounds so ... so grown up."

Merchant Kam laughed, though not in a judging way. He never judged me for anything. I had a keen sense for being judged, and I'd never felt it from him.

"I love Morning Strengths and Postures," I said. "I love what Elda tells us. 'Stand tall and strong!'"

"There is greatness in you," we said together.

"They were saying that then?" I asked. "When you were here?"

"Yes, and I'm glad to know it's still being said."

Later that morning, Novi and I sat on a patch of groile under a thinly clouded sky. He was nice enough to let me sit facing a small view of the ocean, which seemed so far away.

"Let's start with you," I said.

Novi's plan was simple. He would devote more time to studying math, giving extra attention to the material that was most difficult for him. His personal learning schedule would include an hour a day at the Tutoring Clinic, where he would be tutored by a third year student who had won three Excellence Awards in math.

"My target score for my math proficiencies is 96% by the end of the year," Novi said.

"Ninety-six? *Really?*"

"Really," he said.

I stared at him, stunned speechless and more than impressed by his lofty math aspirations. "What was your score on last week's math proficiencies?" I asked him.

"Eighty-five percent."

"*Eighty-five?*"

He just smiled.

"That's almost twice as high as mine," I nearly said. But I avoided the embarrassment and asked the obvious. "Why did you choose math proficiencies as your goal? You don't need any help with your math scores at all."

"I do if I want to get into the Space Program when we graduate."

"Oh, right," I said. "That makes sense."

Novi smiled and said hello to Elda, who had come by to check on us.

"And what is your plan for accomplishing your goal?" she asked me after Novi told her his.

"My plan is to study all the different vocations," I said. "Some I'll learn about on our expeditions. The others I'll learn about on my holophone and in interviews with real people. Then I'll write a short report or give a talk on each of them."

"I think you should write a report on all of them," Elda said. "They'll help with your composition proficiencies."

"But I'm *terrible* at writing Culti," I said.

"Yes," she said, "that's why writing reports will do you well. And don't worry, you won't be on your own on that. We'll schedule an hour a day at the Tutoring Clinic just for your writing skills."

The Tutoring Clinic was the only square building on the island of Vona, a maze of narrow hallways lined with tiny rooms. On the floors were painted bright fat numbers and colored arrows that pointed you to the right place without having to stop and ask someone. No talking was permitted in any public area of the Tutoring Clinic, though I didn't see the need. Every small tutoring room, once the door was closed, let no outside noise pass through its walls.

"How can they concentrate with invisible walls?" I asked Pella after we toured the Tutoring Clinic for the first time.

"They're only invisible looking in," she said. "Once you're inside, you can't see out."

I shook my head in wonder. "Another incredible clarkon invention."

"Oh, those aren't clarkon walls," Pella said. "One-ways have been around a lot longer than clarkon. You've never heard about them?"

"Not until today."

"Unbelievable," she said. "Every day is a new discovery for you. We've been here three weeks and you still see new stuff. I really envy that."

"You do?" I asked. "Why?"

"I love travelling to new places and being amazed. After you've travelled a lot, it's harder to be amazed ... there's less newness."

"That's a tough problem to live with."

"It's a silly problem," she said, "compared to you."

"If I could give you all the newness I deal with every day, I would."

Pella laughed.

"Believe me, you wouldn't want it," I said.

"I don't know. I love adventure. It's the primitive part of your life I wouldn't want, you know, growing up in Bree."

"I wouldn't want it either," I said, "That's why I love being here. Every day is an adventure. Sometimes it's been terrifying, but mostly it's been fun. Amazing, like you say."

"Well, wouldn't adventure be boring if there wasn't a little fear and daring built in?"

"The daring, yes," I agreed. "But not the fear. I've had enough fear for a lifetime."

"Well, if that's true, it doesn't show."

"Really?"

"You're one of the most fearless people I know," she said.

"Do I say that word a lot? Fearless?"

"No, not much that I've noticed."

"That's strange, I haven't been thinking it much either. Fearless used to be my favorite word. I thought it and said it all the time."

"Well, that explains it," she said.

"Explains what?"

"Why you're so fearless. You thought it and said it so much, you became it."

"Think so?"

"I feel pretty certain."

"It got me through some rough times," I said.

"Well, maybe you're ready for a new word now."

"Maybe I am, Pella. I'm going to think about that."

And I did think about it, those few times I had the luxury to think about anything other than making my mind remember all the important parts of what I was learning every day, in school and out.

One morning, while doing Morning Strengths and Postures, I decided on a word, a word inspired by Elda. It was a word that sounded as good as it felt, and it was a feeling that was growing in me.

The word was greatness.

# 14 A NEW FRIEND

The airtram filled up fast with students, taking in at least two at each stop. One of them was Birgard, the boy from Algalon who ruined my first ever sub-orbital landing the day we arrived. He spotted the empty seats near ours and took the one just behind me, his friend taking the seat behind Pella.

Pella's tail swat my leg. She stretched open a data sheet, wrote three words on it, and passed it to me.

"Look who's here," it read.

I erased it with my palm and wrote, "I know. Say nothing. Please."

She pulled another data sheet out of her satchel and wrote on it a line of ancient philosophy, "She who wants friends must herself be friendly."

"Don't want to be his friend," I wrote on the data sheet I still held, keeping it low on my lap and holding it sideways for her to see. It had dawned on me that Birgard and his friend could have been peering over our shoulders all that time.

"Hi, Lin, nice to see you," I heard Birgard say.

"Hi," I said, turning my head for only as long as it took to say it.

"On your way to the Complex?" asked his friend.

Pella shifted herself sideways, facing the boys as much as me. "We are," she said. "The shops and the World Café. Have you eaten there yet?"

They hadn't.

"It's like a food museum," Pella told them. "We can show you how to get there. And if you want, I can tell you about all the foods. I know them well."

To avoid being pulled into a conversation with Birgard, I leaned forward and talked to Nin and Kita until we reached the Complex. But the avoidance was a mere postponement. Nin and Kita took well to the idea that Birgard and his friend spend the day with us.

We headed straight to the marketplace so it wouldn't get put off until the end of the day when crowds would swell as rain blew in. As we passed through the garden, I looked for the adibadi we had seen there before, but I only saw people. Nin talked to Birgard as we walked, and Pella talked to his friend, which left Kita and I with each other. She didn't mind. She loved hearing stories about my childhood.

"I'm here to test drive a Gen 8," I told the clerk in the gadget shop.

"Me too," said Nin.

"Nin and Lin," the clerk said after she verified our parental permissions. "You must be of Welbi stock."

"We are," Nin said.

"You know about the Welbi kings?" I asked the clerk.

"I do," she said. "My father is a historian. Now, here are your eye film and ear pieces. I'll help you with these if that's necessary."

"No, I got it," said Nin.

"I need help with the eye film," I said, watching Nin put hers in. "Though it looks pretty easy."

While Kita was touring Nin around her Gen 8, I was still trying to tap a slimy piece of clarkon film on my eyeballs.

"Is it still there?" I asked Pella as I held up my fingertip.

She squinted and said, "Yes, it's still there."

"I can't even see it," I said.

"You don't need to see it," Pella told me. "Just tap it on your eye. One tap. Believe me, it doesn't hurt at all."

"And be patient," the clerk kindly said. "It's a learning process."

I tried once more to tap the film on my eye, but again, my eye blinked shut.

"I don't know how you do it," I said. "It's like poking your own eye out. It's unnatural."

"Try holding your eye open with your free hand," Birgard said after saying he understood the awkwardness.

I held my eye open and watched my trembling finger. I took a deep breath, held my eye open, and tapped.

After I aptly tapped the other film in my left eye, they quietly cheered for me — my friends and the clerk and an interested stranger standing nearby.

I blinked and looked around me with what the clerk said was augmented vision. Everything I looked at was sharper, brighter, more colorful, and strangely, more *real*.

After the clerk positioned my earbuds and helped me train the Gen 8 to recognize my voice, we followed her to a sitting area near the back of the shop. She led us to a circle of chairs and with a simple voice command lowered a circular wall around us, a wall like the walls in the Tutoring Clinic, which let no sound in or out. We were free to make all the noise we wanted.

Three hours quickly passed inside our wall, where we were everywhere but there. We roamed the world, some of it in Flight Mode over wide mossy canyons and steamy volcanoes and all the tallest mountains, and some of it on foot, inside famous buildings and sports arenas and luxury hotels, where we could walk around as if we were there. It was virtual travel, and I didn't think it could ever be overrated. It seemed as real as life itself.

"How is that possible?" I asked as we walked to the World Café.

"Holographic projection," Pella explained.

"And you can go anywhere? Inside a person's house?"

"No," Kita said. "Only certain places. They're called grid spaces."

"Are there a lot of them?"

"Thousands, probably," Pella said. "Maybe more."

"And who decides which places are grid spaces?" I asked.

"The places themselves," said Kita. "Most are hotels and resorts. They do it to promote tourism."

"Well then Bree should have a grid space," I said.

"You have tourism in Bree?" Birgard asked.

"We do now."

Nin told Birgard the story of how Bree's tourism business quadrupled in one year and how my best friend Mira was mostly responsible because of a newspaper article she wrote about the satellite broadcast petition drive that I started when I was ten years old, not long after my mother tragically died in my arms.

Later, Birgard told me that his own mother had died when he was eight. After knowing that, I couldn't dislike him at all any more. I already had mostly stopped disliking him earlier that day. I think it was after he told me about the trick for putting film in your eye.

We passed by an adibadi who was working in the tree park that stretched long and lush between the shops and the World Café. I wondered if it was the same adibadi I'd seen the week before, and if it was, if he would remember me.

"What's wrong, Lin?" Pella asked me. "What are you looking at?"

"That adibadi," I said. "He's so ..." — I looked back again — "amazing. So much like us. He's odd, isn't he? Odd but adorable."

"Lin's never seen an adibadi," I heard Kita tell Birgard and his friend. "Not until last week."

"I hope he's still here after lunch," I said. "I want to see him again."

"Why don't we go see him now?" Birgard asked. "Just for a few minutes. We can catch up with them at the café."

"If you want to," Pella said, "I'll order for you."

"All right," I told her. "Get what I had last time. You know, that plate of fish from around the world."

"Fish," Birgard said, nodding and smiling. "I'll have some world fish too."

"Great," Pella said. "We'll see you there."

"Did you grow up on the sea?" I asked Birgard as we turned away from our friends.

"No," he said, "but not far. Less than an hour from the beach by Lev."

"Byleb?"

"By *Lev*. That's short for magnetic levitation train."

"Oh, right," I said. "They call it the monorail in Southern Wershonia."

Birgard said something I didn't fully hear. I was entranced by the adibadi, who was cutting branches from a tree less than twenty paces away.

"If he's seen me before," I asked, "will he remember me?"

"Maybe, if you talked to him. But don't be sad if he doesn't. Public adis are trained not to form attachments to people."

"What's a public adi?"

"Adis who work in public places. Private adis are owned by a family."

"And they make attachments?"

"Yes," he said. "They're like a member of the family."

"Does your family have one?"

"We have two."

*Two?* "You're a lucky kid," I said, stopping three paces away.

"Gano," Birgard said in a strong, clear voice.

The adi turned toward us, lowering his giant cutting tool until it pointed to the ground.

"Hello," I said, happy and nervous and searching for a scar below his right eye.

The adi grunted and smiled at me.

"It's him," I said to Birgard. "It's the same adi! He has a scar."

The adi laughed and spoke to me, words I didn't understand.

"He remembers you," Birgard said.

"What did he say?"

"He said 'gano de nu', hello again."

"Gano means hello?"

"Yes."

"Gano de nu," I said to the adi. "It's so nice to see you again."

"Gano de nu," he said.

We laughed together, the adi and me.

"He likes you," Birgard said. "And he knows you like him. Adis are sensitive to that. If you want to be friends with an adi, just be nice to them."

I held out my hand in an offering of friendship. "Friends," I said.

"Fralen?" the adi asked me, his head tilting to one side, his eyes preciously sweet.

"He said 'fruit'," Birgard said. "He thinks you asked for some fruit."

"How do I say friend?"

"There's no one word for friend. Say di ligo tu, I like you."

"Di ligo tu," I said to the adi.

"Di ligo tu," he said to me.

Tears filled my eyes, tears of joy. I'd made a new friend. An amazing friend. An animal friend. A talking animal friend.

"I want to get a video of us," I said to Birgard, "of the adi and me.

Will you—?"

"I already got it," he said. "I've been capturing it all along. I'll send the video to your holophone later."

"You got it all? The adi and me? Talking and laughing?"

"I got it all."

When we said goodbye to the adi, it was a cheerful goodbye. I knew I would see him again, and I sensed he did too.

"You're a good kid, Birgard," I said as we walked to the café. "That was a nice thing to do, taking me to see the adi and capturing the video. I didn't even ask."

"You didn't have to ask," he said. "It's what I would have wanted."

"I wish more people had that attitude."

"You say that like you have someone particular in mind."

"I do," I said. "My father."

"Well, that's no surprise."

"You know about my father?"

"No, I know that most kids want more than their parents want to give them."

"When you first told your father that you wanted to go to the Transition Schools," I said, "what did he say?"

Birgard hesitated. "It was his idea."

"He wanted you to go."

"He insisted that I go."

"What? And you didn't want to?"

"Not at first," he said.

"That's the complete opposite of me. I had to beg father just to let me apply."

"Why didn't he want you to go?"

"Other than the fact that he loves saying no to everything I want just because he can, I think mainly because he has zero interest in the world outside of Bree, and because he's prejudiced against the Continentals and technology and progress generally. And he's not very interested in education, even though my mother was a teacher."

"Nin said your mother died in your arms."

"She drowned," I said. "I tried to save her. But I wasn't strong enough. She actually slipped from my arms. It was horrible, so horrible. And I can't go back and make it different."

"I'm so sorry, Lin," he said, kind and soft. "I hope you don't mind that I asked."

"It's all right. I actually like knowing that you understand. How did your mother....?" I couldn't say the word.

"An industrial accident. Twelve people died in an explosion where she worked."

"That's awful. A senseless accident."

"A senseless accident that didn't have to happen," he said. "My mother was a manager who was supervising an inspection team. She was filling in for a man on vacation. At first I wished that he had died and not her. But the better wish is that it didn't happen at all."

"Right, he probably had kids too."

"He did. I met him once. He came to our house about a year later and apologized, even though it wasn't his fault. He said he was gripped with guilt and thought of my mother every day. He was a nice man."

"I like nice people," I said.

"Me too."

"I'm sorry I wasn't nice to you in the beginning. You reminded me of a boy in Bree who was pretty cruel to me. It wasn't fair to take it out on you."

"So that's why," Birgard said. "Thanks for telling me. I thought—" He stopped himself.

"You thought what?"

"I thought the reason you weren't nice was because you had some kind of chip on your shoulder or that you thought too highly of yourself."

I laughed, relieved not to be talking about our dead mothers. We had arrived at the World Café, and I didn't want us to arrive sad. "I've actually been thinking too *lowly* of myself," I said, "ever since I got here."

"Too lowly?"

"Everyone here is better than me. Better holophones, better families, better culture, better Culti. I could go on."

"Do you think you might be exaggerating?"

"Maybe. Probably. My aunt says I have a lot of my father's traits, and he's a big exaggerator."

We stepped into the World Café, which was mostly empty. It seemed cavernously large as I looked up at the tiered floors of dining tables above us.

"There they are," I said, pointing to a table next to the railing of the top floor.

"A table with a view," said Birgard.

"If you like fish, you're in for a total treat."

As we rode up the clear tube to the top floor, Birgard told me a fish joke his mother liked to tell: "Cook a man a fish and you feed him for a day. Teach a man to fish and you get rid of him for a week."

I finally laughed after he explained that in most parts of the world, men fish for sport because they don't fish for a living anymore and that the men of Algalon like to take weeklong fishing trips just for fun.

I told Birgard some of my father's best fishing jokes. We were laughing when we found our friends feasting on food, food of every possible kind from every place in the world, even Egli, I found out.

## 15 SUNSET PEAK

"Well?" Pella asked as Birgard and I sat to eat.

"I think Lin has a way with adis," he grinned with pride.

"I talked to him," I said, "I talked to him in adi. Or whatever it is, the name of his language."

"It's adi," Kita said, biting into some green thing, "just like you said."

"Some of the words sound like Continental," I said.

"They are," said Pella. "The more you learn Continental, the more easy it will be for you to talk to adis and understand them."

"Did you have adis growing up?" I asked her.

"We had one from before I was born," Pella said. "Ori. She died four years ago. I thought I'd never get over it, but I did ... mostly. I miss her whenever I think about her. We talked about getting another adi, but when Pia was accepted at school here, my parents decided to bring us all to Vona and be a host family. No family adis are allowed in the Residences, so we thought it was a perfect situation."

"I'm sorry she died," I said.

"Me too," said Nin and Birgard's friend.

"It brought you here," Birgard said.

"Right, there's the bright side," said Kita.

Pella smiled and looked at each of us. "Thanks," she said. "Thanks, everyone."

"I wonder what it's like to be an adi trainer," I said. "I can see doing that as a vocation."

"You're too smart to be an adi trainer," Birgard told me.

"Thanks for the compliment, but why do you say too smart?"

"Animal handling is kind of a menial job," he said. "It doesn't require the highest degree of intelligence."

"I don't think my intelligence is too high for an adibadi," I said. "Plus, if I love adis, I would love working with them. Isn't that what they tell us about choosing a vocation? Something we do well and something we love doing?"

Pella leaned toward me from across the table, her wide smile holding some great secret. "There's a big adi-trainer training program at the zoology school. We're going on an expedition there this year."

"When?" I asked. "Do you know?"

"Month after next. Then a month later we're going to the International School of Arts and Sports. I love that place."

"You've been?" Birgard asked.

"Last year," she said. "To see some competitions. You should see the aerialists. They're so graceful and small, but strong. Really strong."

"What's an aerialists?" I asked.

"Aerialist," Kita said. "They're gymnasts who perform in the air using ropes and swings and hoops. They never touch the ground."

"That sounds dangerous," I said.

"They have nets to catch them," Pella said. "But if you think about it, our ancestors lived in trees, so it's kind of natural."

"True," said Birgard. "We were all aerialists once."

"That was the original purpose of the tail," Kita said.

"When we go back to the shop for more Gen 8 fun," Pella said, "we can see some virtual performances."

"I'd like that," I said. "I'd like that a lot."

Pella looked up at the sky through the clarkon dome that gave a perfectly spotless view while shielding all wind and rain and the most violent of storms. "I see some pure sky," she said.

Kita queried her data sheet for a Pure Sky Report. "Excellent pure sky conditions for the next two hours," she said, "then they'll slowly drop off."

We unanimously decided to go straight to the beach.

The crowds at the beach were larger than the week before, drawn, no doubt, to the pure skies. Big patches of the westward sky were cloudless. It was the most pure sky Nin and I had ever seen. We were the only two who had grown up near the equator.

"Have you ever seen the real sun?" I asked of anyone who had.

"I have," said Kita. "But you can't look right at it. It will burn your eyes."

"That's true," Birgard agreed. "You *want* to look at it, but you can't. It's strange."

"I rode up a simulated space elevator once," I said. "They gave us eyeshades because the virtual sun was so bright."

"The sun's a lot brighter in space," said Birgard. "They say the Gen 9s will have better sun protection built into the film. Enough to look directly at the sun for more than a minute."

"That's interesting," Kita said. "I want one already."

"They're inventing a Gen 9?" I asked.

"Sure," said Kita. "There's going to be a Gen 90 some day."

Pella laughed. "I wonder what that will be like."

"A talk-free life," Birgard imagined, smiling as he said it. "All you have to do is think. Think breakfast and breakfast is made."

"Think sleep, and you're instantly asleep," Kita said.

"Think everything you want to say," said Pella, "and your Gen 90 says it for you."

"To the people of your choice," Birgard added, "wherever they are."

"That sounds convenient," said Nin.

"But what if you think the wrong thought?" I asked.

Kita smiled. "If it's a Gen 90, it will probably know which thoughts are wrong. Even if you don't."

"Maybe it will only let you think *good* thoughts," I said. "All the bad or mean ones won't pass through."

"That'd be nice," said Birgard. "A kinder world."

"A kinder world," I repeated, cheered by the thought of it.

The line for the speedboat excursions was long, so we decided to walk along the shoreline and then head over to the shops. We said hello to schoolmates we saw along the way, stopping to talk to a few. Saamta Sio was one of them. As usual, she was less than friendly to me, but she said something that turned out to be a favor to us all.

"Some of us are meeting at dusk on Sunset Peak to watch the sun go down," she said. "Join us if you'd like."

Having lived on Vona for two years already, Pella knew all about Sunset Peak.

"It's the tallest hill on the island," she said. "You can see everything from there. The Assembly Hall, the Residences, the Complex, and if you turn in a complete circle, you see the entire ocean and some of the mainland too. We should go."

We all liked the idea, and Pella called her mother to say we would be late for dinner.

Happy and laughing, we headed to the shops where two Gen 8 demos and a soundproof circle of chairs awaited us.

"I'm dizzy!" Nin cried as we watched the aerialists' performance, video-captured on the special holophones they wore, giving us the entire view and feeling of sailing through the air high above a crowd. We leapt rope to rope, somersaulting, tail-hanging, and landing once upon a fat invisible strand of rope and walking along it, wavering only slightly.

I was queasy, but said nothing. I closed my eyes to make it stop, but the scene didn't disappear. The real-as-life holographic video was being projected from the tiny piece of film stuck to my eye. There was no escaping it.

"I don't know how you can wear your Gen 8 all day," I said as we walked the hill to Sunset Peak.

"I don't understand how you can wear a Gen One at all," Kita laughed. She had tried mine on once and said it made her head sweaty.

"But seriously," I told my friends, "how can you do anything with all that stuff showing in your eye?"

"You can turn off the film any time," Pella said, "with a voice command or a thought command."

"That's convenient," I said. "I guess they thought of everything when they invented the Gen 8."

"Pretty much," Kita agreed.

The walk up to Sunset Peak was not easy for the old, the injured, or the lazy, so an airlift service was provided that took passengers from a station point at the bottom of the hill to a station point at the top, following a route alongside a wide, winding walking path.

Five young boys ran past us, overtaking and passing a 6-person airlift drifting overhead, laughing and squealing as they did.

"Joy squeals," I said to Nin in Welbi.

"Joy squeals," she smiled and said.

I shook my head, feeling I had lost something precious. "We don't joy squeal anymore."

"We're too old for that now," Nin said.

"I suppose so." I watched the boys running wild and happy, turning from time to time to look at the airlift that was well behind them. When they reached the summit they jumped and shouted, arms upstretched, their balled fists punching the sky in celebration of their simple, silly victory.

Tears came to my eyes, I didn't know why, but the feeling in my heart was warm, not sad, so I supposed they were tears of joy. I'd been having more of those lately.

The top of Sunset Peak was wide and flat, a gently rolling field of groile whose outer edges were lined with benches. The benches on the sunset side were packed with people young and old. The air was moist and still and filled with wingless birds.

"Look at those birds," I said to Nin, "they have no wings." I shouted to Pella and Kita who walked six paces in front of us, "How do those birds fly without wings?!"

Kita turned and shouted through her laughter, "Those are transport drones!"

I felt hopelessly stupid.

The drones were delivering food and drinks to people who sat on the benches and who milled about on the groile.

"Hey, girls," said Saamta Sio, who mysteriously emerged from somewhere near. "That was a riot, Lin. You're a funny one."

"It wasn't a joke," I said before thinking.

"What, you really thought the drones were—?"

Kita cut her off. "Thanks for suggesting this place, Saamta. It's really great."

"Sio," Saamta said with a scolding tone. "Saamta *Sio.*" She insisted being called by both names because the Continental word somta, which sounded exactly like Saamta, meant discards, as in litter, trash, or poo.

"Oh, right," said Kita. "Sorry to remind you of that great misfortune."

Saamta Sio glared at her. "Apology accepted," she coolly said. Then, hesitating, she added, "We've saved some spots for Team 10ers. You can follow me, if you want."

"Can our friends come along?" I asked on behalf of Birgard and his friend.

Saamta Sio looked at them. "Sure," she said.

We sat on some groile in front of the sunset-facing benches, where we had a perfect view of the ocean and the violet glow of the sun, which slowly descended behind a medium-thick layer of clouds.

Though I had felt a brisk breeze on our backs when we climbed the hillside, the top of Sunset Peak was free from wind.

"Wind breaks," Pella explained when I asked about it. "All around the field, there's a material that channels the wind upward to the sky."

I squinted. "I don't see any material."

"It's invisible," Kita said.

"Amazing."

"It's the Age of the Invisible," Birgard told me. He explained that after clarkon was discovered, Luratia had entered what scientists called the Nano Age and what almost everyone else called the Invisible Age.

"Does nano mean invisible?" I asked him.

"No, it means one-billionth," he said.

I wanted to ask what a one-billionth was, but Saamta Sio was near, and I didn't want to embarrass myself again.

A water drone passed by, Pella hailed it, and we all got an invisible bag of water that could be eaten after it was drunk dry. The water was good, but the bag didn't taste like anything to me.

"It's a subtle flavor," Pella said.

"Much improved over the old casings," said Kita. "They tasted awful."

"Then why eat them?"

"They're seaweed with added nutrients."

"Oh right, those nutrient things," I said. I thought of everyone in Bree who knew nothing of nutrients and who had never seen a real sunset. "In Bree, the sun sets over some high hills, not the sea."

"That means you have longer days here," Birgard said. "More hours of sunlight."

"You're right," I said. "That's true."

"Am I the only one who feels like we're sitting on top of the world?" Nin asked.

"No," we agreed. We all felt like we were sitting on top of the world.

The sunglow slowly disappeared beneath the ocean, casting vibrant pinks and violet colors across the clouds above and behind us. It was one of the most beautiful sights I had ever seen.

And our long day of fun and adventure ended with an ocean sunset, the first I'd ever seen. The first of many — hundreds, maybe. I was a resident of Vona now. This was my home.

## 16 LINDRI

"So, how is it?" Mira asked when I called to tell her about the Gen 8.

"It's like not wearing a holophone at all," I said. "Because you're not. That's the best thing about it."

"What's it like putting that film in your eyes?"

"Not easy, but better the second time I did it." I shook my head in disbelief. "You won't believe how much *better* you can see with this slimy piece of film."

"Slimy?"

"As slimy as wet seaweed," I said.

"I don't understand how you can see better with it."

"More detail, brighter color, more visual depth, more real."

"What's a visual depth?"

"It means making the close parts look closer and the far parts look farther away."

"Oh ... well," she said, "I'm really happy for you. Supremely happy, as you'd say."

"It's funny, I don't say supremely very much anymore. Or fearless. I'm really changing, Mira, it's strange."

"What'd you expect? You've been there almost a month."

"I guess you're right. Anyway, I have a new word now. Greatness."

"Greatness?"

"Right, greatness. It comes from Morning Strengths and Postures. Every morning Elda says, 'Stand tall and strong, there is greatness in you!' She says it fiercely like that, like it's already true."

"There is greatness in you," Mira said, quiet and thoughtful. "I like it."

"I love Morning Strengths and Postures. You should talk to your father into making the teachers do it at school every morning."

"I don't think it works like that," Mira said. "He's a director, not a dictator. And even if he were, I don't know ... I think a lot of kids here would think it's goofy."

"Maybe so. Maybe they're better to do at the Evolutionaries meetings."

"Some of the kids who'd think it's goofy *are* Evolutionaries."

I saw that that would be a problem, so I abandoned the idea.

"Well," Mira said, "are you going to talk to Merchant Kam about getting Gen 8s for Bree?"

"I don't think the people of Bree are ready for Gen 8s," I said. "No offense."

"I'm not offended. But I'm surprised you said that. You love progress more than anyone I know."

"True, but some kinds of progress aren't right for Bree."

"Why's the Gen 8 not right?"

"First," I said, "the eye film would be a problem, don't you think? Look how much trouble I had learning how to put it in. It's like poking yourself in the eye. Then there's the earbud. You've got two of those, and they just sit in your ear. Losing them is a big problem, even for adults. Everyone would be losing them constantly, especially the kids, and think about how annoying that would be to all the parents."

"Right," Mira nodded.

"And then, I think the Gen 8 would be way too complicated for everyone, even the smart ones, which aren't very many, I'm finding out."

Mira snorted a laugh. "It's just now dawning on you that Breeans aren't the smartest people in the world?"

"So you think so too."

"Without you here," she said, "I feel like I'm suffocating in ignorance and lack of imagination. You know whose becoming my closest friend?"

"Who?"

"Hali."

"That's good," I said. "I've always liked Hali. And he *is* the smartest kid in Bree."

Mira made a kind face of sadness. "He hates that he's not growing yet. He thinks he'll always be short and spindly. I told him the other day how I feel about my bent ear and that there's more to who we are than what we look like. I think that helped him feel better about it."

"Tell him if he doesn't grow, he can always get a growth stimulant implant. The Medical Center on the Embassy Island would give it to him free since Bree's an impoverished region."

"Growth *what*?"

"Growth stimulant implant," I said. "I'll grid you some info on it."

"Grid some info?"

"It's a saying. It means I'll do the research and send it to you."

"Oh. So, tell me one interesting thing about the Gen 8. Something I can understand."

"Well," I thought, "there's the 8-Brain Interface. Eight means Gen 8, brain means brain, obviously, and interface means your brain can communicate directly back and forth with your Gen 8, which means your Gen 8 knows what you're thinking. It even knows what you want."

"Really? Isn't that ... I don't know, creepy?"

"It's not creepy," I said, "it's efficient. Things get done for you. All you have to do is think a thing and it happens."

"That sounds worse. Dangerous, actually. Think about all the stupid things kids think about. Like revenge."

"No, it doesn't work like that. Gen 8s aren't magic. They can't do everything. You program them to do certain things. In your house, mostly. Your Gen 8 is wired to your brain and to your house Central Control. If you're on your airlift on your way home after dark, your house knows when you're almost there and turns on all the lights on your airpad and in your house too."

"You're right," Mira said, "the people of Bree aren't ready for Gen 8s. I don't think they'll ever be."

"It's tragic, really, you're missing out on so much."

"Did it hurt, getting your brain wired?"

"Oh, that's just an expression. They don't put wires in your brain, just a little implant, right under the skin behind your ears. I won't get an implant until I get a Gen 8 of my own."

Mira shuddered, so I thought of other news to share.

"I saw that adibadi again," I said.

"Where?"

"In the tree park where the shops are. He recognized me. And we talked in his language."

"Really?"

"Really. It was so great. He said he likes me."

Mira smiled.

"And he really does," I said. "My friend Birgard said that adibadis are bred and trained to be honest."

"Birgard? I've heard that name before."

"Remember the boy who annoyed me when our sub-orbital was landing on Vona that first day?"

"That's Birgard? I thought you hated him."

"I know, I did for a while, but it turns out he's a nice person. His mother died two years before mine."

"That's a strange coincidence," Mira said. "How did she die?"

"In an explosion at the factory where she worked."

"How awful."

"Birgard said that at least it was painless."

"I'm glad you have a friend who knows what it's like not to have a mother."

"I think he's going to be a good friend," I said. "He speaks Culti slower than anyone. You have no idea how great that is."

"Speaking of Culti," Mira said, "I decided to get serious about learning it, the grammar and everything. I don't want to rely on my holophone to translate my writing from Welbi to Culti. The translations aren't perfect, you know. And if I'm going to interview people, I want to interview them without wearing a Generation One, since it's a total relic and could ruin my professional reputation."

"I understand what you mean, Mira. You want to be known for your great writing, not for being an oddity."

"Exactly," she smiled. "So, I was thinking, maybe you and I could talk in Culti some of the time, when I'm ready."

"That's a great idea," I said in Culti, slow and clear. Then I asked in Welbi, "Did you know what I said?"

"You said, great idea that is."

"Right, maybe you're more ready than you think you are. And I love your idea. It would mean a lot to me to help you with your Culti so you can be a great writer, which I know you will. You're as smart as a lot of my schoolmates."

"That's a nice thing to say."

"It's more than nice," I said. "It's true. And if it weren't true, I wouldn't have said it."

"Your mother used to say that."

"I know. I'm trying to be like her. And I'm trying to be good and kind like the Continentals. It's so easy for them."

"Why do you think?" Mira asked.

"Best I can tell, it's because they're around kindness all the time. Not so much here at the school, but on the Continent, where they grow up. Remember how Elder Evig used to say that love and joy are infectious?"

"He still says it," Mira said, "not that it does much good."

We laughed a short laugh, sad for the truth of it.

"You really have to be around it to know," I said, "but when people work together and everyone's nice and kind and helpful, it's a good feeling. A really good feeling, and you just want more of it."

"That makes sense," Mira nodded. "My parents are nice."

"Right. So you know what it's like. And the more you feel good from other people being nice, the more you want to be nice, and the easier it is. I think after a while it just comes naturally. That's why you're naturally nice. You're patient and respectful and you never hit a boy a day in your life."

Mira grinned. "And you probably won't ever again."

"Not as long as I'm here. Put me back in Bree, though, and who knows? I still get mad at least once a day."

"But you stopped hating Birgard."

"I did," I said. "That's progress. Oh, guess what? I saw an ocean sunset. I've never seen anything so incredibly beautiful. I'm going to send you a video of it. You should get everyone together in the Pavillion some night and project it as big as you can."

"I will," Mira said. "They'd like that. Speaking of the Pavillion, I've been talking to everyone who misses you and they all like my idea of a group holophone call. We could do it one Adri a month, right after Elder Evig's service, here in the Pavillion."

"I'd love it," I said. "That would be early morning for me. And the most people would show up if it were right after service. That's always when we got the most petition signatures."

"How about next Adri then?"

"That'd be good."

"I'll get the word out," Mira said, "and I'll ask Elder Evig to announce it at service."

The next Adri morning I woke early, drank a breakfast drink Mrs. Tria left for me — the sweet kind that was the color of wistberries — and walked to the nearest groile field that had a sunrise view. I had hoped for some pure sky, even a small patch, but a thin veil of clouds stretched across the entire sky, which was typical in the early morning. Still, the sunrise was beautiful, everyone said, almost as beautiful as the video of the pure sky sunset, which Mira showed them while they waited for my call.

When Mira and I connected on our Gen Ones, she projected the contents of her holophone's eyescreen so that everyone could see me. Then she aimed her video eye in their direction so I could see them. Then she turned her holophone's mic volume all the way up, allowing me to hear their voices. With a Gen 8, all of that would have been easier and sounded better and looked more real, but Bree would never have Gen 8s, not in my lifetime, so I put up with the primitive technology. I was with my friends and neighbors, and that mattered more. So much more.

I said I missed them so many times, Mira later told me that they actually believed that I hadn't forgotten them and never would. They liked hearing my stories and seeing all the things I showed them — the transport drones flying overhead, the unusual thinness of the clouds, the roundness of the buildings, the tall pointed upside-down cone of the Assembly Hall, the blue and magenta dew-kissed groile, and the ocean, which was so much wider than the sea.

When I saw that father wasn't there, my heart broke, but only a little. I sensed what I thought was his reason. As much as he was a big storytelling personality that loved standing before a crowd, he was a private man in some ways, and one of those ways was me.

Everyone was stunned that I had befriended an adibadi and talked to him in his own language, so Mira said she would show them the video that Birgard had taken of us. Before we all said goodbye, we agreed to talk again, on the third Adri of every month, a day that became known as Lindri.

## 17 GOOD NEWS AND GROILE

The day after we returned from our camping expedition, Aunt Tala called with good news.

"Kam wants to talk to you," she said. "Something about groile."

My great state of happiness turned to total joy.

"I knew he'd come through," I said, my tail thumping wildly, a habit I hadn't completely rooted out. "Did you know, Aunt Tala, that kids all over the world thump their tails? Elda said it's a universal tendency. You can mention that to father some time if you'd like."

"We'll see," she said. "How was your expedition?"

"The most fun I've ever had. You wouldn't believe the clouds we saw. Thin wispy ones that you can see right through. They call them gossamer types. If you don't know what gossamer means, it means thin and wispy. Did you know that cloud scientists have named 33 different cloud types? Amazing, isn't it?"

"It is," she said, "given that we have only four. Tell me about the expedition."

"We stayed together with our teams, so we'd get to know each other better and learn how to get along and each day we explored a part of the island and taught the team something that we knew well. I liked it all, the exploring and the teaching. We'd sit in a circle on some groile or sand, and each of us stood and talked about a topic of our choice. One day I talked about life in Bree. You should have heard them laugh, and it wasn't mean laughter, Aunt Tala, it was funny laughter. Everyone thinks Bree's a pretty unusual place. I keep learning how much that's true."

Aunt Tala was smiling. "Unusual, yes," she said.

"Then another day I talked about clarkon, and yesterday I talked about progress."

"Progress?"

"They wanted to hear more about the Committee of No Technology and the naysayers, and it turned into a lesson about responsible progress. I can't wait to tell Merchant Kam. It was his ideas I talked about ... you know, when he says that progress that happens too fast can be dangerous."

"I'm glad to hear that, Lin, and I'm sure he will too." Aunt Tala shook her head, grinning as she did. "Speaking of the Committee of Technology," she said, "they're not happy about those super-sweet candies you sent."

"They're called flavor pellets," I said.

"I've been asked to tell you not to send any more."

"Why? They're just flavor."

"I know, I know. But the parents are upset about it. They say it's unnatural and it will spoil their children for sweets."

"Actually," I said, "the flavor *is* natural. It's highly concentrated in nanoparticles that coat every part of the inside of your mouth. Regular flavor just sits in a few places in big fat molecules."

"That's an impressive bit of knowledge, Lin. But you know that won't convince them."

"You're probably right, but this might. After you've had one, you don't want another for a long time. There's a special chemical in them that makes the brain adverse to anything sweet."

"Averse."

"Right. Isn't that clever? They call it built-in addiction prevention."

Aunt Tala smiled that flat smile of hers, where the line of her mouth goes straight across. "Don't send anymore, not until further notice," she said. "And be careful about anything else you send. The new mail clerk has been told to set aside all packages from Vona for inspection."

"Inspection?"

"Yes."

"By the Committee of No Technology?"

"Yes, so be wise."

"All right," I said.

"I'm sorry about all that."

"Thanks, Aunt Tala. Thanks for saying that. Anyway, I love my clarkon dome. You can sleep outside all night and no animals can harm you. It can be raining and lightning, and you can see it all and you're safe inside. What a great invention. I love inventions. Maybe I should be an inventor."

"Hmmm," she nodded, smiling and happy.

"You're in a good mood today," I said. "Did something great happen?"

"No, I'm just glad to see you. I miss you. And I just spoke with the school," she said. "Your proficiency scores need improvement, but other than that, they say you're doing extraordinarily well in every way, given your inherent disadvantages."

"Disadvantages?"

"Being from a rural community and having learned Culti so late in your life."

"I'm not using my instantaneous translator very much," I said.

"I know."

"You know?"

"Counselor Doi told me."

"How does she know?"

"By the sensor chip in your ear."

"I don't understand," I said. "How can—?"

"Your sensor detects certain types of holophone activity."

"Like if I'm in Flight Mode or talking to someone? It knows what I'm doing?"

"Yes, it was stated in the paperwork. You don't remember?"

"I remember that the sensor knows where I am and that it's always reading my vital signs," I said. "But I don't remember anything else."

"Well, I did read it to you."

"I must have forgot. I'm forgetting a lot of things," I said. "There's so much new stuff to remember. Every day, it never ends. Sometimes I think my head's going to explode. But at least they think I'm doing well."

"Extraordinarily well."

I hoped that wasn't because their expectations were low to begin with.

"On Adri we're going to the Complex and the shops," I said.

Aunt Tala laughed. "Your father wanted to know what a Complex is."

"Did you tell him?"

"Yes, not that it made any sense to him."

"And what about the Gen 8?"

"I'll bring it up at dinner tonight," Aunt Tala said. "Kam will be over, and I'll tell your father about how well you're doing in school."

"Thanks, Aunt Tala, you're the best. You want me to have it, don't you, a Gen 8?"

"Yes, Lin, I do. A lot of your learning will be done on your holophone, and it would be good for you to have updated equipment, especially considering your innate disadvantages."

My tail thumped the floor, happy for the fact that she and Merchant Kam were going to work together at convincing father and with some reasons he could hardly reject.

Since the hour in Bree wasn't late, I called Merchant Kam after Aunt Tala and I said goodbye. He had good news too. Bad news and good news. He told me the bad news first, as it always should be done.

"I spoke to an old friend who's an agriculturist," he said, "and groile won't grow in Bree. However, he suggested we consider synthetic groile, which will tolerate any climate conditions."

"What's a synthetic?" I asked.

"It's not a thing," he said. "It's a *type* of thing. It's a man-made fabrication of a natural substance."

"So it's pretend groile?"

"Yes, pretend groile, you could say. But it looks real and functions just as well. And it will never die."

"That's *great* news, Merchant Kam."

"Now, it has to pass the Committee of Technology first, but don't lose hope. I spoke to a few of its members recently, and they're not against the idea. I'm sensing in some of them an attitude of greater leniency. They've taken note of the overwhelming response to the teachers' petition to use holophones in their teaching. The measure was just adopted by the School Council."

"Aunt Tala just told me. It's a day of good news. I wish mother could have lived to see this," I said. "She would have loved holophones, don't you think?"

"More than any other teacher, I imagine."

To stop the sadness that the thought of mother was making, I told

Merchant Kam about our three-day expedition. He was pleased to hear how I taught my modern schoolmates something about progress and using his own wisdom, which he said I had assimilated quite well.

"You have broadened their perspective by sharing with them your life experience," he told me.

"I don't think I know what you mean."

"Think about the fact that you have lived a life without any of the fundamental technologies that they grew up with and take for granted. Your manner of living is as new and different to them as their ways of living are to you. Remember this whenever you feel inadequate about being a simple girl from a small village. You have much to offer them, Lin, and just by being yourself."

"Thanks, Merchant Kam. That really helps."

I didn't know how he knew that I felt inadequate. Maybe I had told him and forgotten. Maybe he knew because he felt inadequate when he was here as a first year student from a backward village. Or maybe my ear sensor was recording all my thoughts and all my speech and transmitting them to Merchant Kam and Aunt Tala and father and—.

*No,* I thought, *that's just plain superstition.* Or, to be exact about it, *paranoia,* a word I learned from Pella during our camping expedition when we were walking under an especially thick cloud of airtrams and transport drones.

"Merchant Kam," I thought to ask before saying goodbye, "what was your Vocational Track when you were a student here?"

"Economics," he said.

"You studied money?"

"I studied the history of economic growth and development."

"And what is that, exactly?"

"It means that over time, the prosperity of a region or a country or a city changes due to many different reasons. Economics attempts to understand these reasons."

"It sounds complicated," I said.

"It is, yes."

"But you're in Bree. After all this education, you went to Bree."

"There was need in Bree."

"Need?" I asked. "Need for what?"

"The maintenance of the flow of goods going in and out of Bree, which is essential to the economy of any community, especially one that is small and remote."

"Remote," I said. "Far away from the rest of the world."

"Far from trade routes, yes."

"Thanks in advance for talking to my father about me getting a Gen 8," I said. "I hope he says yes without a fuss."

"You're welcome, Lin, and I hope so too."

Two days later I spoke to Mira. I had two pieces of news — one good and one great. I gave her the good news first.

"I'm going tomorrow to see my adibadi friend. I'm thinking about becoming an adibadi trainer."

"I see it now," Mira said, "your next Bree improvement project. Importing adibadis to Bree."

"That's not a bad idea, Mira. You laugh," I said, "but I'm half serious. And maybe more serious than that. Bree could use some adibadis. They mostly work outdoors doing things that robots don't do so well. They could clean the beach and repair nets. They could probably fish if you trained them."

"Your father could retire."

"Wouldn't that be great?"

"Adibadis in Bree? Yes, that *would* be great," Mira said.

"I saved the best news for last. It's not technically news yet, but I'm optimistic."

"What?"

"Bree might be getting some groile."

"I thought groile didn't—" Mira held up her hand to quiet me.

"What?" I asked.

"My mother just called me for dinner," she said. "I've got to go."

"Don't tell anyone about the groile. I'll fill you in on the details later."

"I won't mention a word. And don't forget it's Lindri tomorrow."

"Lindri," I laughed. "I like it. I'll talk to you then. And make sure Bissa's there."

"All right. Can't wait. Love you, Lin."

"Love you, Mir."

## 18 How Happy Could I Ever Be?

The next morning 42 Breeans and some curious tourists were waiting for my call at Bree Pavillion.

Father wasn't among them, for the same reason he didn't show up the time before. He wanted to talk privately, just him and me, the two of us. He called me later in the day while I was traveling the world on a Gen 8 demo model at the gadget shop. I discovered his video message as we walked to the World Café for a late lunch. I set my Generation One's eyescreen to 50% opacity so I could see father and walk at the same time. This wasn't easy to do, to look at two realities at the same time, one of them real and necessary to see, the other unnecessary to see but of greater interest.

"Lin," he said, "this is your father." He was standing on the front steps of our rickety wood house in the fishing quarters, and he was smiling. "I've been told you were a big hit this morning at the Pavillion. We're all so proud of you. The tourists are keeping us busy, and Bree's flush with them. There's talk of opening up another place of lodging. Isn't that something?" He cleared his throat. "Your aunt tells me you think you want to be an animal trainer. Not sure what kind of need we have for that around here, but the animal sentinels sure have been testy lately. They failed to predict an unseasonal storm that snuck up fast last week and hit us hard. They slept until the storm'd already reached us. That's raising some concern, of course." Father paused and looked to the ground. "I miss your smile," he said, looking up again. "I miss you. You make me proud, Lin. Very proud. Call when you can." He smiled and said, "I love you, Lin." And then he vanished.

*He loves me.* I was sure I only thought the words, but I had said them out loud.

"Who is 'he'?" Pella asked me.

"He?"

"You said, 'he loves me'. Who is he?"

"Oh, my father," I said. "He called me while we were in the shop. He left the sweetest message."

"Care to share it?" Pella asked. "I'd really like to see him."

"Sure," I said, "I don't see why not."

"Hey," Pella turned and told our friends, "let's go see Lin's father!"

We ducked into a tree-lined alcove not far from where I had first seen my adibadi friend. I projected my father's video message into the empty space before us.

Kita was the first to speak after he disappeared from view.

"He's so handsome," she said.

"And strong," said Pella.

Nin agreed.

"My mother was as beautiful as he is handsome," I told them. "And as smart as he is strong."

"Now we know where you get your great genes," Birgard said.

I hid a smile as I pretended not to hear him.

"What's an animal sentinel?" Kita asked.

"In Bree," I said, "we have a pen of timmins near the center of town. They're darling little animals with big wide eyes and teeth that chatter when they're afraid. Somehow they know when bad weather's coming because they always get nervous before a storm. When a storm's brewing, even if it's really far away, the timmins get jumpy. Some run in a frenzy along the edges of the pen looking for shelter. And that's how people in Bree have been getting weather forecasts for as long as there have been people in Bree."

We laughed as we continued walking, I as much as anyone. From a distance, Bree was hilariously strange, a place that didn't belong in the modern world, which every day felt more like home to me.

When our laughter trailed off, Kita asked me a serious question. "So your father thinks that after all this schooling, you're going to go back to Bree and live a Bree life?"

I had never thought about that, but now that I did, it hit me hard.

"I suppose he does," I said, shocked and stunned, my ears filling with a thick, dull nothing of a noise that drowned out all the sound around me.

Two questions pulled at me, horrible questions that had no easy answer and wouldn't stop asking themselves. If I don't live in Bree after graduation, where would I live? And if I do live in Bree, how happy could I ever be there?

My gut hurt and my mind spun and I slipped into a dizzy daze that made me forget to look for my adi friend as we passed through the tree park.

"Lin," said someone near and loud. The voice snapped me out of my nightmare daydream. "Lin, did you hear me?" It was Birgard.

"No," I said. "No, I don't think so."

"I said the adibadi's not here today. But if you want to, we can come look for him after lunch."

"Oh, I'd like that." I shook my head to wake myself.

"Are you all right?" Birgard asked.

"I'm ... I'm fine."

"That wasn't very convincing."

"Really, no, I'm fine." That's when I noticed we were far behind the others. "Why is everyone so far ahead?"

"Because they're walking faster than you," Birgard said.

"Oh."

"If something's wrong," he said, "you can tell me. Maybe I can help."

"I ...." I couldn't think. I couldn't speak. I was still half-dazed. "I don't ... I'm not ...."

"I'm a trustworthy friend," he said in a chipper voice.

I knew he was trying to cheer me up and somehow that made my mind work better.

"I'll tell you quick," I said. "Just to get it off my mind. But I don't want to talk about it at lunch. Promise you won't tell anyone."

"I won't tell anyone. Ever, if you want."

"I don't know what to do after we graduate," I said.

"Well, if it helps, I don't either. I only think a few of us do. Six years is a long way away."

"I know that," I said, "but it's different for me."

"Different how?"

108

"Bree. You know what Bree's like, at least a little. If I go back to live in Bree after traveling the world, I think it'll be a life of total misery."

"Oh, right," Birgard said with a sympathetic look.

"And if I don't live in Bree, where will I live?"

"I suppose you could live anywhere. Are you worried that you'll pick the wrong place?"

"I'm worried because ... I'm worried for a lot of reasons. If I don't live in Bree, then I'm going to miss everyone I love there for the rest of my life. And it might really hurt my father's feelings. He has no wife and no other children. I worry that if I'm not there he'll be lonely all his life. And I worry that he'll be mad at me if I don't come back to Bree. And right, I guess I am afraid that I'll pick the wrong place. I'm realizing all this now, for the first time. I can't believe I never thought of this."

"Maybe you don't need to think about it. And maybe you shouldn't. It's obviously upsetting you. And what good will it do to try to figure these things out now? There's so much you don't know yet. There's so much that's going to happen in six years that will change everything."

"That will change everything," I said, heartened by the words. "I think you're right, Birgard. I think you're right. Thanks. I actually feel better."

"Glad to help, scholar of Bree."

We picked up our pace and found our friends, who had joined some others and whose laughter we heard when we entered the World Café.

After lunch we parted ways, some going to the beach and some back to the shops. Birgard hadn't forgotten his promise to go looking for the adibadi with me, so we left our friends and headed for the tree park. As we walked, I asked him about his family.

"I have a younger sister," he said. "She was born when I was four."

"Do you get along?"

"We sort of adore each other," he said. "She's bright and funny. Her name is Ingla but we call her Sunshine."

"That's a great nickname."

"It is, isn't it?"

"Do you have one?"

"A nickname? No. My father calls me Gard, but it doesn't mean anything. It's just an abbreviation."

"What's an abbreviation?"

"When you shorten a word."

"Oh, Gard, in place of Birgard."

"Right."

"Does your father miss your mother?"

"Yes," he said, "but probably not as much as your father does."

"Why do you say that?"

"Because my mother died longer ago, and because my father remarried."

"How do you like your father's new wife?" I asked.

"She's great. I liked her from the beginning. I think because she was so good with Sunshine. They love each other, in a real way, like a mother and daughter."

"I'm really happy for her, for them. Insanely jealous and really happy. I'm trying to get my father remarried, but it won't be so easy now that I'm here."

"You're *trying* to?"

"I'm *going* to try," I said. "There's this woman, a wedding planner. She brings people down to Bree to get married on father's boat."

"On his boat?"

"Yes, they think it's quaint. Some people don't want to get married the ordinary way. They want something special. And this wedding planner arranges special weddings. Anyway, she lives in a big city in Similon, but she hates the city. She likes Bree, and I think she likes my father. And he always smiles when he talks about her. I think there's something there."

"Maybe so," Bigard said. "I hope so. I hope it works out for them. And it's good you want your father to marry again and not let your love for your mother get in the way of that. It can, you know."

"I guess so. I miss mother terribly. I thought after all this time, I'd miss her less, but I don't. I think about her every day, every night, every morning. I even dream about her sometimes."

"Good dreams?"

"It's a mix," I said. "Some are good, some are nightmares."

"Nightmares?"

"She's drowning."

"That must be so hard," he said with the right amount of sadness.

"Thanks, it is. But I don't have as many nightmares as I used to. Less than one a week."

"That seems like a lot."

"Really? How many nightmares do you have?"

Birgard thought about it. "Three, maybe four that I can remember."

"In how long?"

"In my whole life."

"That's hardly any at all." I shook my head, happy for him, sad for me. "Were they about your mother?"

"They were," he said. "They all were."

"How did you make them stop?"

"I don't know. I didn't try to make them stop."

"Now I'm jealous of *you*," I laughed.

"You might not be so jealous if you knew ... hey, look who's here," Birgard said, pointing to an adibadi in the distance.

"It's him!"

But it wasn't him. He had no scar under his right eye, and he didn't remember me. And he was a her. Birgard said you could tell by the blonde tuft of hair between her ears.

"She's so pretty," I said.

"Then you should tell her."

"There's a word in adi for pretty?"

"There is."

Birgard taught me more of the adi language, and I made a new adi friend, who I named Lana, after my mother.

Talking and laughing and playing with Lana was the most fun I'd had all day, more fun than being on the Gen 8 and even more fun than talking to my friends in Bree.

As I thought about that in bed that night, and after silently talking it over with mother, I was more convinced than ever that I wanted to be an adibadi trainer.

## 19  FATHER DECIDES

"Want to go groile sliding?" Pella asked when school was done for the day. "A bunch of us—"

"No," I said, "I'm going to call my father."

Kita showed up. "Well, go with us," she said. "You can call him from there and then slide when you're done."

"I'm calling him from Sunset Peak," I said. "So I can show him the ocean."

"We're going to the North Shore," said Kita. "There's ocean there."

"No, I want to show him the *whole* ocean, 360 degrees."

Kita nodded. "Who are you going to Sunset Peak with?"

"No one," I said.

"Sounds lonely."

"I don't want to be distracted. Talking to father isn't the easiest thing," I said.

"You do know that Sunset Peak's a half an hour from here on foot," Kita told me.

"It's about twenty minutes, actually," said Novi, who stood nearby.

"Still," said Nin, "it's aways away."

Kita asked, "And what if you get there and your father doesn't answer?"

"You're bent on convincing me," I said to her.

"I'm bent on *protecting* you."

"Protecting me from what?"

"A lack of fun. You've been so serious today."

"It's true," Pella said.

"I've been preoccupied," I told them.

"Whatever it is," Nin said, "maybe we can help."

I scanned the faces of my friends, and thought it all over. I didn't want to be alone. I didn't want to walk twenty minutes just to leave a video message, and then miss out on groile sliding on top of it. The North Shore was the opposite direction of Sunset Peak.

"If I go with you," I finally said, "promise to give me peace and quiet while I'm talking to father. If you want to protect me, that's how you can do it."

"Agreed," said Kita, who took me by the hand. "Let's go, everyone!"

In fifteen minutes, we were at the North Shore. I stood under the tall, sweeping branches of a swykaff tree, far enough from my friends not to be bothered by them, but close enough to feel that I wasn't alone. I took a deep breath and called father.

He smiled when he saw me.

"Father, it's Lin!"

"You chose a good time to call," he said. "Just closed up the Boat Rental. My workday's done."

"I found a beautiful spot to call you from," I said, spanning the horizon through my holophone's video eye. "They call this the North Shore. We go groile sliding here. Do you see my friends?"

"Yes," he said. "And look at the size of those waves, will you."

"These are ocean waves. Next time I call I'm going to stand on the highest spot on the island and show you the ocean in all directions."

"I'd like that, Lin." Father sat down on the edge of the Second Pier, where tourists gathered day after day to rent boats and listen to his exaggerated real-life stories. "Your aunt says you're doing well in school and with the Trias."

"I guess I am," I said. "My proficiency scores weren't so great compared to my schoolmates, but Elda said that's because they had a different education than me. And my Culti's getting better every day. Mr. Tria said I'm a natural at languages, and that's saying a lot, because he's a linguist."

"A linguist?"

"He studies languages. He speaks eight different languages, one of them Welbi."

Father raised his eyes and shifted his leg.

"I'm giving a big talk at the end of the week," I said. "And then another in three weeks."

"Are you," he nodded. "And what are you talking about?"

"The first is on medicine."

"Medicine," he said.

"I interviewed a doctor and some nurses at the Medical Center, the one where I went when I broke my arm. They were really nice. It's a good profession, but it's not for me."

"Just as well," father said. "Bree already has a doctor as it is."

"Right, well … after that, I'm giving a talk on food science."

"Food science?"

"More precisely, food science as a vocation."

"I see," he said, though I knew he didn't.

"I don't know much more about it than you do, not yet," I said. "Next week we're going to the Food Sciences Lab. A lab is a place where scientists experiment and invent things. Food scientists make food better."

"Well, how food can be improved on, I don't know. I think nature has done its work quite well."

"Pella said she's going to record my talk. I'll send you the video, and you can learn what I find out."

"I'd like that, Lin."

"It's a big audience," I said. "The entire first year class will be there and all the teachers and some others, I don't know who. I'm getting nervous. Maybe you have some advice."

Father smiled and took in such a large breath of air, his chest rose and he grew taller. "Advice," he nodded, squinting to collect his thoughts. Then he rattled off some of the best advice he'd ever given me. "Look for the friendly faces in the crowd and let your eyes linger on them a half minute or so before looking for the next friendly face. Pass on by the unfriendly ones and reason when you see them that they're having a bad day. Practice as much as you can and keep your sentences simple. Your audience will enjoy your talk better if you don't make them work too hard at understanding it. And wherever you can, add some humor, as much as you can without overdoing it. Try to get them laughing with your opening line. A humorous opening will get you off on the right footing every time."

"Thanks, father. I feel less nervous already. I'm going to do everything you said."

Father smiled at me, pleased and proud. This was it, the perfect moment to ask.

"Thanks for giving permission for me to try out the Gen 8 holophone," I said. "I was on it again yesterday at the gadget shop. It can do so many things that will help me with my schoolwork. And you know how disadvantaged I am, being from the schools of Bree. Not that they're bad, they just don't teach as much current material as the schools in Northern Wershonia. Nin's getting a Gen 8, and almost everyone else has one. And my Generation One is totally outdated. There's a huge difference between the one and the eight. I don't want to be disadvantaged by that too. And so ...." Father was smiling so widely, I lost my concentration. In the silence, I choked up. I couldn't ask. I couldn't just straight out ask.

"I've already decided," he said. He was quiet for a long space of time, half-squinting, half-nodding, impossible to read.

My heart raced, my tail twitched.

Then he said, soft and kind, "Your aunt and Kam made it clear to me that it would do you well to have a number eight."

"So, yes? You're saying yes?"

"I'm saying yes."

"Father, you've made me so happy! So, so happy!"

"I'm happy you're happy," he said. When I calmed down, he surprised me more. "Kam said you should have one of those sheets too."

"A data sheet?"

"Yes."

"Really?"

"Yes."

"Thank you, father. Thank you for letting me be here. Thank you for everything."

"You're welcome, Lin," he said, his eyes filling with tiny tears. "Not a day goes by that I don't regret the decision, and not a day goes by that I don't miss you terribly."

"But we have holophones and can be with each other this way."

"That's true."

"See? Technology can be a great thing."

Father nodded, but said nothing.

"I heard someone got married on your boat," I said.

"Yes, and we have another wedding in a few days and more later in the season."

"She's nice, the wedding lady."

"Wedding planner."

"She's very nice. I've always liked her."

Father smiled. "She arrives in two days."

"I have a friend," I said. "His name is Birgard. He's from Algalon. His mother died when he was eight."

"Mmm."

"She died in an explosion — you know, suddenly, like mother. Anyway, it's been great to talk to him about it. To have a friend who really understands what it's like."

"I'm glad to know that," father said.

"And guess what?"

"What?"

"His father remarried three years ago. To a really nice woman. They're very happy together. Very happy."

"That's good," father said.

I searched for the next right words, letting an awkward silence pass as I fidgeted with my trinketless tail.

"Lin, is there something you're trying get at through the back door?"

"Well, it makes me wonder if you'll ever get remarried."

"Ah, no woman in Bree would put up with me."

"But the wedding planner."

"I hardly know her."

"But you like her," I said. "And she likes you."

"We do business together. Nothing more."

"But she doesn't like the city. Maybe she would be happy in Bree. She's been there at least ten times."

"All for business and nothing more."

"Well," I said. "Will you at least think about it?"

"About marrying a woman I hardly know?"

"About marrying a woman who you like and who likes you."

"Marriage is not a simple matter, Lin. It's far more than liking someone."

"But liking each other is a crucial foundation. That's what the Trias said."

"Have you been talking to them about this?"

"No," I said. "I've only slightly mentioned it to Birgard. Only him. That's all. It's true."

Father tried to hide a smile.

"What?" I said.

He shook his head.

"What?" I said. "What are you thinking?"

Father hesitated and then said, "It's good to know you're not against the idea."

"Of you getting married?"

"Yes."

"I'm not just *not* against the idea," I said. "I *want* you to. I think you'd be a lot happier. You have a lot of years to live, and I don't want you to be lonely."

"I understand."

"I'm really glad you're not against the idea, either," I said. "You're not, are you?"

"No," he said. "I'm not."

When father and I said goodbye, I called Mira.

"You won't believe the conversation I just had with father."

"Good or bad?"

"Good. Great. Supremely great. He was the nicest to me as he's ever been. *Really* nice. And he finally agreed—"

"He agreed to the Gen 8?" Mira asked, her whole face smiling, as if the good news was hers.

"Yes, how did you know?"

"Just a guess. I can't think of anything else that would make you this happy."

"Him getting married would make me happy. We talked about it. He's not opposed to the idea."

"Of getting married?"

"Yes. Maybe to the wedding planner."

"Oh," Mira smiled.

"Will you do me a favor and keep an eye on them? She's going to be there in a few days."

"What? You want me to spy on your father?"

"I want you to notice how they are with each other when you see them together."

"That sounds like spying."

"No," I said, "spying is sneaking around."

"I think technically you can spy without sneaking. It's about the motive. Watching someone without them knowing—"

"Well, what I'm asking, if it *is* a motive, it's not a bad one. It's for a good cause."

"What good cause?"

"My father's future happiness."

Mira laughed. "I can't believe we're having this conversation."

"I know," I said. "We never argue."

"I don't think it's arguing."

"Well ... then never mind I asked you." I tried to hide my disappointment, but it was difficult. All my elation had nearly disappeared.

"Sorry, Lin," Mira said. "That wasn't nice. You called with good news. And just so you know, I'll tell you whatever I notice between your father and the wedding planner."

"Thanks, Mira. You're the best. I was starting to feel sad, but I feel better now."

"Good. Well, I have some news that will make you feel even better."

"What?"

"We're going to get groile," she said. "The Committee of Technology approved it."

"I had a feeling all along they would. I'm so happy for you, for all of Bree."

"My father said he thinks they approved it because word got out, and all the tourists knew about it. He said that put extra pressure on them to do the right thing."

"Your father always loved technology," I said.

"He likes it more than most. I love him for that."

"I hope you get it soon, while the weather's still good. Maybe I should call Merchant Kam and find out."

"Maybe you should."

"And to thank him," I said. "He's the one who made this happen."

"You deserve a lot of thanks, too, Lin. This was your idea in the first place."

"I'm so unbelievably happy," I said. "And I don't even live there."

"That's because you care."

"I love Bree."

"I know."

"I think I always will."

"I'm sure of it," Mira said. "So, how's school these days?"

"It's starting to get hard. I have to give talks in front of a big audience two or three times a month."

"Every month?"

"Yes, they singled me out. Everyone has to give three big talks a year, but some have to give more. I'm one of them."

"Why?"

"Different reasons. For me, Elda said it's to improve my Culti. For one of the boys on my team, the shy one, it's to overcome his fear of public speaking."

"Oh, that makes sense," she said.

"Pia says that if something's hard for you, they make you do a lot of it, sooner or later."

"Ouch."

"I know, but it's good."

"The price you pay for an excellent education."

"Right." I shook my head. "I can't believe father said yes. It's still sinking in."

"You won't be Gen One Girl anymore."

"Probably not. I'll have gone through two nicknames in just a month."

"Maybe they'll just call you Lin after this."

"I guess that'd be all right."

"Where are you?"

"The North Shore," I said, "the best place on the island for groile sliding."

"It looks fun. I envy you."

"I haven't even been yet. I've been talking since I got here."

"Well, you should go. You can talk to me anytime."

"You're right. You're a good friend, Mira. You're a good person. I've always known it, but from a distance, I see it more."

"Thanks, Lin. That's a nice thing to say."

"If it weren't true, I wouldn't have said it."

"Your mother used to say that."

I smiled at the thought of her. "I know."

"I'm glad about your Gen 8," Mira said, "and I'm glad that you're there, even though I miss you every day."

"I miss you too, every day."

After we said goodbye, I took off my Generation One — grateful that in a week's time, I'd never have to wear it ever again — and joined my friends for some groile sliding and a joyful celebration of the greatest news I'd gotten since we first arrived five weeks ago.

A lot can happen in five weeks. Big things. Things that can change a girl's life forever.

# 20 THE LUCK OF LIFE

Elda glared at me for the sixth time since our tour of the Food Science Lab began and held up that many fingers. Six reprimands. Anyone who got more than ten in a day was sent to a counselor for some lecturing.

"I never thought I'd see a machine that makes food out of nothing," I had innocently whispered.

Though I hadn't meant it to be funny, forbidden laughter rose up around me.

On vocational expeditions like this one, we were allowed to use our holophones for essential, pre-approved purposes. I was permitted to use my new Gen 8 for translation since the scientist was a fast talker and used a great number of words I had never heard before. The Welbi language had no equivalent of many of those words, and my instantaneous translator fed me meaningless tones in their place. At times I heard more tones than actual words, and I couldn't help but laugh. That's what got me my first five reprimands.

At the end of the tour, we ate a lunch of fresh-made machine food in a spotless food-tasting room that echoed every spoken word. As much as we tried to behave ourselves, it wasn't the quiet lunch Elda had asked for. I'd never heard an echo before, and everyone else already knew the fun that echoes can be. In the end we agreed that the joy we had was worth every reprimand we got for it.

Mysteriously, mid-way through lunch, the reprimands stopped, though not from any improvement in our behavior.

While we waited outside for one of the farm techs to tour us around the vertical farms that grew on the west side of the island, Pella speculated that Elda was backing off on the discipline since so many of us were close to the ten-reprimand mark.

"Why would she do that?" I asked.

"To cut us a break," she said. "Pia told me they'll do that in the first year, especially on the vocational expeditions."

"Put a bunch of teenagers in a room that echoes," Kita said with her toothy grin, "and you're just asking for trouble."

"Teenagers," I said.

"Teenagers what?" said Pella.

"We're teenagers now."

Nin laughed. "You just now figured that out?"

"It just dawned on me for the first time," I said, "in a really real way. When I was younger, I couldn't wait to grow up."

"Well, I have great news for you," Pella said. "You're growing up every day."

"You're right," I said. "We all are."

"Some days a little, some days a lot," said Kita.

"And some more than others," I said, glancing over at Saamta Sio, who was holding court with the rest of Team 10.

Novi looked over at me and mouthed words I couldn't understand. I shrugged and shook my head. He left the half of Team 10 he usually spent time with and walked over to say, "Are you ready for tomorrow?"

"I'm ready," I said. "We're meeting tomorrow to talk about our personal goals," I told the girls.

Novi said to me, "Your talk yesterday was good. Really good."

"Thanks," I said. "I give credit to the doctor and nurses at the Medical Center. Interviewing them wasn't hard at all. I just asked questions, and they did all the talking. They all agreed with me that I don't have a future in medicine. So I've definitely ruled out one vocation. This is going a lot easier than I thought."

A friendly, smiling farm tech showed up and led us through a tidy maze of circular rows of spiral garden towers that seemed to touch the clouds when looking up from below.

Pella nudged me. "Look," she said. She pointed to an adibadi who stood mid-way up a nearby tower.

"I see an adibadi," I said to the farm tech. "Do they work here?"

"They do," he said.

"How many adis do you have here?" I asked.

"Between 25 and 30 on any given day," the farm tech said.

My jaw dropped open. "And where do they stay at night?"

"There are four abodes around the perimeter of the gardens."

"Can we see them?" I asked. "The abodes?"

"I'm sorry," he said. "I'm not permitted to do that."

Elda smiled at me. "Don't be disappointed, Lin. We're going to spend some time with adibadis at the Zoolology school."

"When's that?"

"About three months from now."

"Three months," I complained to Novi the next day. "I wish it was sooner."

"Well, if it helps," he said, "I have to wait two years for our Space Center expedition."

"I guess it does help, even though you've been there before."

Novi grinned, and in that moment, he seemed familiar. Like a brother or a friend I'd known most my life.

"So let's start with you," I said.

"My latest math score is up by two points," he said.

"Congratulations. If you keep that up every month, you're going to meet your goal."

"You're right."

"So, anything else?"

"No," he said, "I'm the simple one here, remember? I've already got my entire life figured out and my goal is completely uncomplicated."

"That was the most polite way anyone's ever made fun of me," I said.

He grinned again. "My mother taught me good manners."

"She did. It shows. You're a lot like the Continentals."

"When we lived at the Space Center," he said, "most of my friends were Continentals."

"How lucky for you."

"I feel lucky."

"You do?"

"I've had a better life than you," he said. "I don't mean that in a—"

"I know how you meant it."

"Good. And my life isn't better because of anything *I've* done. I was born into it."

"Really? You think so?"

"If I were born in Bree like you, I never would have lived at the Space Center, I'm sure of it."

"I'm sure of it too."

"That's why I admire you," he said. "Because of where you come from and where you are now."

"That's nice for you to say."

"It's true. Anyone would agree with me."

"Except Saamta Sio," I said. "She's never liked me."

"I kind of feel sorry for her."

"*Sorry* for her? Is that what you said?"

Novi nodded.

"Why?" I asked.

"Because her father's a big diplomat and her mother's a celebrity—"

"What kind of celebrity?"

"She was a famous singer. Not any more, but when Saamta was young, she was. Everyone knows her, all over the world. Saamta's parents met at a Delorian resort. He was an ambassador and she was a singer, and they met and fell in love."

"I didn't know any of that," I said. "But how can you feel sorry for her, a life like that?"

"Her life wasn't that great."

"Are you kidding me? She's lived a life of total privilege."

"With parents who ignored her," Novi said. "They gave her everything but their attention. When you saw pictures of Saamta, she was always with a different nanny."

"What's a nanny?"

"A girl who's hired to take care of kids."

"Saamta's parents didn't take care of her?"

"Not really. They were too busy."

"How do you know all of this?"

"From newspapers and the grid streams," Novi said. "Stories about Saamta's family are all over the grid. She has a younger brother who was always getting in trouble."

"So Saamta's famous too."

"Yes, but not in the best way. And what if she didn't want to be famous at all? She didn't have any choice."

"We don't choose who we're born to," I said.

"That's why I feel lucky."

"I understand now. And now that I know about her, I feel sorry for Saamta too."

"I don't think she's very happy," Novi said. "And I think she's trying to be a big person like her parents. It's a lot of pressure."

"Maybe I should start feeling lucky," I said. "My life could have been a lot worse than it is."

"Look at it this way. You're famous too, not as much as Saamta, but more than me, and what you're known for is pretty positive and inspiring."

"You think so?"

"I do."

"I want to be positive and inspiring," I said. "It's not always easy."

"My father says that it's more important what you're becoming, day after day, than what you are right now in time."

"That's great advice."

"My father loves giving advice. Fortunately, I agree with a lot of it."

"My father loves to give advice too," I said. "And unfortunately—" I stopped myself, choosing to go a better way. "His latest good advice was about talking in front of an audience."

"I guess he would be an authority on that."

"He would. He is."

Since he asked, I told Novi father's advice. He liked the humor part.

"Well," he said, "since we're on the subject, I'm ready to help you with your talk on food science."

"All right," I said, "I thought I would start with the line, 'Being from Bree, where we know nothing of food science, I never thought I'd see a machine that makes food out of nothing.'"

When Novi laughed, I knew it would be a good talk.

## 21 MY CERTAIN CALLING

The next day at Morning Circles, Saamta Sio caught me staring at her, not once or twice, but four times. She was angry or hurt by it, I couldn't tell which. Her indignant glares were hard to read.

I remembered being stared at my first days here, certain that the starers were judging me, silently laughing at me, thinking cruel thoughts about me. When Pella told me that some were just curious and some felt sorry for me for breaking my arm or for the great misfortune of having been born and raised in Bree, I didn't believe her. But I believed her now.

"We have a change in our learning plans today," Elda said after we finished our Morning Strengths and Postures.

"We're not doing the atom thing?" I asked. I'd been waiting days for this day, which Elda had described as going on a virtual 3D journey on our holophones deep inside an atom.

"No," Elda said. "Not today."

I groaned my disappointment. Gen 8s made any kind of learning fun, and I'd never seen an atom before.

"We're going to West Park to learn about the sun," said Elda. "There's a wide patch of pure sky today. So power on your holophones and follow me." She took one look outside and turned and said, "And turn on your sun filters. I see direct sunlight."

We bounded out of the Assembly Hall, shouting our happiness to be learning outside on a pure sky day. There wouldn't be many of them left. The storm season was coming.

Pella showed me how to turn on the sun filter of my eye film. "You can set it from one to ten," she said. "Ten lets you look directly at the sun."

I set it to ten and, for the first time in my life, I stared at the sun. *The* sun, with my own eyes. I couldn't wait to tell Mira.

"I saw the sun!" I said when I called her early the next morning. "My Gen 8 lets you look right at it. Right at it. The sun!"

"What does it look like?" she asked.

"A round glowing ball, just like it does when you go up the simulated space elevator."

"That's it?"

"Yes," I said. "It's not beautiful or anything. I guess what's so great about seeing the sun is that you're looking at the sun. But I wasn't disappointed."

"Did it hurt?" Mira asked.

"No, but it could if you look at it too long. There's a sun filter in my eye film. But even when you set it to the highest number, you still can't look at the sun for more than a minute. Your eyes would burn. So you look at it, look away, and look at it again. You just keep looking away and ... you get the idea."

"You're the only girl from Bree who's ever seen the sun with her own eyes."

"I'd video record it for you," I said, "but it wouldn't be the same as seeing it yourself."

"I'll see the sun someday," Mira smiled. "Somewhere. Somewhere north."

"Novi said that when you look at pure sky, you're looking at infinity."

"Infinity?"

"Yes, you're looking at space, and space is infinite in all directions."

"Really?"

"That's what the space scientists believe."

"So we'll never run out of space," Mira smiled. "I guess that's good."

"You would have loved school today. We were learning about science — really technical science stuff — sitting outside, not in a classroom. It reminded me of the Teaching Rock back when we were in Nature School."

"I'd like to learn outside again," Mira said. "There's only one thing about school I don't like, and that's sitting in a schoolroom all day long."

"I was thinking, maybe the teachers should petition to have some classes outside. Their other petition went so well."

"Mmm," Mira grinned, tapping her chin with her kipper-ink pen. "That's a *great* idea. Now that they can use holophones, they could teach anywhere."

"And you'd be learning more, not less."

"We would, we could. You're right about that, Lin."

"You'd learn more and have more fun doing it. It's a win-win."

Mira laughed. "Win-win doesn't really work like that," she said, "but I know what you mean."

"And the teachers might like being outside too."

"You're right, they probably would. I'm glad you said that. *That* makes it a win-win. There's something in it for the teachers too." Mira nodded, smiling and hopeful. "I'm going to talk to my father about it."

"You should," I said.

"I will."

"If you need my help—"

"No, thanks," Mira said. "I'll get Hali to help me."

"Are those new? All those kipper-paper notebooks?"

Mira looked at the shelf behind her, neatly lined with newly hand-made kipper-paper notebooks. "I've been writing more than ever since you've been gone," she said. "I'm entering some stories in a national competition."

"Oh, that's great news. What will you win if you win?"

"Money," she said, "not much, but even better, the winning stories are published in a book that all the schools make their students read—"

"Except the schools in Bree, probably."

"Yes, but I'm going to change that. And then there's also a mention in the Strellin paper, and my father said that if I win, it will help me get into the university."

"Which university?"

"The University at Clud," Mira said. "I want to get my degree in journalism there and get hired at the *Reporter*."

"That's convenient. The university and the newspaper office are in the same city."

"My thinking exactly."

"If they don't hire you," I said, "I'll be surprised. They've already published two of your stories. That's a huge advantage."

"I hope so," she said.

"I'm really happy for you, Mir. You've got your future so figured out."

"I have a plan, anyway."

"My schoolmates here talk about colleges and universities and which ones they want to go to."

"I definitely see you going to college," Mira said. "Are there any you like?"

"Any that teaches adibadi training," I said. "There's more than one."

"You really want to be an adibadi trainer?"

"I'm feeling pretty sure. I know I won't be a food scientist. It's complicated work and boring on top of it. Did you see the video I sent you of the towering gardens?"

"Yep. I liked the view of it from a distance, where you see the Food Science Lab sticking up in the middle of the gardens. I like the juxtaposition of the fake food being made in the lab and the real food growing the natural way."

"You said juxtaposition in Culti," I said.

"There's no word for it in Welbi. It's a great word. Hey, do you mind talking in Culti for a while? I need some practice."

"I'd love to."

"Your Culti's so good," Mira said after a while. "I'm amazed. Maybe you should be a linguist like Mr. Tria."

"I've actually thought about it," I said, "But I think I'm starting too late. Some of my schoolmates already speak three or four languages."

"That's hard to believe."

"The trick is, they started young. Anyway, I'm starting to learn Continental now. Did you know di Ana means 'to the good' in Continental?"

"What does 'to the good' mean?"

"Nothing, really, I just like the way it sounds. It's something an old philosopher would say in their ancient ways of saying things."

"The kids still slide on the groile every day," Mira said. "They love you for it. So do the parents. Kids aren't addicted to their holophones like they used to be."

"See, *that's* progress. *Good* progress. Responsible progress. I'm thinking of being a responsible progress promoter, if being an adibadi trainer doesn't work out."

"Being a what?"

"Responsible progress promoter," I said.

"What kind of vocation is that?"

"Technically, I'm not sure, but I'd be working out of the embassies, so maybe International Diplomacy. Novi thinks I might have to study education or maybe science."

"Science," Mira said, "I don't know about that. I don't see you as a scientist. You're more a people person."

"An adibadi person."

Mira laughed while I grew sad.

"What's wrong?" she asked.

"We haven't gone to the Complex the last two Adris. Now that Nin and I have Gen 8s, there's no reason to go to the gadget shop to use the demo models like we used to. And we can get World Café food anytime we want from food transport drones, and the beach there is great, but there's a good beach a lot closer to the Residences. No one wants to go to the Complex anymore. And that's where my two adibadi friends are. I miss them."

"Then go yourself."

"That's no fun."

"I'm sure there's someone who would want to go with you."

I thought about it. "You're right, Mira. There *is* someone."

Birgard, of course, who I hadn't seen in two weeks. I called his holophone after Mira and I said goodbye.

"Want to go to the Complex on Adri?" I said. "I haven't been in two weeks, and I miss my adi friends."

He said, "Well, that's funny. I've been missing my Lin friend."

I didn't know what to say to that, and I laughed nervously. "Does that mean yes?"

"Yes," he said, "it means yes."

Birgard and I met that Adri and took an airtram to the Complex. We talked about everything — our proficiency scores and how our personal goals were going and his little sister and my father's attitude about remarrying. When we arrived at the Complex, we headed straight for the tree park, where we saw no adibadis working. None, anywhere.

"We came all this way," I moaned.

"Don't be disappointed," Birgard said. "The adi and his handler might be taking lunch. Why don't we get something to eat and come back?"

"Great idea," I said. "I'm in the mood for a flavor pellet."

We turned and strolled to the World Café, where we each had a pellet of our favorite sweet fruit, ate a lunch of world fish, and then had another pellet of our favorite dessert.

Our mood was great when we arrived back at the tree park.

I grabbed Birgard's arm the moment I saw the adi, shouting louder than I should have, "He's there! Look! He's there!"

"He is," Birgard laughed. "And I think we're in luck. See that man standing near?"

"Yes."

"I think that's his handler."

The adi's handler was a friendly, stocky man with a handsome face and a sense of humor.

"You remind me of my father," I told him.

"Well," he said, "as I don't know the man, that could be a compliment or an insult. Judging from the likes of you, though, I'm inclined to be complimented."

"It was a compliment," I said. "You remind me of his better qualities. My name is Lin. I'm from far away, the furthest part of Wershonia from here. We have no adibadis there. I never saw an adi until I got here."

"My name is Hennit," the animal handler said.

"And I'm Birgard, from Algalon. I was practically raised by an adi."

"Ah, then you're fluent in adi," Hennit said.

"I am. I've been teaching Lin. I've never known a girl so fond of adis as her. She's thinking of being an adi handler herself."

"Is that right?" Hennit said, sizing me up. "A small thing like you?"

"I'm still growing," I said. "And I have great Welbi genes. So they say."

"You're in school here, I take it."

"We are," said Birgard.

"We're first year students," I added.

"Well, that would account for the petiteness of your build," Hennit said.

I asked him, "Is it important that adi handlers be strong?"

"It helps, though it's not required."

"Part of my learning this year is to interview professionals and give a talk to my schoolmates about their work. Could I interview you, Hennit?"

"Well," he smiled, looking down at his feet. "I've never been interviewed before."

"It's not difficult," I said. "I ask questions and you answer them. They're questions about your work, so I'm sure you'll know all the answers."

Hennit laughed. "Well, if I'm sure to know all the answers, how can I say no?"

"Then you will?" I asked.

"Yes," he said, "I'd be pleased to."

After planning to meet the following Adri at that very spot, Hennit excused himself and disappeared behind a neatly trimmed tallbush, a bush named for its extraordinary height.

Birgard and I stayed until the cloudy sky grew dim, talking and laughing with the adi until we were exhausted. Then we sat on a trellised bench and watched him weed the garden.

"He's so adorable," I said. "Oddly adorable in his odd adi way. Oddi. I finally thought of a name for him. Oddi."

"Adi?" Birgard asked. "That's not very original."

"No," I said. "Oddi. O-D-D-I. Oddi. Because he's so odd."

Birgard laughed. "Oddi," he said. "I like it."

I dreamt that night of Oddi and Lana, my first two adibadi friends, the first of hundreds. I was an old woman in the dream, and I was a world famous adi trainer who had worked with genetic engineers to extend the lifespan of adibadis. I had adopted Oddi and Lana, who were 125 years old but still as bouncy and playful as when they were young. I traveled the world with them, visiting children in backward places who had never seen adibadis and probably never would have. Their laughter was what I heard when I woke the next morning, feeling more certain than ever that I had found my calling.

## 22 BIG NEWS

The following Adri, I woke up happy. It was the day of my interview with Hennit, the adibadi trainer, and it was a Lindri.

"Hi, Lin!" shouted the people gathered at Bree Pavillion.

"Hi, everyone," I waved. "Notice anything different about me?"

Hali did. He didn't miss much. "You're not wearing your holophone," he smiled. "Or so it appears."

"That's right," I said. "I'm wearing a Generation 8 holophone. No eyescreen."

"Then how do you see?" someone asked.

"With a film in my eye," I said.

Some fell to murmuring.

"I'll let Mira tell you about the Gen 8," I said. "We have more important things to talk about, and my time is short. I have an interview today."

"What kind of interview?" Bissa asked.

"I'm interviewing a man who works with adibadis," I said.

Two in the crowd spoke one-word questions, one on top of the other.

"Adibadis?"

"Why?"

"Part of my school work is to interview professionals about the work they do. It's to help me decide what I want to do for a living. But I already figured it out. I'm going to be an adibadi trainer."

"You already decided?" Bissa asked. "*Before* your interview with the trainer man?" She was always a stickler for details.

"I've been deciding for a while," I said. I told of my days at the tree park talking and playing with real, live adibadis. "The girl adis have a blonde tuft between the ears. They're adorable. The boy adis are too.

You would love them. And so, I've decided that the perfect profession for me is to be an adibadi trainer. I would travel back and forth from Bree to the Continent, coming back with adibadis for the people of Bree and then I—"

I was interrupted by hollering and clapping and some shouts of joy for the news that Bree would finally have adibadis like the rest of the civilized world.

"I would train the adis for particular kinds of work," I said when it was quiet again, "and I would teach new adibadi owners how to talk to their adi."

"That's great news," said Koppi Dun, and many agreed.

"Congratulations, Lin," said some.

"Thank you, Lin," said others.

"To tell you the truth," I told them, "I didn't know how I was going to be happy living in Bree after six years here. But this is the perfect solution. Now I can live happily in Bree and travel the world. And it would all be part of my work. It couldn't be more perfect."

After everyone shared the latest news of their life and we all said goodbye, Mira wanted to talk to me privately.

"Everyone really likes my idea," I told her. "I'm surprised."

"Surprised? Why?"

"I knew that the kids of Bree would be happy about owning adibadis so they wouldn't have to do so many chores, but I didn't think the parents would be this happy too."

"I think the tourists are having a positive influence on everyone," Mira said. "Everyone but the naysayers," she giggled. "They're all bent sideways about the big crowds of tourists and the lax regulation of the contraband they're bringing in."

"What kind of contraband?"

"Those big screens that unroll from a tube and show videos of outer space or sports performances. I love them. Everyone does. Even the Sheriff. He's not enforcing the ban. He lets the tourists use them, except without sound. He's banning the sound, but nothing else."

"What a victory," I said. "Even the Sheriff's coming around."

"So now that kids know about the better generations of holophones," Mira said, "they all want them."

"Uh, oh."

"Yep," she said, "I kind of agree."

"Well, we'll see how that turns out. Anyway, I have to go. I'm meeting Birgard at the tram station."

"Birgard?"

"He didn't think I should go alone," I said. "And he loves adis as much as I do. He's fluent in adi."

"I know," she said. "You told me. I think more than once."

"Oh. Well, I've never talked to so many different people every single day as I do since I've been here," I said. "It's hard to keep track of what I tell who."

"I understand, I just—" she stopped herself.

"You just what?"

"No," she only said.

"You can't do that, Mira, start to say something important and then hold it back. Now I really want to know."

"I didn't say it's important."

"Well, you know I'm going to be wondering about it for the rest of the day. It will ruin my concentration for my interview."

Mira laughed. "I was just going to say that I think you're sweet on Birgard."

"I'm not sweet on Birgard."

"And the way you talk about him, I think you're sweet on Novi too."

"I'm not sweet on Novi. I'm not sweet on anyone. I'm just trying to survive here."

Mira was still laughing when we said goodbye and she disappeared from sight.

I walked to the tram station, wishing she hadn't said what she said. Instead of gathering my thoughts for my interview, I was worrying. Did Birgard think I was sweet on him? Did Novi? I wished it didn't matter to me, but it did.

"You seem nervous," Birgard said about midway to the Complex.

I had been staring out the window at a sub-orbital in the distance touching down on one of the landing pads along the South Shore.

"Nervous?" I asked.

"You're so quiet," he said. "It's not like you."

"Oh. I guess I have a lot on my mind."

"Anything I can help with?"

I thought about it and gave myself some advice. *Talk about something positive, it will relax you.* It was good advice, the kind mother would have given me. I wondered if somehow it came from her.

Birgard laughed as I told him about the morning Lindri holophone call I had with everyone in Bree. I told him of the big news I shared about my future profession and how surprised I was by their overwhelming joy for the idea.

"I'm glad you know now," he said.

"Know what?"

"What you want to do when we graduate."

"Thanks, Birgard."

"And I'm glad you're not nervous anymore."

"You can tell?"

He smiled, his resemblance to my least favorite boy in Bree coming into sharp focus. "I can tell," he said.

"I'm glad you turned out nice," I said. "And I'm glad you like adis."

"Same here," he said.

The interview with Hennit went better than well. It was the best interview I'd had so far. The longest and the most interesting and the most fun. Birgard planned to go to the shops while I talked to Hennit, but Hennit said he didn't mind if Birgard joined us, and I didn't see any problem with that. Hennit spent his entire lunch hour and more time after that telling me every wonderful thing there was to know about being an adibadi trainer and handler.

After Hennit left to have have lunch, Birgard and I played with Lana, who I had learned that day was 14 years old and who would live another 60 years or more.

"Sad," she said when it was time to go.

"Sad," I said to her.

We shared a smile as Birgard looked on. Then we left her and made our way through a thickening crowd to the World Café.

"Someone called during the interview," I said. "They left a video message. Do you mind?"

"No," said Birgard.

I thought the words *retrieve messages* and waited for my Gen 8 to play the message. After no response, I thought the words again, and again, and a fourth time. I gave up and retrieved my messages the old fashioned way. "Voice command," I said to my Gen 8. "Retrieve messages. Opacity 50%."

I heard Birgard chuckle. "Were you trying all that time to thought command?" he asked.

"Yes," I said. "I don't think my holophone likes my thoughts. It never works for me."

"Are you thinking in the right language?"

I paused the video message that had just appeared. It was my aunt's face, her mouth half-open, her face unhappy. "It doesn't matter what language I think in," I said to Birgard. "It's programmed to recognize Culti or Welbi."

"Maybe that's the problem."

"What?"

"Two languages," he said.

"Really?"

"Sometimes that can cause the thought command to malfunction. That happened to a man my father works with after he got a Gen 8. They made an adjustment to the settings, and then it worked fine. If you want, we can go to the shop after lunch and tell them what's happening."

"Great idea," I said. "Thanks. Now, back to my aunt."

Ten words out of her mouth, and my happy day was ruined.

## 23  BIG TROUBLE

Aunt Tala was furious.

"What's this I'm hearing about you bringing adibadis to Bree?" she said, all stiff and miffed and pacing the floor. "Tell me this is just a rumor, Lin. A misunderstanding."

I paused the video, stopped dead in my tracks, and swallowed hard.

"I'm going to need a flavor pellet," I told Birgard.

He turned around. "What's wrong?"

"I think I'm in big trouble."

My favorite flavor pellet did little to cheer me up. As weak from stress and hunger as I was, I could barely eat lunch, I was so queasy.

"I'm easy to quease," I told Birgard. "Did you know they sent me on four simulated sub-orbital landings before we came to Vona? Not one, or none, like everyone else."

Birgard laughed, not seeming to mind my dour spirits. His laughter made me feel a bit better, so I went on with my whining.

"Though I felt no less queasy on the fourth landing than the first," I said, "I told them I was ready. I couldn't stomach a fifth landing, and I was convinced it wouldn't have helped. And I half-believed that on the day of the actual landing I'd be so overcome with total joy that I'd hardly feel the queasiness and maybe not at all."

"And?"

"The joy made me feel more queasy, not less."

"Is that why you were so cross with me?" Birgard asked.

"Maybe. That and the fact that you reminded me of someone I'd been mad at for a long time. But I wasn't cross with you, I was just annoyed."

"Seemed cross to me," he said.

"Well, if I came off that way, I apologize. I'm nice to you now."

Birgard nodded his agreement and smiled. "You're eating," he said.

"I feel a little better. I think it helps to talk about our troubles. And I know if I don't eat now, I'll be a wreck later. Stress is depleting, you know."

"If I can help with your stress, let me know."

"Thanks," I said. "Will you call my aunt for me?"

"Sure."

"No, no, that wouldn't work. I wish it would, but...."

"You're nervous about calling her back," Birgard said.

"Supremely nervous. But when? And where?"

"Where?"

"Where to call her from? Location matters to me. You know, my surroundings. It affects how I feel."

"I think that's true for everyone," he said. "Maybe you need to call her from a place that gives you peace and strength or whatever will—"

"That's brilliant," I said. "And I know just the place. The waterfall near Sunset Peak. Will you go with me?"

"Sure. I've never been there."

"Pella's family took me there last week. You're in for a treat."

Birgard grinned. "See how it pays to be helpful?" He pushed away his empty plate of world fish, leaned back in his chair — shifting until it molded just the way he wanted — and patiently waited for me to finish eating.

Before heading to the waterfall, we went to the gadget shop, stopping along the way to say hello again to Lana in the tree park.

"Wish me luck," I told her.

"Good," she said.

"Lana, that's a terrible habit. You can't just say 'good' to everything you don't understand. Some people might say the most horrible thing to you, and you say 'good'. It's not...." I shook my head and half-smiled.

"Good," she said.

"For the first time ever," I said to Birgard when we turned and walked away, "I felt like a mother with a misbehaving child. And it's true, you can be mad at a child, but love them no less. I kind of loved her more, actually, when I was scolding her."

"I saw how she smiled at you," Birgard said.

"Maybe she loves me too."

"Maybe so."

"They *do* love people, don't they?"

"They do."

"In their odd adi way," I said.

He laughed. "Yes, in their odd adi way."

The pretty clerk was at the shop, sweet and friendly, glad to see us again. She wasn't surprised to hear of the trouble with the thought command of my Gen 8, and in less than ten minutes, it was working normally.

"That was an easy victory," I said.

"Victory," the clerk nodded with a smile. "That's an interesting way of looking at it."

"Wish me luck?" I asked her. "I have a nerve-wracking call to make."

"Then good luck," she said. "May it have the very best outcome."

"I like nice people," I told Birgard as we left the shop.

"Me too," he said. "She really cheered you up. Just what you needed."

"Just what I needed," I said, pushing away every thought of Aunt Tala with memories of the waterfall we were about to see.

"Unbelievable," Birgard said when he first saw it.

"I know a special place," I said. "There won't be any people there. How are you at climbing?"

"Not bad."

He was as good a climber as me, and we soon stood on a broad rock outcropping about midway between the very top and very bottom of the waterfall.

"That's got to be about 400 emins high," Birgard said. "Maybe 500."

I scanned the distance. "Four or five hundred," I said.

"Don't you think?"

"I don't know. I'm still trying to figure out how big an emin is. Back in Bree we use thurstins."

"Really? Thurstins? I didn't know anyone still...." Birgard's voice trailed off.

"Thanks for stopping yourself from insulting my culture," I said.

Birgard just smiled, and, silent for a while, we took in the beauty of our surroundings — the tall, flowering cliffs that exploded with color, the graceful cascade of pink-tinted water, the white foam of the water where it crashed into the swimming pond far below, and the scent of sweetmoss that grew beneath our feet and that was made even sweeter with a squish or a step.

"We could have a waterfall in Bree," I said when I began to feel nervous. "We have a cliff like this, steep and tall and close to the sea. It's the perfect place for a waterfall. It would make Bree more beautiful and it would bring more tourists."

"I thought you said Bree didn't have enough lodging for the tourists it already has."

"It doesn't," I said. "That's why we need more lodging."

Birgard laughed. "You have a big eye for improvement."

"Everything needs improving," I said, "sooner or later."

"And the sooner the better, right?"

"Exactly."

Birgard laughed again.

"I guess I better call her," I said. "I feel a chill in the air."

"Stand tall and strong," Birgard told me. "There is greatness in you."

We smiled at each other.

"I'm going to go explore and give you your privacy," he said. "Call me when you're done and good luck." He turned away and turned back again. "And don't forget."

"There is greatness in me."

"There is," he said. "I've seen it all along." He grinned and turned and scampered away.

I slid my sweaty palms against my back and tried to still my trembling tail. I was surprised by the intense dread I felt, and I hoped it was all for nothing. Just a mild scolding, nothing more. Nothing precious taken away from me.

"Hi, Aunt Tala," I said when she answered.

"Don't even think about amending the truth of what happened," she said. "I heard for myself your exact words, Lin, and I'm very disappointed."

"What did I do that was so bad?" I asked.

"You honestly don't know?"

"Not really. Not the exact thing."

Aunt Tala was momentarily speechless. She stared at the floor, pacing, her face contorted in a familiar expression. "You acted irresponsibly and impulsively. Did you stop for one minute and consider the consequences of what you told everyone?"

"No," I said. "It just came out. I was happy about it. I didn't think it would be such a big deal."

"Well, it *is* a big deal."

"Does father know about it?"

"Yes."

"Does Merchant Kam?"

"Yes, they all know, everyone who matters."

"Is father mad at me?"

"I can't tell. He's too busy standing up for you."

I smiled. "Standing up for me?"

"Yes. He's been inundated with irate calls. The Mayor, members of the Village Council, half the Committee of Technology it seems, and others." She shook her head.

"Which others?"

"I wouldn't rattle off a list for you even if I knew. But I will say this, I too have been getting calls, not calls of complaint," she rolled her eyes, "but calls of gratitude and—"

"Gratitude?"

"Don't find joy in that, Lin. A lot of people believe that you or Kam are going to start importing adibadis to Bree any day now. Some are already making plans to expand their business. Koppi Dun called to order three. Then, after I took great pains to explain to her that adibadis are never coming to Bree, she called back to order a fourth."

"Don't say never, Aunt Tala, and I didn't tell anyone they'd be importing any day. I said in the future, after I graduate."

"Yes, and do you see how a plain truth is so quickly distorted by wishful thinking?"

"I guess so."

"This is why you have to be careful about what you say to people.

You have to think about what they're going to do with that information. Most will take you at your word, as implausible as it may be, and some will take what you say and embellish it any which way, according to their own wants and wishes."

I was silent while she took a breath and turned to pace in the opposite direction. *This isn't so bad,* I thought. She's been a lot angrier at me than this.

"Listen to me well," she continued. "You *must learn* to think about the consequences of what you say to people. It's as important as thinking about the consequences of what you *do.* Especially, and I'm sorry to say it, to such a dimwitted bunch as the people of Bree. Do you understand that?"

"Yes," I laughed.

She glared at me — an it's-not-funny glare — which did nothing to stop my laughter.

"I'm sorry," I told her. "I'm laughing because it was funny what you said. The dimwitted bunch."

Aunt Tala flashed a smile.

"I understand what you're saying about the consequences of what I say," I said. "I'm going to work really hard at getting better at that."

"Good," she said. "And you have to stop meddling in the affairs of Bree. You live there now. You need to leave Bree in peace."

"But I only want to help. A lot of people want adibadis. They've told you themselves."

"Yes, we want a lot of things, but whether or not they're fitting for Bree is not for you to decide. And it's not for you to make any pronouncements on whether Bree ever has adibadis. Do you understand that?"

"I think so."

Aunt Tala stopped pacing and let out a heavy sigh.

"I know you mean to do well, Lin, but your impetuousness can be damaging."

"What's impetishness?"

"Impetuousness. It means acting without thinking, being impulsive."

"Is Merchant Kam mad at me?"

"No, he's not mad at you."

"That's good."

"Now," she said, "you're going to have to make a public statement and apology."

"You want me to tell everyone I'm sorry? I guess I can do that."

"There's no guess. You *will* do it. Let's talk tomorrow. Call me as soon as you wake in the morning. And Lin, don't talk to anyone in Bree until then."

"Not even Mira?"

"No one."

As soon as we said goodbye, I called Birgard to say I had finished.

"Did you get the rain alert?" he said when he returned to my spot.

"The what alert?"

"The rain alert. It's going to rain."

"There's a rain alert on the Gen 8?"

"Yes," he said, "and some other weather alerts you might want to know about. The rainy season's coming."

On the airtram back to the Residences, Birgard showed me how to set four different weather alerts on my Gen 8: the rain alert to warn of likely rain, the wind alert to warn of heavy winds, the sand alert to warn of blowing sand, and the lightning alert to warn of cloud-to-ground lightning.

"What about cloud-to-cloud lightning?" I asked. "I want that alert too."

"There's no cloud-to-cloud alert," he said.

"Why? That's the best kind."

Birgard was confused. "The best kind?"

"The best for lightning shows."

"Lightning shows?"

"Haven't you ever watched lightning?"

"Not intentionally," he smiled. "Is that a Bree thing?"

"Before holophones, that was our best form of entertainment."

"Entertainment? Really?"

"Yes," I said. "If you watched a good lightning show, you'd probably love it."

"Then I hope to sit and watch one some day."

"I wonder who I can talk to about getting cloud-to-cloud alerts."

Birgard laughed and said, "We're visiting the Meterology School in two months, why don't you ask them?"

"That's a great idea," I said.

"I was joking, Lin. I didn't mean that seriously at all."

"Doesn't matter. Great ideas come in many packages."

He choked on a laugh he tried to hold back, and then changed the subject.

"You didn't say how your conversation went with your aunt. By your mood, it seems it went well."

"It didn't go bad," I said. "Not as bad as I was expecting. But I have to call her early in the morning to figure out how I'm going to make this right. The people of Bree think they're going to get adibadis any day now."

"Is that why you're in trouble?" Birgard asked.

"Oh, I never told you, did I?"

The rest of the way home, I told Birgard about what I said that morning about importing adibadis to Bree and how the dimwit people of Bree thought that meant it was going to happen immediately and how my father got angry calls from the Committee of No Technology.

"Committee of No Technology?" Birgard asked.

"You don't know about them?"

"No, but I think I want to."

"Believe me, you do."

We laughed so loud at my stories — which needed no embellishment — nearby passengers hushed us four times before we disembarked at the Residences.

And my mood was good again as I walked through tiny raindrops under a darkening sky to Residence 26.

## 24  THE APOLOGY

"I just talked to the Mayor," Aunt Tala told me the next morning. "He wants you to issue a clarification and an apology to everyone. And he wants you to do it immediately."

I wiped my bleary eyes. "Clarification?" I said. It was too big a word so early in the morning.

"He wants you to say in plain language that you did not mean what you said about bringing adibadis to Bree."

"But I did mean it. Not *now*, but in the future."

"I'm not haggling over details with you, Lin. Forget about the future for now. This is about present time. So, let's be clear, you're going to tell everyone that you nor Kam nor anyone else will be importing adibadis to Bree. Period."

A long yawn came over me.

"Lin, pay attention," Aunt Tala scolded. "This is serious."

"I know, I know. I'm just—"

"You have no idea the trouble you've caused."

"You told me yesterday," I said. "You don't have to repeat it."

"It's grown worse since yesterday."

"It has? How?"

"That's not important now."

I yawned again, a long yawn, yawned in total innocence.

"Lin! What's gotten into you?!"

"I'm tired. I didn't sleep well last night. We had a bad storm. And then I had a nightmare."

Aunt Tala tightened her mouth, which stayed shut for a while. In her silence was sweetness. Not a lot, but enough.

"All right," she said. "Here's what we're going to do. I'm going to tell you what to say. I want you to write it down, and I want you to say every word as written. Nothing more, nothing less. Exactly as written."

"But what if I don't agree with—"

"Your agreement has nothing to do with this. This isn't about what you want to say or don't want to say, it's about what you are required to say."

"Required by who?"

"By the powers that be."

"You? The Mayor? Father?"

"Lin. Don't fight me on this. It will only make the ordeal more difficult."

I was too tired to argue. "All right. What do you want me to say?"

"Good." She cleared her throat. "Hello, people of Bree."

"Oh, wait," I said. "Before you start, I just thought of something."

Aunt Tala took to pacing as I commanded my Gen 8 to translate her words to text and send the text to my data sheet.

"Now I don't have to write with my hands!" I said with an enthusiasm she didn't appreciate.

"Good. People of Bree," she began, "I know you were happy to hear of my interest in bringing adibadis to Bree...."

"People of Bree," I said ten minutes later in a video message that was sent to every holophone in Bree. I held up my data sheet. "By the way, I'm reading these words from my data sheet. Here's what it looks like. I'll tell you all about it sometime."

I yawned a small yawn, the smallest I could make it, and continued reading.

"I know you were happy to hear of my interest in bringing adibadis to Bree. Let me emphatically state that this was nothing more than an expression of my own wishes. And wishes are wishes and nothing more. It is not true that I will be bringing adibadis to Bree. And nor is Merchant Kam or anyone else. I repeat, there will be no adibadis in Bree."

I had to bite my tongue to keep from adding, "not for now."

"I repeat, Bree is not getting any adibadis. None. I apologize for the confusion this has caused, and I'm sorry to all of you who believed what I said. I'm sorry to all of you who got their hopes up.

My statement—" I didn't want to say this part, but I promised I would "—was careless. It was said in haste, and it was never true. So, again, I say, Bree is not getting adibadis. Please don't call my father or the Mayor or Merchant Kam or anyone else about this. Bree is not getting adibadis." I wiped a tear that had started to fall. "Thank you for understanding and getting back to a peaceful, profitable, enjoyable tourist season."

"Profitable?" Mira asked when we talked later that day.

"Aunt Tala made me say it. I told her it wouldn't sound like me."

"That part didn't, but some of it did."

"Do you think it helped?" I asked.

"Your video message? Probably. It's what everyone's talking about."

"How's father? Have you seen him?"

"He's telling his stories on the Second Pier," she said, "just like always."

"That's a relief. I really don't get what all the fuss was."

"That's because you're not here."

"So it was pretty bad?"

"I wouldn't say bad," Mira said. "Really, it was hilarious, if you ask me. The Mayor had an emergency meeting this morning. I sat outside the hole in that far corner of the wall of his office, pretending I was waiting for my father."

"Your father was in the meeting?"

"Not this one," she smiled.

"And what'd you hear?"

"That Brister Liggan was threatening to write an article about it."

"How did *he* find out?"

"I'm not sure," Mira said, "but every good journalist has his sources."

"It wouldn't have been my father, would it?"

"Who knows? So the Mayor was all upset. He said, 'I can see the headline now, *Adibadi Mayhem: Young Girl Dupes Entire Town with Adibadi Rumor'*. He was mad when he said it, but a bunch of men laughed. That made the Mayor even more mad. He said, 'I'm not going to let that di Ana girl ruin our reputation again!'"

"He did?"

"Yes. Then someone said, 'I thought we were done with her!' and someone else said, 'No, you said it wrong. We thought that *she* was done with *us!*' It went on and on like that."

"I can't believe they brought me into it," I said.

"Well, you are the one who started it."

"I guess you're right."

"Then the Mayor said he was going to take matters into his own hands. He called Brister Liggan and begged him not to report on this — oh, how did he say it? — this *embarrassing ordeal.* The Mayor said there was a better story. The story of Bree getting groile. He told Brister Liggan it would be a great photo opportunity. You know, darling pictures of kids sliding on groile."

"I wonder what Brister Liggan said to that."

"I don't know," Mira said, "but he didn't take the bait on the groile story, obviously, because the next thing the Mayor said was that he'd pay Brister Liggan not to write the adibadi story."

"I don't see what's so bad about the adi story," I said. "Any article about Bree is good for tourism."

"Well, all I know is that the Mayor doesn't want people laughing at Bree."

"I guess you're right. There's been enough of that already. Hey," I said, "I got some really bad news last night."

"What?"

"The rainy season starts two months earlier here than in Bree."

"It does?"

"Yep, next month. We don't have many pure sky days left, not like the ones we've been having."

"Is that what's making you so sad?" Mira asked.

"A lot's making me sad," I said. "I had to give a speech that Aunt Tala wrote for me, and I disagreed with most of it. And I had a great interview with Hennit, the adibadi trainer, and now I want to work with adibadis now more than ever. But if the powers that be won't let me import adis to Bree, then what do I do? Where would I live? I don't know if I could be happy in Bree if I'm not working with adis."

"Just because you told everyone that Bree's never getting adibadis, doesn't mean it's true. A lot can happen in six years."

"You're right, Mira. I should stay on the bright side."

From the patch of groile where I sat, I saw the lone figure of Saamta Sio walking slowly up a nearby hill. Saamta Sio was never alone, never, so I saw this as a chance to talk to her in private.

"Mira, I have to go. Keep me informed of any new developments."

"All right. Love you, Lin."

"Love you, Mir."

Saamta Sio had disappeared behind a tall patch of thick, flowering bushes that had cozy benches tucked into little alcoves on the other side from where I was. I took the fastest route, and found her sitting on one of the benches, her face in her hands, her shoulders bouncing. I was unsure of what to say and hoped that the right words would come when I needed them.

"Saamta Sio, is that you?" I said with a tone of surprise.

She wiped her face, looked up, and frowned when she saw it was me.

"What are *you* doing here?" she said.

"I came to sit and clear my thoughts," I said. "It's so quiet and private here. I'm sort of having a bad day. It looks like you are too."

"That's no business of yours," she said, blinking her eyes tight as if to squeeze tears out of them.

"You're right," I said. "But since I'm here, do you mind if I sit down? I've been wanting to tell you something."

"What kind of something?"

I wondered what mother would have said. "I want to apologize," I said. I was so pleased with the words I had to force myself from smiling.

"Apologize?"

"Yes," I said. "I haven't exactly been kind to you since we first met, and there's no reason for it."

She stared at me, speechless.

"I'm not asking that we be friends," I told her, "although I wouldn't mind it. I just don't want to be enemies."

"Why are you saying this now?"

"Because this is the first time you and I have ever been alone together. I wanted to tell you before, but it didn't seem right with other people around." I was still standing, and I didn't like looking down at her, so I asked again, "Do you mind if I sit down?"

She scooted to one end of the bench to make room for me.

"Who said anything about enemies?" she asked.

"I guess that was a harsh way of saying it. I meant unfriendly. There's been unfriendliness between us, and I don't want there to be."

"Then be nicer," she said.

"I am, starting today."

"And stop staring at me."

"Do you want to know why I've been staring lately?"

"Why?"

"I never knew anything about your life," I said. "I knew your father was a diplomat, and that was it. I was jealous of you for having a father who did great things. Lately I learned the truth about your parents and your childhood, and now I feel so bad for being unkind to you. I thought your life was so great, but now I know you've suffered tragedy just like me. That's why I've been staring at you. I feel sorry for you."

"I don't want your pity."

"I don't think it's pity," I said. "I think it's compassion."

"Did someone put you up to this?"

"No."

"Did you know it's my birthday tomorrow?"

"No," I said. "Is that why you're sad?"

Saamta Sio stared at me, and I saw her whole face change. Her bottom lip trembled, her eyes filled with tears, her ears drew back.

"Has something bad happened?" I asked.

She buried her face in her hands and started to cry. I reached in my satchel for a tissuecloth and stuffed it in one of her hands.

She held it up with two fingers, examined it with crinkled eyes, then sniffled and said, "What's *this?*"

"It's a tissuecloth," I said. "To wipe your tears."

"Is it self-cleaning?"

"I don't know what that means, but it *is* clean, I can assure you that. My aunt packed a lot for me since I—" I decided to say it "—since I cry a lot."

Saamta Sio wiped her eyes with the back of her hands and gave back my tissuecloth. "Thanks, but ... thanks," she said.

I took it and wiped my own eyes, which had started to tear. Why, I wasn't sure. Maybe it was her rejection of my tissuecloth, maybe it was the kindness in her thanks, or maybe it was the fact that anytime I heard the word birthday I was reminded of mother's drowning. I wiped another stream of tears and tried hard not to cry.

"And why are you having a bad day?" Saamta Sio asked me, her voice a bit softer.

"A lot of reasons," I said, "but I'm most sad right now because birthdays make me sad. My mother died two days before I turned ten. Ever since, the joy of birthdays has been ruined. Mine or anyone else's."

"Two days?"

"Yes. My tenth birthday was completely uncelebrated, and ever since, on my birthday, I only think of mother."

Saamta Sio shook her head. "My parents have been away on my birthday six times. Six out of thirteen. That's almost half."

"Away?"

"Traveling somewhere. For father, it's on business, but my mother has no excuse. She could at least drop her fun and visit me for a day."

"Or they could take you with them on their travels," I said.

"They took me once and hated it."

"Really? They told you that?"

"They didn't have to say it," she said. "I don't believe most of what they say anyway."

"I can't believe they completely forgot your birthday. How awful."

"They never forgot," she sniffled. "They always send me big stupid presents."

"Well, that's not so bad."

"Yes, it is. My mother loves to shop. My birthday's just another reason for her to buy stuff. One year she sent me an ear trinket, the jeweled kind you'd give an old lady. When she came home, she was so happy to find out I didn't like it. Now it belongs to her. I think she meant it for herself all along."

"That's pretty bad."

"I know. And that's just one example."

"See?" I said. "You have a tragic life like me."

Saamta Sio half-smiled and looked out at the ocean. "White caps," she said. "The weather's turning."

"So I've heard."

Our ear chips buzzed, low and slow. It was the ten-minute alert. Ten minutes until the start of afternoon class.

"Ear chips still amaze me," I said.

"That's no surprise," she grinned. "I guess we should go."

"Right."

"Though I really don't feel like it."

"Me neither," I said.

"But...."

"What?"

"I do sort of feel better," she said.

"Good. I do too."

Without saying a word, we smiled, stood to our feet, and headed down the hill to the West Park, where an afternoon lecture on Wershonian history awaited us.

"You never told me why you're having a bad day," she said as we walked.

I told her the whole bringing-adibadis-to-Bree story, and I told it well. I wished father could have heard it. He would have been proud, I think, for making Saamta Sio laugh so hard she cried. Mother would have been proud, too. That day, which started so terribly, I made a new friend.

## 25 THE NETS

"I can't believe you made Saamta Sio laugh," Pella told me later that night as we sat in her sleepingroom and watched fat raindrops splash upon her ceiling, which she set to tenebri zero for total invisibility.

"It's so great," I said. "A heavy stone has been lifted from my back."

"Why was a heavy stone on your back?"

"It wasn't. It's a saying. It means that I'm relieved that she and I finally talked. I actually kind of like her. I think she likes me too. Isn't that great? I was worried we'd be enemies. And I don't want to be enemies, not with her, not with any person."

"I don't know why anyone would," Pella said.

"Her birthday's tomorrow," I said. "I think we should do something special for her. She hasn't had the best birthdays in her life."

"That's a good idea. Do you have something in mind?"

"All I know is what we do in Bree. When you turn ten, everyone writes a birthday wish and puts it in a big bowl. Then you stand up on a table and read all the wishes out loud in front of everyone and they clap and laugh. Some of the wishes are funny and some are serious. But the serious ones can be good too, now that I think about it."

"Well, let's do that, then," Pella said. "We can message everyone in Team 10 and tell them to write a wish for her and bring it to Morning Circles tomorrow."

We wrote a message and sent it out from Pella's data sheet.

"Since time is of the essence," she said, "I used an urgent alert."

"What's that?"

"It beeps the ear chip of everyone you send a message to, so they know about the message right away even if their Gen 8's powered off."

"That sounds helpful," I said. "You'll have to show me how to use it."

154

"I will. You can only use ten urgent alerts a month. That's the first thing you should know."

"Ten? Why?"

"So people don't abuse the privilege. Think how often your ear chip would beep if everyone who sent you a message thought it was urgent."

"Right," I said.

The night sky flashed white but no thunder could be heard through the soundproof walls and ceiling.

"Father said the nets are going up tomorrow," Pella said. "Do you know about nets?"

"I know about fishing nets."

Pella laughed. "Not fishing nets. I'm talking about storm nets."

"What do you do with a storm net?"

"*We* don't do anything, the robots do it all. They put up nets all around the island, with the help of some adis."

"Robots and adis working together," I said. "That's kind of funny. I don't know why. Maybe it's the mix of old and new. Adis are so ancient, and robots are so modern. Adis are born and robots are made."

"Robots do have birthdates," Pella said.

"Are they celebrated?"

"No, not that I know about."

"Are adibadi birthdays celebrated?"

"Yes, if they're owned by a family."

"I wonder if Hennit celebrates the birthdays of Oddi and Lana. And I wonder if they've ever worked with robots." I imagined Lana giving an attentive group of robots their work assignments and Oddi keeping them in line.

"Probably," Pella said. "It's pretty common with outdoor projects. Anyway, you'll like the nets. They cover public places, like the Residence Commons and a lot of the parks and some of the walkways and beaches. Sunset Peak has a really big net. You can sit under it in a storm and you're totally protected."

"I can't believe a net can protect you from a storm."

"It shields rain and deflects wind."

"Like a clarkon dome?"

"Yes," Pella said, "But they're made of woven clarkon nanoribbon. It folds up like a piece of fabric. That makes nets easier than domes to put up and take down."

"Say again what they're woven from."

"Clarkon nanoribbon."

I wrote the words on my data sheet.

"Some call it nanofabric," Pella added.

I wrote that word too.

"I'm going to ask Merchant Kam about getting some nets for Bree," I said.

"That's a good idea."

A brilliant streak of lightning exploded long and white across the black sky, splitting into hundreds of tendrils that stretched further than we could see.

"Oooo," we cooed.

"I love watching lightning," I said.

"Me too."

I sunk deeper into the sittingcushion in the corner of Pella's immaculately kept sleepingroom. "Thanks for talking with our translators on," I said. "It's so great to speak Welbi. It relaxes me."

"We should always be relaxed," Pella said. "Father says we make bad decisions when we're stressed."

"I know a lot about stress, and he's right about that. Although I'm less stressed than I used to be, which is odd because I have more problems than ever before. The language, the technology, all the new people, my low proficiency scores, what I'm going to do when we graduate. There's more, but I'll spare you."

"I think you're doing great with it all. My parents do too. They think you have a strong character."

"That's nice of them to say."

"So whatever your proficiency scores, you always have that going for you. And that's important. It's why we're here. To build strong character."

"The people in Bree don't seem to care about character," I said. "They're just ... surviving, I guess."

Pella glanced over and smiled. "Maybe that's another way you'll change Bree," she said.

"Maybe. I think everyone would be happier if they had more character. More maturity." I closed my eyes and saw Bree — my house, the beach, the pier, the marketplace, and Merchant Kam's office, the only place in Bree kept as tidy as the buildings and homes of Vona. "Your family is so neat and clean and organized," I said.

Pella laughed. "To tell you the truth, we think you're kind of messy."

"Really?"

"Not you," she said, "your sleepingroom. It's always disheveled."

"What does disheveled mean?"

"It's an adult way of saying messy."

"Did your parents say that word about me?"

Pella nodded. "But they said it in kindness. Don't be hurt by it. You're not are you?"

"No, I don't think so."

"My father said it's because of your culture."

"Everything wrong about me is because of my culture," I said. "Being born in Bree is like a curse."

"At least you weren't born in Egli."

"You're right, Pella. That's a curse, being born an Egli slave. Being from Bree isn't *that* bad. It's more of a ... a massive lifetime annoyance."

The sky flashed white.

"I've been thinking about getting a tail trinket," I said. "Do we need parental permissions for that?"

"Probably," she said, "we'll ask my parents."

"I want a small one like yours. The big ones are way too showy."

"My rule is, if you can see a tail trinket from 20 emins away, it's too big. Ear trinkets too."

"How many people tall is 20 emins?" I asked.

"What size person?"

"A grown man."

Pella tapped on her data sheet. "About four and a half men," she said.

"Novi's going to write a formula for my data sheet that will instantly calculate how many people tall any measurement of emins is. I think he's tired of me asking him all the time."

Pella giggled.

"He loves writing formulas," I said. "He's practically a genius. I'm so glad he's my goal partner. He's been helping me with my math."

"That's nice of him. Although you know that's what the Tutoring Clinic is for."

"I know, but those rooms make me claustrophobic, and I'm already going to the clinic for so many other things."

"Mmm," she hummed with a nod of compassion.

"I could feel bad about that," I said, "but really it's Bree's fault. I was a good student in Bree, one of the best."

"Well, if the adibadi training doesn't work out in Bree, you could improve the educational system there."

"I hadn't thought of that."

"A lot of graduates work to improve education," Pella said. "It's a worthy cause."

"I think my father would like that. My mother was a teacher."

"Do you have any video of her?" Pella asked.

"No, she died before we had holophones."

"So your aunt is like your mother now."

"I suppose so. She treats me that way, though a lot less sweet and gentle than my mother was. A lot less. She's so much like my father." A sadness came over me. "I really miss them," I said. "As much as I like being here, I miss them terribly."

"We'll have to talk them into visiting. A lot of families come right after the final Proficiencies. The school puts on a lot of events. That's when we have the circum-island races."

"Oh, right," I said, "that boat race that goes around the island. I've read about that. Anyone can enter."

"Maybe your father would."

"No, that'd be a bad idea. He owns one boat, and it's really slow. And I wouldn't want him to enter any race he doesn't stand a chance of winning."

"But he could rent a speed boat. That's what most people do who live far away."

"No," I said, "that wouldn't work either. Those boats are too modern for my father. Too bad there's not a storytelling contest."

"Why don't you suggest it? They're always looking for new ideas."

"Really? Who would I suggest it to?"

"Ask Elda, she would know."

"I will," I said. "Maybe that would lure him here."

"And he might win."

I smiled. "I know. That's the real selling point. I'm going to ask Elda about it tomorrow."

"It's nice what we're doing for Saamta," Pella said.

"Sio. Don't forget. She hates being called just Saamta."

"I would too if my name meant dirty."

"Does Sio mean anything in Continental?" I asked.

"No."

"That's good. That could be even worse. What if Sio meant face?"

"Dirty face," Pella grinned.

"What if it meant sleepingroom?"

"Dirty sleepingroom. That would be your name."

"I know," I laughed. "That's why I said it."

"Good, then I think your feelings weren't hurt too bad."

"No, I blame Bree for my messiness. It's a messy place. Muddy and mossy. Broken buildings, torn windowscreens, moldy corners. It's dusty when it's dry and musty when it's wet."

"There's something else you could do for Bree. Self-cleaning surfaces."

"Self-cleaning, that sounds good. How do they work?"

"Special nanocoatings," Pella said.

"Where do people get them?" I asked her.

"I don't think you can. They're applied during the manufacturing process."

"Can you buy a bucket of nanocoating and paint it on things yourself?"

"I'm not sure. I don't keep up with the forward edge of nanotech, so for all I know, maybe you can."

"Forward edge of nanotech," I nodded. "I like the words you use. I learned the meaning of innovation yesterday. It's another word that doesn't exist in Welbi. I guess Southern Wershonains aren't very innovation-minded."

"Not technologically, but they are in other ways."

"Really?" I thought about it. "I can't even think of one."

"Southern Wershonian folk music is considered a world treasure," Pella said. "All the music schools teach it. And most people really like it, even though it's ancient. It's pretty, don't you think?"

"I suppose so. It's triumphant, my father says."

"Triumphant, right," Pella smiled.

"And what else? What other good things are there about Southern Wershonia?"

"You have fish drying techniques that food scientists haven't ever been able to improve. And the peaceful reign of the last Welbi monarchs inspired the the better governments of Northern Wershonia."

"You know more about Wershonia than I do," I said. "Where'd you learn all this?"

"History class."

"So maybe being from Bree isn't entirely bad."

"Not entirely. I hope you don't see it that way."

"To be honest, I do, but a lot less than I used to."

"I think you're going to do great things for Bree," Pella said.

"You think so?"

"I'm positive."

I shuddered with the hope that she was right. Despite its hopeless backwardness, I would always love Bree. And wherever in the world I would ever live, I would miss it, the place and the people. I knew that now.

## 26  BIRTHDAY WISHES

The next day a tradition was born.

At Morning Circles, Saamta Sio was not the last to arrive as she commonly was. She was the fifth to show up.

"Oh, no," Pella said when she saw her approaching. "Saamta Sio's here."

"Someone needs to detain her," I said. "Any volunteers?"

After a long silence, Kita spoke up. "I will. She's my goal partner."

"Good," I said, "that's the least conspicuous. Keep her as long as you can."

As Pella read the wishes our teammates had sent to her data sheet, I wrote each one in my best handwriting on a piece of kipper-paper I had made myself years ago in Bree. I had brought a whole stack of it to Vona, ignorant of the facts that they don't write on paper here at all and if they did, it wouldn't be on ragged-edged paper made of kipper seaweed. In my secret embarrassment, I hid my stack of kipper-paper in my sleepingroom, certain it would never once find a useful purpose over the next six years of my life.

"All right, that's everyone," I said, holding seven wishes in my hand.

"No," said Pella, "there's one more. Elda sent one."

"Perfect," I said when I'd written Elda's wish. "These are great wishes. Some are funny and some are serious, just like we asked for."

We folded each wish and put them all in a bowl, not a round, dirt-color wooden one as we always used in Bree, but a square bowl, the kind that folded up flat when you didn't need it and snapped open when you did. The square bowl was light blue and shiny, and as we thought, the light blue made the pink of the kipper-paper look even pinker and the shininess made the rough seaweed texture look expensive and exotic.

"Beautiful," said Pella as we stood back and admired it.

"And festive," said Nin. "I think she's going to love it."

"I hope so," I said.

Then I hid the bowl behind our pile of satchels — mine made of lidden ox leather, Nin's made of faux celerwox hide, and Kita's and Pella's made of a lab-made fabric with 20 pre-programmed colors and patterns that they could change with a simple voice command.

"As you all know, it's a special day," Elda said after we finished our Morning Strengths and Postures.

Elda called me forward, and I presented Saamta Sio with her bowl of wishes, which she read out loud — surprised and happy — through stifled tears. When all the wishes had been read and thank you's sufficiently said, Elda announced that we would be learning outside that day, at a place of Saamta Sio's choice.

Though we didn't know it at the time, we had just pioneered a Vona birthday tradition. By the end of the school year, every student's birthday was celebrated in their team with a bowlful of birthday wishes — handwritten on kipper-paper — and a choice of where their team would learn that day, anywhere within reason.

On the day of my birthday, three weeks later, I chose Sunset Peak. It was deserted and still and lovely that morning, freshly cleansed from an evening rain that had cleared off before sunrise. Every type and shape of cloud filled the sky. Some were clouds I had never seen in Bree. We sat in a circle on a patch of blue, self-drying, synthetic groile.

"It's dry!" I laughed. "Completely dry!"

"After a rain, if it's blue, it's dry," Pella said. "If it's magenta, it's wet. That's the Vona rule, as far as groile goes."

"I like it," I said. "From a distance, just by color, you know exactly what the groile conditions are."

"Power on your holophones," Elda said. "We're going to watch the formation and movement of a hurricane, from inside of it, *as* it."

"That sounds fun," Nin said.

"It is," said Pella. "Pia showed it to me once."

Just then a large transport drone landed on the north side of Sunset

Peak. Eight robots rolled out on their wheeled feet and four adibadis followed behind.

"Look, Lin," Pella whispered. "They're here to put up a net."

"Pay attention, everyone!" Elda shouted. "And keep your opacity at 100%! You're about to become a hurricane!"

With four adibadis nearby, it was almost impossible to pay attention to the hurricane, even though it was everywhere I looked and everything I was. Some laughed and some squealed as the wind we were grew stronger and wilder and our movement across the ocean quickly picked up speed. We were a hurricane barreling toward a nearby coast and most of us were loving it, but not me. I didn't want to be a hurricane. I wanted to watch the adis put up the net.

The hurricane stirred massive waves that tumbled furiously toward a marina. The girls gasped and the boys laughed as we approached a madly bobbing tangle of boats. They were so small and innocent and hopelessly doomed. I braced myself for the impact and instinctively closed my eyes when the first of the boats was ripped to pieces. More boats were ripped, and I kept my eyes shut, even though I could still see the scene. Bits of boats flew around us in a howling, swirling frenzy of destruction. We hit land and sent sand and stones flying, uprooting every tree we passed, leveling every house and building. We left total chaos in our wake and could see nothing but spinning bits of debris against blurry gray air. Then the gray went black and the whooshing, snapping wind turned silent. Our shouting stopped, but some still laughed.

"Destruction is not a laughing matter," Elda said when our eye film self-adjusted to 0% opacity.

I looked over to the robots and adis. They were putting tall poles into the ground.

"I hope this helps you appreciate the work of our weather scientists," Elda went on. "They can predict storms weeks in advance and subdue the most severe hurricanes. The hurricane we just experienced shows the damage that would have been done a hundred years ago. With today's technology, not a single boat would have been destroyed. Our weather scientists have saved thousands and thousands of lives and have very nearly eradicated the destruction of property.... And now, seeing that I've lost your attention, we'll stop for lunch."

While we waited for the food transport drones to arrive, I walked over to the net-raising enterprise.

"Hey," I heard from behind. I turned to see Saamta Sio.

"Hi, Sio," I said.

"Sio," she laughed. "No one's ever called me that."

"Maybe they should. What were your parents thinking," I asked, "naming you Saamta?"

"It's a name from my mother's family. There's a long stupid reason behind it. I'll tell you about it someday."

"I'd like that," I said.

"I want to thank you again for giving me the best birthday I ever had. I still think about it. This morning I kind of relived it all over again."

"Really?"

"Really," she said. "And I hope this is your best birthday too."

"It is so far. And it's not over yet. There might be more great moments."

"A few of us are staying after class to watch the nets go up and see the sunset," she said. "You should join us. We'll turn it into a birthday celebration."

"Count me in," I said. "I'm headed over to watch the adis right now."

"You and me and everyone else." Saamta Sio gestured behind us. Elda and our teammates were following close and far behind.

We sat on patches of blue groile and watched the robots and adis silently working, each knowing what to do. Elda said it was a lesson in teamwork and cooperation.

"When we work together cooperatively," she said, "things get done better and more quickly, which leaves more time for the enjoyment of life."

*A win-win,* I thought.

"Maybe I could bring cooperation to Bree," I said to Pella, my eyes on the adis.

"How?" she asked.

"Not sure yet. I'll have to think about it. Look," I pointed, "there's a robot talking to two adis. I wonder what he's saying?"

"Probably giving them instructions," said Pella.

"A *robot*," I said, "telling an *adi* what to do? That doesn't seem right."

I heard Saamta Sio's staccato laugh two people over. She leaned forward and looked at me. "It's right," she said.

"But robots are robots," I said. "Machines. Adis are practically people. Birgard said their brains are a lot like ours, just smaller. Why don't *they* order the robots around?"

"Because robots are smarter than adis," Novi explained.

I didn't believe him. "Smarter than adis?"

"Way smarter," said Saamta Sio.

"A lot of robot series are smarter than us," Novi said.

I asked him, "How can they be smarter than the people who made them?"

"Because the people who made them wanted super-smart robots and found out ways to do it."

I opened my mouth to ask another question that hadn't yet formed. In the silence, Mira called. "It's Mira," I said.

"Take some distance if you take the call," Elda told me.

I took the call and whispered, "Mira, hold on. I'm taking some distance." I leapt to my feet. "See you all later," I said to Team 10.

A safe distance away I found a blue patch of groile with a better view of the robots and adis. I reduced Mira to 30/50 —30% size and 50% opacity — and slid her to the left side of my visual field.

"Where are you?" she asked after singing a short, funny birthday wish.

"On top of Sunset Peak with Team 10 watching adis and robots putting up a net. You should see what I'm seeing."

I captured an image of my visual field and sent it to Mira's holophone. Within five seconds she got it. My Gen 8 told me so in a friendly voice that sounded like mother's.

"That's what I see on my little pieces of eye film," I said. "Can you believe it?"

"I'm so small," Mira said.

"You're at 30%."

"And half invisible."

"That's 50% opacity."

"Why?"

"So I can see the adis."

"You'd rather see—" Mira stopped herself and smiled. "You've seen my face all your life. Of course you'd rather see the robots and adibadis. They *are* more interesting."

"Don't take it personally, Mira. Everyone does it."

"Makes the person they're talking to small and half invisible?"

"Yes," I said, "all the time."

"Isn't it confusing to be looking at two things at once?"

"No, you get used to it. Novi said that some people have something in every corner of their visual field."

Mira smiled and shook her head. "I'm more convinced than ever that Bree will *never* be ready for Gen 8s."

"I don't know," I said. "You should never say never. Not about anything."

"Maybe in the rest of the world, but here? I'm not convinced. Anyway, I called to cheer you up in case you were homesick. But I don't think you are."

"Not today," I said. "I loved your video message this morning. I watched it while I was still in bed. It was hilarious. It was a great start to a great day. Thanks for thinking of me."

"We're all thinking about you today."

"I know," I said. "My aunt and grandparents called, Bissa called, Hali called, and so did Jabe di Groot. And my father called early this morning. He asked me what I wanted for my birthday, can you believe it?"

"I believe it," Mira said. "It *is* your birthday, and he's been really happy lately. Brister Liggan wrote a big story about people getting married on his boat. His boat marrying business is booming now."

"It was a great story," I said. "I read it on my Gen 8. I was so happy Brister Liggan actually took my advice!"

"Advice?"

"Didn't I tell you? I sent him a message and told him that I had an idea for a story."

"That was your idea?"

"Yes, it was Brister Liggan's best story ever, don't you think?"

"It was pretty good," Mira said. "I have some news you'll love. The wedding planner's in town. Four couples are getting married this week and there are more after that. Koppi said the wedding planner booked a room at Dun Inn for the rest of the month."

"The rest of the month?"

Mira nodded.

"And are they together, she and my father?"

"I've seen them together."

"Were they laughing or acting sweet in any way?"

Mira squinted and smiled. "Mmm-yes, actually. I kind of think so."

"She's really nice, you know."

"She seems nice," Mira said.

"I'm going to try to get father to come in Rasa."

"I thought you said he would never visit you there."

"I know," I said, "but there are competitions here that month, and one of them is a storytelling competition. That was my idea too."

"You change things more than anyone I know."

"Things are meant to be changed," I said. "That's what progress is, one change after another, along positive lines."

"Along positive lines?"

"That's what Mrs. Tria told me. Not all change is good change. Change for the sake of change can actually do damage. That's why progress is change along positive lines. She kind of lectured me about it."

"I'm glad you finally have a mother," Mira said. "As much as she's a mother to you."

"She's more a mother to me now than Teacher Hana was after mother died. And she's just as nice and unbelievably smart. So is Mr. Tria. It's so refreshing to live with mature adults. You have no idea what the kids of Bree are missing out on."

"I have a sense of it," Mira said.

"Pella told me that her family thinks I'm messy."

"Messy? As in 'progress is messy'? Are you still saying that all the time?"

I laughed. "I'm probably saying it more than ever. But they meant sloppy messy. You know, untidy. And I realize, Bree's one messy place. And it's not very beautiful. Not as beautiful as it could be. The only flowers you see in Bree are the ones that grow on their own out in the mosswoods and on the back hills of Mount Tantrill."

"Or that sit in the water buckets at the marketplace," Mira rightly added.

"So I've been thinking, since the groile's been such a success, maybe we can get some synthetic flowers for the edges of the footpaths. I think people are happier when there are flowers around."

"I'd like more flowers," Mira smiled. "I'm sure a lot of people would. You should ask Merchant Kam."

"I will," I said. "Want to see the adis and robots?" I asked.

"Sure."

I video-captured the scene and explained to Mira what nets were.

"The adis are putting the poles in the ground," I told her, "and the robots are lifting the net."

"Look how long their arms are," Mira said of the robots.

"They're called extension arms."

"Adis are so amazing."

"More amazing than robots," I said.

"I hope we get them in Bree."

"I do too. I'm going to try my hardest."

"What are you asking your father for your birthday?" Mira asked.

"A tail trinket and a clarkon raincape. And now that he's in such a good mood, I'm going to ask him for a bunch of parental permissions that have been piling up."

"What kind of permissions?"

"I've been keeping a list on my data sheet. I'll read it to you: a small golden tail trinket, I told you that already ... two fragrance implants, one in each arm ... purple ear trim, just a little along the outer edge ... a brain training utility for my Gen 8 that will teach me math and languages while I sleep—"

"While you sleep?"

"Yes, isn't that amazing?"

"Isn't that cheating?"

"Cheating how?"

"You're sleeping."

"And what's cheating about that?"

"I'm not sure," Mira said. "It just seems like you're getting around the rules."

"What rules?"

"Rules of fairness."

"People do brain training all the time," I said. "It's not unfair. If there's any unfairness, it would be to children whose parents *won't* let them do brain training."

"Parents let their kids learn like that?"

"Yes, and parents do it too. Mostly to learn foreign languages and prepare for meetings. Mr. Tria told me himself."

Mira shook her head. "I don't know if you should ask your father about that one."

"I don't see why not, especially if it helps with my proficiency scores."

"But he's so ... traditional about things. I'd be careful."

"Well," I said, "I thought about all that, and I decided to be bold and ask for what I want. He won't say yes to everything, so I have to give him some things to say no to. Plus, it's my birthday, so I'm going to ask for it all."

"Is there more on your list?"

"Three things. A library of music that I can listen to whenever I want, that's another Gen 8 utility ... and permission to go on two off-island expeditions, one to the island of Wri'wat Ko, where they study weather science, and one to the top animal science school in the world. All the best adi trainers graduate from there."

"I'm sure he'll say yes to that."

"Me too," I said. "I can't wait to go."

"Well, good luck with your list. I hope he says yes to all your favorite ones."

"Thanks, Mir. Our lunch is here. Have I ever shown you what food transport drones look like?"

"Yes, but I'd like to see them again."

"And you can see the water bots too."

"They do look like wingless birds," Mira said.

"They're kind of darling from a distance, don't you think?"

"Kind of. But the adis are more darling."

"More darling than anything."

"Well, I'll let you go. Happy birthday. I hope you have fun with your friends."

"Thanks, Mira. I hope I get to play with the adis when they're done working."

Mira said goodbye and disappeared and I walked back to my spot between Novi and Pella, where we ate and laughed and watched the adis and robots until the net was up and they were done.

As the adis walked toward their transport drone, I waved my arms and shouted to get their attention. Two of them looked over at me, and one of them smiled. I increased the magnification of my visual field and saw a scar below his right eye.

"Gano de nu!" I shouted.

"Gano de nu," I saw him say.

Kita stood near. "You just told him 'hello again'," she told me.

"I know," I said. "He's my friend. His name is Oddi. O-D-D-I, as in oddly adorable."

Pella and I begged Elda to make the adis stay, but she said it wasn't in her power to do so.

*At least I saw him*, I told myself when they boarded the transport drone and disappeared below the horizon. I tried not to be sad, but for a while it was impossible. It being my birthday, I did my best to push the sadness away, which was easy to do in the company of friends.

When the school day was done I called father, who was chipper and talkative and got tears in his eyes when he heard how great a birthday I was having. When I asked him if he would visit in Rasa and bring his wedding planner friend, he grinned and said, "We'll see about that." When he asked me what I wanted this year for my birthday, I asked for everything. And to everything, he said yes — the tail trinket, the raincape, the fragrance implants, the brain training, the music, the weather expedition, and best of all, the animal science school expedition, where I was certain I would study after graduation.

# 27 Zoo U

They called it Zoo U, but I didn't know what a zoo was, so I called it Animal University.

"If you're going to say it like that," Kita said, "you should say Animal U."

"But U is just a letter," I told her, "and not the most interesting one. If you're going to use a letter, Z is a better choice. *Z University*." Everyone laughed, everyone but Kita. "See?" I said. "It *is* better. Zoo U ... Z University. There's no comparison."

Kita threw her hands up. "I give up," she told me, "you're hopeless."

"Hopeless?" I asked.

"Hopeless," she said. "You'll hopelessly never be culturally cool. All my efforts with you go nowhere."

"Good," Novi said. "She's great the way she is."

"He's right," said Saamta Sio. "Lin's a rare nonconformist. Don't try to turn her into one of us. The world needs *more* independent thinkers, not less."

"Well said," Pella nodded.

Kita smiled at me, her teeth all of perfect length. "You know I was only kidding, Lin."

"I know," I said. "I knew all along."

I looked out a window of the ultra-speed and saw a mountain range, thickly forested in all the shades of purple, violet, and magenta.

"Elda," I asked, "how much longer?"

"About half an hour," she said from behind me.

I wiggled in my seat and fidgeted with my new tail trinket, which only slightly took my mind off my swirling stomach.

As I had feared, our one-and-a-half hour flight on the ultra-speed was making me queasy. It flew high and fast and the only thing it had going for it was a solid floor, which spared me a view of the ground. Being a 12-passenger ultra-speed, it was large enough for all of Team 10 plus Elda, with three seats to spare. I took a seat furthest from the windows, which no one minded. Everyone wanted a window view. Truthfully, I wanted one too but I couldn't do it. The excitement of the day was making my queasiness worse. So I looked now and then out one window or another, which, from where I sat, only gave a view of distant horizons and mountaintops.

Pella caught my eye. "Happy?" she asked.

"Out of my mind happy," I said. "There's not a word in any language that could describe it."

I had researched the Animal University so long and so well, I knew much of what the robot guide told us on our tour through its History Hall, where suspended panels showed the earliest videos ever taken of the place. These videos were hardly watchable — flat, dingy, two-dimensional, and practically colorless.

We were greeted by a man with an old, crinkly face and a young woman who was short and stocky like an athletic boy. She wasn't pretty, but she had vibrant eyes and a permanent smile, which gave her a kind of beauty that even Nin envied. And Nin, everyone agreed, was the prettiest girl in our class.

"You can tell she loves her work," I whispered to Pella. "You can see it on her face."

The young woman welcomed us and told us she was a graduate student and the old man was a professor, and they would be touring us today around the university.

"And I understand there is one among you who is interested in pursuing an education in animal husbandry," she said.

My heart skipped a beat. "That would be me," I said.

"Good," she smiled. "Now follow us, everyone. We're on our way to the nurseries."

Even though they smelled bad, we didn't want to leave the nurseries, where we got to hold and feed the newborns. A small oskiwat cub took a liking to Saamta Sio, who held it like a baby and walked it like a mother, patting its back, whispering in its ear, rocking it gently.

The reptiles I didn't care for and refused to touch.

"He's harmless," Novi said when he offered a young lizard for me to hold. "Look, no teeth."

"He's slithery and creepy," I said. "You can have him. I'm more of a mammal person."

I pet or held every furry species at least once, going back to my favorites and giving some of them names. The most adorable was a newborn celerwox, the fastest land animal in the world. She sat in my palms and looked at me with fat black innocent eyes. She opened her mouth wide as if to roar, but the smallest squeak fell out.

"The celerwox," the graduate student stopped and said when she passed by, "they're the fastest runners and the fastest growers. She'll be about your size in a year's time."

"How do they grow so fast?" I asked.

"It's in the genes," she said. "The fastest growers live longer and pass their genes on."

I asked her, "Why don't the slow growers live long?"

"Predators typically go after the smaller, younger, weaker celerwox because they're an easier catch. The more quickly a celerwox grows, the more able it is to outrun a predator. The speed of the celerwox is its greatest defense."

"There's something I've wondered for a long time," I said. "Since predators are always killing innocent animals, why don't people kill the predators until they're all gone?"

She unsmiled and almost frowned and said to me, "I understand your sentiment, but it really doesn't work that way. If you're interested, I'll tell you why while we walk to the labs."

I wasn't interested, but I didn't want to be rude, so I said that I'd like that a lot. And I did my best to pay attention as we walked along the edge of an enormous, misty meadow of tall grasses and wildflowers and small, winged creatures. In the near and far distance, roaming freely, were the most animals I had ever seen in one place. I shuddered knowing that in six years, this is where I would be living and learning.

The professor led our group through the lab and did all the talking while the graduate student stayed near me. After I asked, she confessed that she was giving me special attention because of my interest in zoology.

"I want to train adibadis," I told her.

She smiled and nodded her head. "That's nice," she said.

"Are we going to see some adis today?" I asked.

"I'll make sure we do. Now, let's hear what he's saying."

"Zoology," the professor said, "is the science of animal life. Zoologists study the anatomy of animals, their life cycles, habitat, behavior, distribution, and their relationship to their environment, to people, and to each other."

I didn't know what an anatomy was, and I would have never cared to, but it was a foundation of every zoologist's training, and it was the next part of our tour of the lab, and so I was doomed to find out.

We were led through a large door with a sign on it that read "Virtual Dissection Lab".

"What's a dissection?" I asked the graduate student.

"Look," she smiled, gesturing to a table with a large animal sprawled out on its back, completely still, as if dead.

"Ooo," I heard from the gaping mouths of my teammates first to get there.

"What is it?" Nin asked as she stepped toward the table. "Oh!" she cried when she saw. In disgust, or something like it, she turned away.

I was the last to arrive at the table, curious to know what was so captivating. Everyone but Nin was staring intently at the animal, some smiling, some not. The belly of the animal was cut fully open, its insides grotesquely shimmering greens and yellows and every putrid color in between. I looked to the ground and took a deep breath and tried to see in my mind something beautiful to make the ugliness go away. The horror of what I saw was so great, I thought I might pass out.

I looked at Pella, who stood on the other side of the table. She was staring at me.

"What's wrong?" she silently mouthed.

I put my hands to my belly and made a face of sickness.

"Oh," she mouthed. Her head fell a little to one side as she gazed at me with the most compassionate sweetness I had ever seen from a girl my age.

I looked down at the ground again, standing frozen, listening to the professor talk about organs and vessels and how great it is to have virtual dissection because way back when he was a zoology student they had to cut open real animals. I clutched my belly with one hand and my mouth with the other and ran from the room.

Elda and the graduate student found me in the hallway hiding in a recessed door that said Faculty Only. My muffled crying must have given me away. The sight of them turned my crying to sobbing.

Elda knelt at my side. "Lin, what's the matter?" She wasn't mad at me — I had no sense of that — she was soft and kind.

"I'll get some tissues," the graduate student said.

My hands and face were sopping wet, and all I that tried to say got lost in the sobbing, which had let up only a little.

"Is there something I need to know about?" the graduate student said when she returned with two thick tissues.

"Tell us what's upsetting you," Elda said.

"The dissection," I said through my sobs.

"Do you not like seeing it?"

"I hate seeing it."

"You know it's not a real animal," the graduate student said. "No animals are harmed here in any way."

"It's not that," I said. "I know it's not real. But it looks real and it's ... it's horrific."

"Oh, dear," I heard the graduate student say under her breath.

"I'm really sorry," I said. "I'm sorry I made a scene."

"You've done nothing wrong," the graduate student said.

Her kindness made me cry more.

"Is there something else bothering you?" Elda asked me.

"No," I said, "I just ... I wasn't expecting that. If I'd known, I would have ... I wouldn't have looked. Now I can't get the sight of it out of my mind. I hope I don't have nightmares from it."

"Well, we'll just wait out here until they're done in there," Elda told me. "And if you want, we'll talk to the professor to see if there are any other surprises we need to be prepared for."

There *was* another surprise, and it was worse. It was the second worst surprise of my life, the first being mother's death.

"What do you mean it's required?" I asked the professor when he talked privately with Elda and I.

"Anatomy is a fundamental learning requirement for everyone pursuing zoology," he said.

"But I don't want to pursue zoology," I said. "I want to train adibadis."

His face turned grave and his eyes turned sad and he let a silence pass before he softly said, "All adibadi handlers, trainers, and breeders are required to hold a zoology degree."

"A zoology degree? I have to study zoology to be an adibadi trainer?"

"Yes," he said.

"I have to look at animal insides to be an adibadi trainer?"

"I'm afraid so."

"I have to look at the insides of adis?"

He pursed his puckered lips. "Yes," he nodded.

"Isn't there something ... some way around that? An exception?"

"Well, that's not for me to say."

"Can you ask someone?"

Elda took my arm. "Lin," she said.

I bristled at how she said it, so sad and stern and final. It's over, she was telling me. Those are the rules and there's nothing you can do.

"Then I can't be an adi trainer," I said to the professor. "I can't look at a dissection, not even a fake one. It's impossible. I don't have the stomach for it." Tears fell from my eyes, and I hoped they would make him feel sorry for me and think of something that could be done.

"I am deeply sorry," was all he said.

The rest of the day was ruined. All the great moments that I would treasure forever — like seeing a new litter of adibadi babies and playing with 13 adi toddlers and watching an actual adi training class and running with a pack of young celerwox through a meadow of violet grasses that grew so tall they tickled our knees — were hollow and bleak and steeped in heartbreak.

Pella stayed close by my side and Kita tried to make me laugh every chance there was. I did laugh a few times, especially when she put her head in the open mouth of the world's most feared predatory animal.

He had a paw on a smaller animal he had just mauled. The savage scene was prominently displayed in the holographic zoo that we roamed at the end of our stay.

"Animals shouldn't eat other animals," I said as we walked to the ultra-speed for our return flight to Vona.

"People eat animals," Novi said.

"But not so much anymore," Pella said. "On the Continent, we grow all our meat in labs. Fish is the only exception."

Elda overheard and told us that in the wild, larger animals have always eaten smaller animals and that's just the way it was.

"There's much we've been able to do to alter nature," the graduate student said, "but when it comes to the predator-prey relationship, there's little we can do."

I shook my head at the cruelty of life. I had a lot to say about it, but I kept quiet. We were 20 paces from the ultra-speed.

Elda held me back, ushering my teammates to board ahead of me. The professor and graduate student said a friendly goodbye to each of them as they piled into the ultra-speed.

When I was the last one standing on the boarding dock, the professor and graduate student smiled kindly and said they were certain I had a bright future and to bear in mind that my revulsion to dissection might pass.

"It has happened before," the professor said. "When my father was a child, he got faint at the sight of blood. And yet he became a veterinarian, one of the best surgeons of his day."

"So you see," said the graduate student, "this may be nothing more than a phase that you grow out of. Don't give up hope. Be patient. I won't be surprised to see you here in six years, and I hope I do."

I managed to smile even though I had no hope and was an emotional mess and on the verge of crying all over again.

"Thank you," I said. "You've been really nice about this. That means a lot to me."

I stepped inside the ultra-speed, took the same seat I sat in that morning, and watched from the nearest window what little I could see of Animal University, its sprawling meadows, and the buildings that I would never, I was sure, step foot in again.

## 28  A MYSTERY UNRAVELING

Mira knew as soon as she saw me.

"What's wrong?" she asked.

I just cried.

"I thought you were going to the animal school yesterday," she said. "Did something happen? Did you not go?"

"I went," I said. "It's not that."

I tenebri zeroed my sleepingroom ceiling only to see a dark gray morning sky. It was so depressing I tenebri tened it back to full opacity.

"Then what's upsetting you?" she asked me.

"My future is ruined."

"Ruined how?"

"I'm not going to be an adibadi trainer."

"You're *not?* Why? You were so—"

"Because to be an adibadi trainer you have to look at animal insides, and I can't do it, Mira. I can't do it."

"Animal insides? What are you talking about?"

I told Mira what dissection was and that every adibadi trainer had to do it as part of their schooling and how the school won't make exceptions to that rule, not even for a girl from Bree who loves adibadis more than anything else.

"That *is* tragic," Mira said, shaking her head for the longest time.

"I don't know how I'm ever going to get over this," I said. "I don't know if I can even go to school today. I'm so depressed, Mira. I feel like I've lost everything."

Mira stared at me, half-squinting. She was thinking, thinking before she spoke. I had always admired her for that. "So what will help you most," she finally said, "sympathy or common sense?"

"Both if you can do it."

Mira smiled. "All right," she said, "I'll start with the common sense."

Already I felt a little better.

"First, you *will* get over this. No one's better at getting over tragedies than you. Every tragedy you've ever suffered, you got over. Every single one. Right?"

"Right," I said.

"And think about this. Every time something really bad happens, something good always happens again. Every time. There's goodness in your future. Maybe today. Maybe a bunch of times today."

"Maybe so. I know everyone at Morning Circles will be nice to me. You should have seen how sad and sympathetic they were when we flew home yesterday. They care about me, Mira, like real friends, not just schoolmates. I can't tell you how great that is."

"Then you should definitely go to Morning Circles. And I know you. When you're sad, you do better when you're with other people. Being alone just makes all your bad feelings worse."

"Mmm," I nodded. "Thanks, Mira."

"You seem better," she said.

"I am, except for...." I tried not to cry, but the urge was too strong. Mira waited patiently while I cried some more.

"What?" she said when my tears let up.

"I have to give a talk at the end of the week."

"But you're doing great with those."

"I know, but this was the big special one I was actually looking forward to giving, the one on animal training."

"Ohhh," she said, shaking her head again.

"I had a great talk planned, but now it's ruined. And I don't know what to say now."

"I wish I knew what to tell you."

"Thanks, I know you do. I'm going to talk to Elda about it. Maybe she'll give me an extension."

"What's an extension?" Mira asked.

"That's when you have to do something at a certain time and they let you do it later."

"I hope she says yes."

"Me too," I said. "Mid-term break's next week. Maybe she'll give me an extension to the week after."

"Mid-terms? Already?"

"Yes, a whole week of no classes and sleeping in."

"It's so strange," Mira said. "We just *started* school."

"How's teacher Gwin? Is she—?"

"Yes, everything they say is true. She snorts and spits in a tissue, right in front of everyone."

We laughed, Mira more than me.

"We have a big math exam in two weeks," Mira said. "Hali's tutoring anyone who needs it for an argen an hour."

"That's pretty enterprising."

"He's smarter than anyone I know."

"I hope he gets out of Bree like you," I said. "I hope he doesn't waste his intelligence."

"Me too," Mira agreed.

"Encourage him."

"I don't think he needs encouragement. He's already talking about the University of Clud."

"Good," I said. I shook my head.

"What?"

"Mira, I don't know if I'll ever be able to look at an adi again without crying."

"You will," she said. "You will. It's just a matter of when. And to tell you the truth, I haven't been convinced that adibadi training is your true calling. Isn't that how you say it? Calling?"

"Yes. Novi says the same thing, and Birgard too. They both think I have a better intelligence than what animal training requires."

"That's exactly what I think."

"Well, you know me. What do *you* think my true calling is?"

"I think for you it's more than one thing," Mira said.

"That's not very helpful."

"I wasn't done. I think your calling is to do what you do best, which is to change things and to inspire people to think about new possibilities."

"That's not really a vocation, though."

"Sure it is," she said. "They call it advocacy."

"Advocacy?"

"You don't know what advocacy is?"

"No," I said. "How do *you* know?"

"From Hali. He's been studying history on his holophone. We were talking about you one day, and he said that you're an advocate."

"What's an advocate?"

"A person who stands up for a cause. There are a lot of them in history. They're really great people, you'd like them. Look it up on your holophone: advocate."

"But is that a vocation?"

"I'm not sure," Mira said. "You should ask Elda."

I decided to ask Elda after Morning Circles.

"Advocacy," she said. "Give me a few days to look into it."

A few days seemed like a long time to wait, but when I complained to Mrs. Tria about it, she gave me a lecture on impatience. I didn't mind, though, she had a way of lecturing that didn't feel like scolding and left me feeling a little wiser afterward.

And waiting a few days gave me a reason to call Merchant Kam.

"Do you know anything about advocacy?" I asked him when he said he had time to talk to me.

"What kind of advocacy in particular?"

"I don't know. What I'm really wondering is, is advocacy a vocation?"

"It is not a vocational track," he said, "if that's what you mean."

"That is what I meant. There's not an advocacy school?"

He laughed. "No, none that I know of. People who are advocates are from any number of professions. Law, education, journalism, government ... those are a few that come to mind."

"So if I want to be an advocate, I have to be something else first."

"You can be from any profession," he said. "What exactly do you want to advocate?"

"I'm not sure, I haven't gotten that far yet. I definitely want to advocate for progress, though. I do know that."

"You realize, don't you, that you're already an experienced progress advocate."

"I am?"

"Look at how Bree has progressed because of you. Holophones and groile. You inspired the teachers' petition for holophonic teaching. We have flower-lined paths now because of your relentless push for them."

"Flowers that will never die," I said with pride. "Aunt Tala said everyone loves them. They're beautiful, aren't they? She sent me some video."

"Yes, they are. And you continue to advocate for Bree's progress." Merchant Kam smiled like a proud teacher. "And so you see, Lin, you're a natural advocate. You need no training in advocacy. None whatsoever."

"Oh."

"You sound disappointed."

"I was hoping there was an advocacy school," I said.

"Now the last I heard, you wanted to be an adibadi handler."

"I did," I choked. "But I'd have to study zoology, and I can't handle the dissection."

"I see," he said.

"I asked them if they could make an exception, but universities don't make exceptions."

"Exceptions of that nature, no."

"So now I'm back to the beginning."

"Beginning?"

"Figuring out my vocational track."

Merchant Kam gave me a lecture on patience, and like Mrs. Tria's lecture on impatience the night before, it wasn't scolding and it made me feel a little wiser in the end. I hoped the wisdom would stick. It was dawning on me that I had a problem with impatience and that it could get me in trouble. They both had said so, with actual examples.

"The announcement you made that you were bringing adibadis to Bree was made in haste," Merchant Kam said. "And that caused you and others no small amount of anguish."

"Right," I said. "But even though I won't be an adi trainer in Bree, I still think we should have them."

"Lin, be patient with that too."

"Why?"

"Adibadis are expensive to purchase, to import, to house, and to feed."

"They are?"

"Yes."

"But we're an impoverished region. Maybe we could get them at a discount or for free even."

"I doubt that."

"We could at least ask."

Merchant Kam held up a hand, pointing upward at nothing, and grinned. "Do you see?" he said.

"What?"

"Advocacy. You were advocating."

I thought about it. "I guess you're right," I said. "So advocacy is wanting something and trying to get it or make it happen."

"Yes. That's what advocacy is."

"I like advocacy."

"I believe you have a future in it, to a greater or lesser extent. And how much and in what way is up to you."

"I think I'm getting over it," I said. "I can't believe it."

"Getting over...?"

"The tragedy of not being an adibadi trainer. Maybe my friends are right. I have a different kind of intelligence."

"Your intelligence is still forming," Merchant Kam said. "Remember that. And it will continue to all through your teenage years. In a sense that means you're somewhat of a mystery to yourself."

"I *do* feel like a mystery to myself."

"I did too at your age."

"You did?"

"Yes. That's why I advise patience. Give yourself time to develop. Think of yourself as a mystery unraveling."

"I'm a mystery unraveling. I like that, Merchant Kam. I like that a lot."

"We're a mystery unraveling," I said to Pella after dinner that night when we sat in her sleepingroom watching the rain and lightning, talking in our native languages with our translators on.

"That sounds interesting," she said. "Tell me what that means."

We talked late into the night about the mysteries that we were and what we knew we *didn't* want to be when we grew up and what she knew about advocacy and how my latest efforts to get my father to visit in Rasa were going.

"He keeps saying, 'we'll see,' which isn't a no," I said. "Father's quick to say no if he's against an idea. That means there's hope."

"I love hope."

"Me too. And no matter how hopeless a situation seems, we should still have hope, because you never know what's going to happen next."

"You're right," Pella said.

"Life is a mystery unraveling."

"Just like us," she smiled.

"Yes," I said. "Just like us."

## 29 DIPLOMATIC BONES

A week later I saw an adibadi and I cried.

It was the first day of mid-term break, and since the cloudy skies were dry, we went to the North Shore for some groile sliding. We were happy, even me. I had been granted a two-week extension on my talk on vocations in zoology, and I had mostly gotten over the blow of learning that I didn't have a future in adibadi training.

But then, on our great day of fun, I saw him, an adi in the distance. He was clearing away debris from the beach that had washed up in a sea storm. He was alone and hunched over and the sight of him brought back all the sadness I had felt that day at Animal University.

I sat on a nearby patch of groile, pretending to make a call, my back to my friends.

"Lin," I soon heard someone say from behind. It was Pella, who walked past and turned to look at me. "Are you laughing or crying?"

I didn't have to answer.

"You're crying," she said. "It's the adi, isn't it?"

I nodded and buried my face in my hands.

"Can I sit down?"

I nodded again.

She sat close and said, "I'm so sorry." As we sat silently, shoulders touching, Pella swayed us side to side in a slow, steady show of caring and kindness.

"Thanks," I said, wiping my face with a tissuecloth the graduate student at Animal University gave me extras of. When my face was dry, I held it up. "This is amazing," I said. "You can use it for the longest time. It can do what 20 tissuecloths from Bree can do."

Pella giggled.

"I'm serious," I said. "Twenty, maybe more. Bree's so impossibly primitive, Pella. It annoyed me when I lived there, and it annoys me now. And it's really going to annoy me when I go back. We're never going to have adibadis in Bree. Never."

"You shouldn't *ever* say never," Pella said. "A wise woman once told me that. I think it was you."

I laughed. "Well, believe me, Bree's an exception. A big, hopeless exception.... It's so unfair, Pella. I had my whole life figured out, a life in Bree I could live with. A happy adibadi future."

"You have a different happy future. Just because you don't know what it is yet, doesn't mean it's not there for you."

"I *can* see myself being an advocate, but where, and for what?"

"Bree needs an advocate," Pella said, "desperately. You could always start there."

"Progress in Bree will always be too slow and too difficult. Every little thing I suggest — great things, useful things, things that will make life better for everyone — they have to be approved by the Committee of No Technology." I held up my tissuecloth. "Even these harmless tissuecloths that work at least twenty times better than what they have now, the Committee has to talk about and vote on. It's ridiculous."

"Do the people of Bree want progress?"

"Yes," I said, "most of them."

"Then *they* should vote, don't you think?"

"Yes, they should."

"Maybe you should change that."

"My father would hate me for it."

"What? Why?"

"Because his naysayer friends would blame *him* for all my revolutionary activities. They've done it before. My father has never been nicer to me than since I've been here. And you know why?"

"Why?" she asked.

"Because I'm here now. I'm not there stirring up trouble that he gets wrath for."

"You really think so?"

"I know so," I said. "My aunt told me herself."

But Aunt Tala was only half-right about that. There had been another reason for all of father's niceness. The tourist season. And now that the tourist season was over, the joy of his life — telling stories to his adoring crowds — was suddenly gone. I did my best not to expect the worst.

"Hi, father!" I said the next day in a video message. "You think we have bad skies in Bree? Look at these clouds! They're called angry clouds, and they're going to rain buckets later on. But don't worry, I'm safe. I'm in my sleepingroom, showing you the clouds through my invisible ceiling. Anyway, there are some permissions I need. Not for stuff, just for two off-island expeditions. So you'll be getting a call from the school. Aunt Tala said that you've been resting from a grueling finale to the tourist season. I'm so happy for your all your successes and all the weddings on your boat! Have you thought anymore about visiting in Rasa? I know you would win the storytelling competition, and I think you would like walking on soft, violet sand. I'm giving a big talk next week. I'll send you the video. We're off this week for mid-terms, so you can call me any time during the day. My day, not yours. I love you father. And call me soon, I miss you."

Days passed, and he didn't call. I phoned Aunt Tala to find out what was going on.

"No, he hasn't been too busy," she said. "He's not fishing at all. He's horribly depressed and keeping to himself."

"Because tourist season is over?"

She frowned a sad smile. "Yes, I'm sure that's why."

"Just like last year. I hope this isn't long and awful. We need to do something."

"I'd be careful about meddling, Lin."

"I'll be careful," I said. "Will you give me the number of the wedding planner?"

"The wedding planner? Why would you want to call *her?*"

"To invite her to come to Vona with father in Rasa. If she likes the idea, she might talk him into it."

"No," Aunt Tala said.

"No what?"

"No number."

"You know I'll just get it from somewhere else," I said. "So you can save me the trouble. Even though it's mid-terms, I'm busy. We still have to study, and I have a big talk to write. Why are you laughing? I'm serious."

"And who do you think will give you the wedding planner's number?"

"Brister Liggan or Koppi Dun."

"Koppi?"

"The wedding planner stayed at Dun Inn when she was there last month."

"You're incorrigible," Aunt Tala said.

"Is that good?"

She smiled as she said it. "Mostly no." Then she coughed up the wedding planner's number. "I'm doing this because I trust you," she said. "And the wedding planner — Gilden is her name, *please* don't call her wedding planner, that would be terribly rude."

"All right."

"Gilden has said many times how much she wants to meet you. I think she might like hearing from you. But don't be pushy."

"Pushy?"

"Don't push your agenda of inviting she and your father to Vona and the matchmaking I know you're doing."

"I—"

"I know what you're up to. And if you love your father and don't want to destroy any kind of future they have, whatever that may be, don't be pushy. Invite her to Vona, be polite about it, and accept whatever she says. Do you understand that?"

"Accept whatever she says. Don't be pushy."

"Good," she said.

"They *do* like each other, don't they?"

"Like each other? Yes. They have a nice camaraderie. They make each other laugh. Whether they have romantic feelings or not, I don't know. I would err on the side of no. So, no, they do not have a romantic future as far as we know. Let's go with that for now."

"All right, I can live with that."

"And Lin, when you call her, call when it's morning there at Vona.

Don't call her any later than your lunch hour. That would be disrespectful."

The next morning, I called the wedding planner. Just as Aunt Tala predicted, she was pleasantly surprised to hear from me. She was about as nice as I expected, almost as pretty, and a bit on the gossipy side, especially about the most important topic of our conversation.

"Your father," she said, "he's a lovely man. You must so proud of him."

"I am," I said.

"He's a man with a kind heart, hidden beneath all his bravery and bravado. I sense that few people see his gentle nature. He thinks it's unmanly, so he conceals it. My husband — I lost him six years ago — he was a strong man with a gentle heart, just like your father. Strength and gentleness, they're wonderful qualities when combined in a single person."

"They are," I agreed.

"He adores you," she said. "He lights up when he talks about you."

"He does?"

"You don't know?"

"No," I said, "I guess he conceals that too."

"You see?" She raised her brow and shook her head.

I couldn't keep my eyes off her ears, which were painted four shades of teal that perfectly complimented her green-gray eyes, which were quite pretty though her face was fairly plain.

She leaned forward as if to whisper a secret. "You need to know, then," she said. "He's *very* proud of you, Lin. He's proud of your achievements and he's proud of your ... oh, how did he say it? Your willful determination."

"I can be willful," I smiled. I was glad that was out in the open. If I came across as pushy, she would understand. "Speaking of willful," I said, "I have something to ask you. A couple of things, really."

"Yes, dear, what is it?"

"First, I want to invite you and my father to visit me at Vona in late Rasa. That's when school ends and all the families come, a lot of them, anyway."

"Well," she said, smiling a soft sadness, "that can be a busy time for me. Everyone wants to get married during the dry season, can you blame them?"

"No."

"Has your father made his travel arrangements yet?"

"No, not yet. He kind of hasn't completely said yes. I think if you decided to go with him, he would jump at the chance."

A bout of shyness came over her. She stammered some non-words and looked away for the very first time since we had been talking. *Always maintain excellent eye contact*, I remembered Elda saying one day.

"You don't have to decide now," I said. "I just wanted to ask you."

"I appreciate the invitation," she said. "We'll see what Rasa has in store for me."

*We'll see?* That's what father always says. I tried to hide my disappointment. "Good," I smiled. "I also wanted you to know that father can get a little blue after the tourist season ends. I think it's from sudden extreme loneliness, you know, after all the big crowds. The crowds are a joy to him."

"And he is a joy to them as well. He's a unique and inspiring man, especially to city-dwellers."

"I'm glad to know that," I said. "Anyway, it's heartbreaking to see him so unhappy. Maybe you could call him and cheer him up. I know it would make him happy, to talk to you."

"Is this your second question?"

"Yes."

"You're a lovely girl, Lin. I see how much you care about him."

"I do care about him. I want so much for him to be happy and unlonely. First he lost mother, and now he's kind of lost me."

"I understand your meaning," the wedding planner said. "And it's good that you've told me this. I assumed he was a man who was always in a crowd, surrounded by people."

"No, not when the tourists leave. Everyone in Bree has already heard his all stories, some a lot more than once."

"I've been missing your father's humor," she said. "I will most definitely call him."

"Thank you, Gilden. Aside from my mother, there's never been anyone he's liked as much as you."

She mumbled and averted her eyes, smiling and bashful.

Three days later, I called Mira with good news.

"I just talked to father," I said. "He called me, his mood was good, almost great. And you know why?"

"The wedding planner professed her love to him?"

"No, but there's hope. More hope than ever. She called him. He went on and on about it. I asked her to promise not to tell him I asked her to, and I think she didn't. He kept saying, 'how nice of her to think of me'. He likes her, and she likes him. And they might come visit me, together."

"They might?"

"They haven't said no, so I'm hopeful. And she *likes* Bree, can you believe it? That's one big problem in finding father a wife that I don't have to deal with."

"Well, I didn't think you'd get this far with it," Mira said. "What a surprise. I'm happy for you."

"Thanks, Mira."

"It's really cheered you up. Last time we talked, you thought your life was over."

"I know," I said, "a lot can happen."

"A lot does happen, all the time."

"And sometimes it goes your way."

"And sometimes it doesn't."

"And when it doesn't," I said, "we have to make a different plan."

"A better one."

"Hopefully. I still don't know what I'm going to be studying in six years."

Mira laughed. "That sounds kind of crazy."

"Crazy? How?"

"The way you said it. Like it's the end of the world that you don't know what you're going to study in college. You're only 14."

"You're right, you're right. I'm still a mystery unraveling. I keep forgetting that."

"A mystery unraveling?"

I told Mira about my conversation with Merchant Kam and what he said about our teens being a time of discovering who we are.

"That's good advice for you," Mira said.

"I know, everyone keeps telling me I have an impatience problem."

"You also have a drama problem."

"What's a drama problem?"

"That's when you take any little thing and make it a big thing, bigger than it really is, and get all upset about it."

"Really? I do that?"

Mira grimaced. "Yes."

"For how long?"

"For as long as I've known you."

"My father does that," I said, half-dazed.

"Maybe that's where it comes from."

I laughed. "I can blame him."

"If you want."

"Well, thanks for telling me and not being mean about it."

"Thanks for listening and not being mad about it."

"I'm *not* mad," I realized. "That's really great."

"And now you know something more about yourself. You're a little less of a mystery now."

"I wish a better part of me unraveled. A more interesting part."

"But at least you unraveled," Mira said. "If you unravel a little every day, after a while, you'll figure out what to do with your life."

"I think you're right."

"You said you were going to ask Elda about being a professional advocate."

"I did. It's not that simple. There isn't an advocate school."

"But there's a diplomacy school, isn't there?"

"There is," I said. "We're visiting the embassy in a couple of weeks."

Mira tapped her chin with her kipper-ink pen. "Think about that. Diplomacy school."

"I have. I don't have the temperament for it. Aunt Tala told me."

"She did?"

"She told me I don't have a diplomatic bone in my body."

Mira laughed. "That's kind of ... direct."

"You know Aunt Tala."

"Well, I still see you working in some embassy-type job."

"I love embassies," I said. "Crossroads of the world."

"That's poetic. Who said that?"

"I did. Just now."

"It's good."

I smiled. "I love you, Mira."

"I love you, Lin."

"Keep an eye on my father?"

"I will. And Lin, when you go to the embassy, forget about what your aunt said. Maybe you do have some diplomatic bones, but they're still growing."

"You think so?"

"Who knows you better than me?"

No one knew me better than Mira, not Aunt Tala, not father, not even me, really. I was still a mystery to myself. But I was a mystery unraveling. And I promised myself to unravel at least a little every day.

## 30  TWENTY-TWO PERCENT

The day after our tour of the embassy, I called Mira with the best news of my life.

I had to wait until morning to call because of the time difference between us, but waiting gave me a whole night to sleep on my decision — to help me be sure it wasn't just another fleeting fascination, to use the words of Mrs. Tria. She had told me at dinner the night before how important it was to take time and go slow when we're making major life decisions.

When I woke feeling *more* certain about my decision, not less, I was overjoyed.

I tenebri zeroed my ceiling to watch the brightening of the early morning sky. Fat raindrops splat on the roof, slow and steady. A deep calm filled me. I was certain, I was so certain.

"Lin! I was about to call you," Mira said. "How was your day at the embassy?"

"Better than great," I said. "You were right, that's where I belong, doing embassy work. I've decided, Mira. I've decided!"

"So, tell me then."

"I'm going to work with Egli slaves. Can you believe it?"

"I can believe it," she said. "You've always liked them."

"I met some yesterday. They were in a language class learning Culti. I told them I've only been learning it less than three years, and look how well I speak it now. One girl told me it was encouraging to hear that."

"Congratulations. You're really happy," Mira said. "Happier than the day you got your Gen 8."

"I know I can help them. And they really need help. Not enough people care about Eglians or even understand what they've been through. Since I'm from Bree and had the life I've had, I can understand them better than anyone."

"That's true."

"The counselor at the Expatriation Center said she could tell the Eglians took a liking to me. She said I had a special fondness for them and that it showed. I'm going to interview her next week."

"The counselor?"

"Yes," I said, "and I'm going to interview a citizenship lawyer and Mr. Tria."

"Citizenship lawyer?"

"They're really called expatriation lawyers, but I like citizenship lawyer better."

"Me too. Are you thinking about being one?"

"Maybe. To work with Egli slaves, I could be a lawyer or a counselor or a language teacher. That's why I'm interviewing Mr. Tria. He's a linguist, and he says I have a gift for language."

"You do," Mira said. "But I don't think you'd be the best language teacher, to tell you the truth."

"Why do you say that?"

Mira smiled. "Think about it. If it takes a long time to learn a language, it takes a long time to teach it. If you want to teach a foreign language, you need to have stellar patience. And your—"

"Right," I said. "I see what you mean."

"I think you'd make a good lawyer."

"I do too, but I'm not so sure I'd like it. Lawyers don't spend as much time with the Eglians as the teachers and counselors do. And they have a lot of meetings and do a lot of paperwork. Kita told me all about lawyering. Her father's a lawyer, so she's practically an expert. She said lawyers have to be sticklers for details or they could make a big mess of things. That's why she said she's doubtful that I have a future in law since details aren't my strong suit and I can be rebellious like her. She said that as a compliment."

"And you're still thinking about being a lawyer, after all she told you?"

"Yes," I said. "It's a prestigious profession that could open a lot of doors for me. And if I was really good at it, I could become a judge someday. Can't you see me as a judge?"

"Sitting in the highest chair in the courtroom and telling people what to do? Yes, I can see that."

"Judging is more than just that. They keep order in the court, they listen impartially, and they make sure the accused is getting a fair trial. That's the part I like best. Fair trials."

"Well," Mira said, "good luck with that, your future plans."

"Oh, speaking of the future, I have more great news. The Trias want to take me all over Northern Wershonia during Travel School."

"What Travel School?"

"That's our new nickname for the Excursion Months, the three months we're not learning on campus."

"Oh, right, when you travel the world."

"Right. That's why I call it Travel School. I came up with it, and now all my schoolmates are calling it that. Most of them, anyway."

"You and nicknames," Mira said. "Whatever happened to yours?"

"What? Broken Arm Girl and Gen One Girl?"

Mira nodded.

"No one calls me that anymore. And I'm glad, actually. I want to be Lin. Just Lin. Although … Birgard still calls me scholar of Bree sometimes. That's nice."

"Birgard," Mira said.

"What?"

"Oh, just the way you said it."

"I said it perfectly normally," I said.

"Yes, but with a lilt in your voice."

"Lilt? What lilt?"

"It's subtle, but it's there," Mira said.

"I think you're imagining it."

"Suit yourself," she smiled.

"As I was saying, the Trias have been all over Northern Wershonia, and they think I should get acquainted with it. They want to take me through every country and see the big cities and the countrysides and the big ports of the North Coast."

"Sounds great," Mira said. "And you'll be there three months?"

"Yes, father has to approve it first, but why wouldn't he?"

"Right, why wouldn't he? It's not Waturi, where you could get kidnapped."

"They only kidnap wealthy kids, but I get your point."

"Northern Wershonia," Mira said. "I'm insanely jealous."

"I'd be too."

"Well, I hope your father says yes without a fight."

"Have you seen him lately?" I asked.

"Not since you and I talked last."

"Well, he'll say yes eventually. I have to go *somewhere* for Travel School, and it might as well be Wershonia. And since Bree's impoverished, he doesn't have to pay."

"You're right," Mira agreed. "He'll say yes."

Two days later, father said no. I called Aunt Tala in tears.

"Lin, I'm so sorry to hear that," she said. "What did he tell you? What were his reasons?"

"He told me he doesn't know the Trias and what kind of people they are ... and that three months is a long time ... that he wanted me home ... that I belong home ... and whatever kind of learning that's done on vacation shouldn't be too important to miss out on ... and what kind of school goes on all year without a break anyway?"

"Oh, dear," she said.

"It's not vacation," I said. "It's Travel School. It's required. I don't understand why he doesn't get that. I never told him I'd be coming to Bree after our final proficiency tests. Did you?"

"No, I didn't."

"Well, he thinks that my school year is over after finals."

Aunt Tala shook her head. "He had to have known you wouldn't be coming back to Bree. It was in the paperwork he signed."

"Well you know how father is with paperwork," I said.

"He told me he read it all."

"Well, either he didn't or he forgot all the parts he didn't like."

"That would explain it," Aunt Tala said.

"Is his mood still bad?"

"He's coming out of his depression more quickly than last year."

"Has he talked more to the wedding planner?"

"I'm not sure," she said.

"I was going to ask him about her. I was going to ask him about a lot of things, but I brought Travel School up first, and when he said no, I couldn't wait to get off the call. I don't want to argue with him, Aunt Tala. I don't want him to be angry at me, and I don't want to make him sad. I just want him to be happy."

"I know you do," she said. "I'll talk to him, so don't fret about this. You have enough to handle, and your grades are suffering."

"I know."

"Seriously suffering."

"You don't have to rub it in."

"I don't want to rub it in," Aunt Tala said. "I want you to recognize the gravity of the situation."

"Gravity as in grave?"

"Yes, it's grave. You have two more months to bring your proficiency scores up."

"Three."

"Two. Trust me, it's two. I talked to the school. They have to be improved *before* final proficiencies."

"You know why they're so bad," I said.

"Why your scores are bad?"

"Yes. I've had a rotten education. They don't teach you anything in Bree. All my schoolmates went to great schools, honor schools some of them. I'm having to catch up with them *and* in a language that's still new to me. Do you see how unfair it is?"

"It is unfair," Aunt Tala said. "It's a great disadvantage and handicap, and the school knew that when you were accepted. That's why you're being graded on a different metric than all of your schoolmates."

"I know about that. They're increasing my scores by an average of 22 percent."

"So you understand, then, how serious the issue of your scores has become."

"I don't think I'm doing so bad."

"Sixty-three percent on your math proficiencies?"

"Right. Add 22 and you have 85 percent."

"No, Lin. The 22 percent has already been added in."

"I don't understand."

"Add 22 to 41 and you have 63. Sixty-three percent."

"What!?"

"Lin, the scores you're given already include the 22 percent."

A heavy rock of doom dropped in my belly.

"No," I said.

"Yes."

"No, no, no. There must be some kind of mistake."

Aunt Tala shook her head, all solemn and serious. "Is that what you've been thinking all along? Have you been adding 22 percent to your scores every month?"

I swallowed hard. "Yes," I said.

"Oh, dear."

"Don't be mad."

"I'm not mad.

"My heart's beating really fast," I said, "and not in a good way. I think it's going to explode."

"It's probably a panic attack. Take deep, slow breaths, remember?"

I breathed as deep and slow as I could. My heart felt less explosive, but I didn't feel any better, and I didn't feel more calm. I felt doom and dread and the heartbreak of a broken future.

"I'm 22 percent more stupid than I thought," I cried. "There goes law school."

Aunt Tala's eyes opened with wide surprise. "Law school?"

I mumbled between sobs, "I was going to tell you ... I'm thinking of going to law school ... it was supposed to be good news ... really good news ... I'm going to work with Egli slaves ... I decided on my career."

"What? When did all of this happen?"

"The last few days." I dried my face with an Animal University tissuecloth. "I decided the day we went to the embassy."

"Well, that's ... interesting. I wasn't expecting to hear that."

"I was all happy about it, and now my happiness is ruined because of 22 stupid percent. Twenty-two stupid percent."

Aunt Tala sighed her sympathy, long and slow, and then she smiled. "I have an idea," she said. "I'm going to schedule a conference with you and I and the school. We'll explain this misunderstanding and devise a highly focused tutoring plan for you."

"I hate those tutoring rooms. They give me nightmares."

"We'll explain that too. I'm sure they would be willing to grant a special exception where you can be tutored elsewhere."

"All right," I said. "It's not too late to turn things around."

"No," Aunt Tala said, "not at all. I have complete confidence in you."

"You do?"

"Yes, I do."

"Please don't tell father."

"I won't," she said, "I promise."

"Only tell him good things for a while."

"Only good things," she smiled.

I wiped some tears and held up the tissuecloth. "Have I told you about these yet?"

"No."

I told Aunt Tala about the Animal University tissuecloths and asked her if she would mention them to Merchant Kam and find out if he thinks we could get them imported to Bree without too much fuss from the Committee of No Technology.

"That's a matter you should take up with him yourself," she said. "Why don't you give him a call? He might have some good advice for you regarding your studies and your scores."

"All right," I said. "That's a great idea."

"Good," Aunt Tala smiled. "Good."

"Thanks, Aunt Tala. Some days you're just like a mother. Kind and sweet and smart. Every one needs a mother. Especially the ones who are hurting the most and who've had the most difficult lives. That's why I want to work with escaped Egli slaves. I can be a kind and sweet motherly person in their life. Most of them are young, you know. They escape and they're free, but then they're like orphans in a big, scary world. They have no one, not until they find a host family, and sometimes that takes a while."

Aunt Tala brushed away a tear. Instinctively, I held out my tissuecloth. It took a full few seconds to realize that she was there and I was here.

"Did you see what I did?" I said.

"You offered me your tissuecloth."

"That's how real you look in a Gen 8. Really real. It's kind of spooky, actually. I hope you get to try a Gen 8 sometime."

"Oh, I plan to. Some day."

"I miss you, Aunt Tala."

"I miss you, too, Lin. You make me very proud. You're a good girl and you mean well and you have a big heart and a feisty intellect."

"And I'm going to get my scores up," I said with more confidence than I actually felt. "I have to or else my whole future is ruined. The future I've been working so hard for."

Aunt Tala was still smiling when she faded from view, leaving me alone in the darkness of dread.

I thought of mother and tried to see her face, to feel her love, to hear her say that everything would be all right and I would get my scores up and father would come around and say yes to Travel School. When that made me feel no better, I called Pella, even though she was just a room away, for some comfort and consoling and understanding sympathy.

"Don't worry about your scores," she said after I told her the story. "I'm going to help you. We all will."

"We?" I asked.

"Me, my family, the team."

"But I don't want them to know," I said.

"You don't have to tell them the embarrassing details."

"I guess you're right."

But in the end I did tell them the details, at lunch that day. We laughed and laughed, and it's true what they say, that laughter is medicine. My dread disappeared, and in its place I felt confidence. Not confidence in me, so much, but in my situation. I had the smartest friends a girl could have, friends who cared and who promised to help and said they believed in me.

And since they believed I could get my scores up, it was easier for me to believe. Most days I mostly did.

# 31  THE IDEA DREAM

Two days later I called Merchant Kam.

"Yes, I've spoken with your aunt," he said. "I'm sorry to hear there was confusion in your mind about your actual scores."

"Twenty-two percent confusion," I said.

Merchant Kam smiled and nodded knowingly. "We're optimists, you and I," he said, "and as such, we can make trouble for ourselves."

"Trouble? How?"

"We prefer to see life as being better than it actually is. Sometimes we're right, but often we're not."

"Oh. Is there a way I can be right more often?"

"There is," he said, "by making a habit of questioning what you believe to be true and then being willing to accept unpleasant facts. Then you will be the best kind of optimist. A practical optimist."

"Is that what you are? A practical optimist?"

"I strive to be."

"I'm going to strive to be too," I said. "Especially if it will stop me from making stupid mistakes like this."

"Good."

"I'm supremely stressed, Merchant Kam. I don't know *how* I'm going to get my scores up. I know I will — I have to — but I don't know how. I was hoping you had some advice for me."

"I've been giving some thought to it," he said, "and yes, I do."

"Merchant Kam gave me great study advice," I told Pella later that morning as we walked to school. "Look, I wrote it all down on my data sheet. Pages and pages." I held it up for her to see.

Pella took a long, squinted look. "Either that's written in Welbi or you have terrible handwriting."

"It's in Welbi *and* I have terrible handwriting," I said. "So I've been told."

"Fortunately that doesn't matter anymore," Pella told me. "Before Gen 4s, everyone wrote. Now it's totally optional. My grandmother told me that when she was in school, they were graded on handwriting ability."

"Really? That's not very fair. What if you were born with bad handwriting? Some people are, you know. As hard as they try, they can't get over it. It's like trying to make your tail longer or your ears taller. You can't do it. You're stuck with it."

"And what if you're born terrible at math?" Pella wondered. "Do you think that's the same thing?"

"Probably not," I said. "Math can be learned. But tails can't be grown, not by a mere act of will."

"You're pretty smart for having such low proficiencies."

"Thanks, Pella. Shows you how much my scores are the fault of my paltry education."

"So what did he tell you about improving your scores?"

"He said I need to use every resource available. And one of them is brain training while I sleep. He told me about certain brain training modules that would help me most. I thought I'd go to the gadget shop tomorrow to get them. Want to come?"

"You don't have to go to the shop," Pella said. "You can get them straight from the grid."

"I know, but I want to go to the shops anyway. I want to see my adi friends. I've been missing them."

"Oh. Well, I hope they're there when you go."

"Me too," I said. "It would be good to know before I went. Remember that adi trainer I interviewed? Hennit? He would know. And I have his number. I'll call him. What a great idea."

"Glad I could help," Pella leaned close and said.

I laughed. "I guess I shouldn't congratulate myself like that. It's not very ...."

"Humble."

"Right."

"What else did Merchant Kam tell you?" Pella asked.

"He said to definitely talk to someone about my phobia of the tutoring rooms."

"Phobia?"

"It's a Culti word. You don't know it?"

"I don't think so."

"It's a certain kind of fear," I said. "An exaggerated fear. The kind of fear that gives you nightmares about the most harmless things."

"Like tutoring rooms."

"Right," I said. "So I'm going to ask the Head Teacher if I can be tutored somewhere else so I can benefit better from it. That's how Merchant Kam said I should say it. To benefit better."

"That sounds good."

"Then he said that since I'm a social person, I would probably learn better in a group than alone with a tutor. So he told me to go to as many study circles as I can in the subjects I'm having most trouble with, which is all of them."

Pella laughed and said, "I'll go to some math circles with you." She skipped and landed soft on her feet, a habit of hers when her mood was bright, which was more often than anyone my age I'd ever known.

For the next three weeks, when I wasn't sleeping or schooling, I went to study circles, which met at our favorite nature places like Sunset Peak, Powder Beach, and the North Shore. I loved study circles, and I couldn't wait to tell Merchant Kam and Aunt Tala about it.

I called her first. She was working in his office and had time to talk.

"Bree kids should have study circles," I told her. "They make learning more fun. Except there's one catch: you have to like who's in the circles. If people in the group don't get along, it can be a complete drag."

"A complete drag?" Aunt Tala asked.

"It's an expression. It means awful. I'm following all Merchant Kam's advice, and it's actually helping. I'm more certain than ever that I'm going to get my scores up."

She set down her papers, nodded, and smiled. "Lin, you have no idea how happy I am to hear that."

"Will you tell father and Merchant Kam?"

"Of course."

"You're having dinner with them tomorrow night on Merchant Kam's boat. He told me so."

"About that," she said.

"What?"

"It's going to have to wait."

"Why?"

"Kam's grandfather passed away."

"When?"

"Kam just learned of it this morning," she said. "He left this afternoon."

"How long will he be gone?"

"I'm really not sure."

"This is terrible, Aunt Tala! Terrible!"

She frowned an intense displeasure. "I want to believe that you're saddened by Kam's family tragedy, but I fear you're only concerned for yourself."

She was right, and I was quiet.

"Will you please try to exercise the smallest measure of unselfishness?" Aunt Tala said. "Kam is torn up by this. He had a very close relationship with his grandfather. This is a great loss for him. Certainly you can understand."

I thought of losing mother and how that tore me up and how it tears me still. "I understand," I said. "It is a terrible tragedy, and I feel really bad for him. Do you think I should call him and tell him how sad I am?"

"You let me handle that. I'll tell him for you. All right? Is that clear?"

"It's clear," I said.

"Good."

"He was going to help you talk father into giving permission for my Travel School travels."

"I know," she said.

"I don't think you should do it by yourself, do you?"

"No. It's best that Kam be involved."

"So what are we going to do?" I asked.

"Be patient."

"I hate patience."

"Lin."

"I'm sorry. It slipped out."

"You're just going to have to wait. I'm sorry to say that, but that's how it is."

"How long do you think I'll have to wait?"

"I really don't know."

"A few days? A week?"

"It may be longer."

"Really?"

"Travel School is three months away," Aunt Tala said. "What's your hurry?"

"I don't know. Impatience, I guess."

"You're going to have to put up with the uncertainty of not knowing."

"I don't like uncertainty."

"You don't have a choice."

"All right." I said. "I'm sorry for being impatient. I know it's unbecoming."

"Unbecoming?"

"That's what Mrs. Tria says about bad behavior."

Aunt Tala smiled. "I can see she's having a good influence on you."

"She is. All the Trias are. If father could only meet them, he would probably give his permission without you having to talk him into it."

"Mmm," Aunt Tala nodded.

Little did I know, an idea was born.

As I slept that night I had a dream. Not a nightmare dream, and not just a good dream.

It was an idea dream.

## 32  THANK YOU BRISTER LIGGAN

"I had an idea dream last night," I told Pella on our way to Morning Circles, "and it's about your family."

"An idea dream?" she asked.

"You know, when you have a problem and then you have a dream that gives you an idea for how to solve it. Sometimes it's a bad idea, but sometimes it's a good one. This one I think is good."

"You solved the problem of your bad proficiency scores?"

"No," I said, "it's about the Travel School permission problem. In the dream, my father met your family. We were standing in our house — ours, here — and father was charming and made your parents laugh and he liked you all and then he said to me, 'of course I'll grant permission for you to travel with the Trias. They're a wonderful family.'"

"You dreamt that last night?"

"I did," I said. "I think if my father met your parents, he would instantly like them and then give his permission."

"What does he say about visiting in Rasa?" Pella asked.

"Nothing. No 'yes', no 'no', just 'we'll see'. But really, I was thinking about a holographic meeting. You and Pia and your parents and I could synch up our Gen 8s, then I could call father and project him here."

"That *is* a good idea," Pella said.

"I'm glad you think so. But it's only half an idea, the second half to be exact. I have to come up with the first half, which isn't going to be easy. He needs to be in a good mood when we do it," I said, "and his mood hasn't been good lately."

"That's the first half?" Pella asked. "His *mood?*"

"Yes, haven't you noticed? When it comes to parents and asking them for something, mood is everything. Mood and timing."

"I guess you're right. More with some parents than others."

"Right," I said, "yours hardly at all."

Pella didn't disagree. "So, your father," she said, "how do you get him in a good mood?"

"Good grades might help, but that wouldn't be enough. Plus, I'd rather not wait that long. Proficiencies aren't for another 19 days."

Pella laughed.

"But even if that didn't seem like a long time," I said, "which it does, good grades wouldn't be enough. He needs to be a lot happier than good-grades-happy before I'm willing to let him meet your parents." I watched a cluster of airtrams pass overhead and thought of all the things that made father happy. Brister Liggan came to mind. "I know what I'll do. I'll call Brister Liggan and ask him to write an article about father. A really good one. That would work."

By the time we had reached the Assembly Hall, I had formed a simple plan, and early the next morning, I called Brister Liggan.

"And what kind of article did you have in mind?" he asked of my question.

"I thought *you* might have some good ideas," I said.

"None come to mind. Has your father done anything newsworthy of late?"

"I don't know. I don't think so."

"Then why write an article at all?" he asked. "The tourist season is months away. It's far too early to begin promoting it."

"I have a different reason."

Being a reporter, he was curious what this reason was, and it couldn't hurt to say. I knew Brister Liggan liked father and I knew he liked me and would be sympathetic to my cause. I told him all about my Travel School parental permission problem and how father always grew sad after tourist season ended.

"So there's two reasons, really," I said. "It's to cheer father up so he'll be more happy and so he'll give me permission to travel with the Trias. It's officially part of my schooling, but he doesn't understand that. I'm not sure why."

Brister Liggan smiled. "If he needs cheering up," he said, "there are other ways."

"Do you have any ways in mind?"

"I could pay him a visit. Been wanting to."

"He considers you a good friend," I said. "I think a visit from you would make him really happy. *Really* happy."

"Good, then."

"How soon could you go?" I asked.

"Oh, I think toward the end of next month I could get away."

"The end of next month? That's way too long. He's sad *now*. Terribly sad."

"Yes, I see your point. My time's not all my own, but I'll see what I can do."

"It's for a good cause," I said.

Brister Liggan's eyes took on a faraway look, as if recalling some fond memory he and father once shared. He shook his head and chuckled. "No one makes me laugh like your father," he said.

"You have no idea how much it would mean to me if you went this month if not sooner."

"Then I'll get there this month. Even if I have to make it short."

"You've really made my day, Mr. Liggan, thank you."

"You're welcome," he said. "And how are you getting along in school?"

"Pretty good. I love it here. I love modern culture, and I love being a modern girl. I have a Gen 8 and a data sheet and a tail trinket and ear color and six embedded fragrances, three on each arm, and a ceiling I can make invisible whenever I want, and on Adri I'm going to start using those brain-training programs that teach you while you sleep."

"Interesting," he said.

"And I've made some adibadi friends and I've been on an ultra-speed and I've eaten food from everywhere in the world, even fronli intestines that are grown in a lab but taste just as good, and some say even better."

"I should write an article about *you*."

"Me?"

"Yes," he said. "A follow-up story. The last our readers knew of you, you had just been accepted to the Vona School. I'm sure they'd be eager to know about your new life there. And we've got a great angle. Simple girl from Bree living in high-tech society. It would make for a good human-interest story, a cultural study in contrasts. Now, I would only write it with your consent."

"Do you think it would cheer father up?"

"I do," he said, "and make him proud. And I would interview him too, of course."

"This seems too good to be true."

"Take some time to think about it."

"No," I said, "let's do it."

Brister Liggan kept his promise. On a drizzly afternoon four days later he called me while Birgard and I were visiting Lana in the tree park.

"Good news," Brister Liggan said. "My editor likes the story idea. We've got an Adri 24th publication date."

My tail thumped wildly. "That's a week and a half from now," I said.

"Yes, so I'll need to schedule an interview with you as soon as possible."

"And what about father?"

"I have time early next week to go to Bree," Brister Liggan said. "A friend here at the paper owed me a favor, so I gave him one of my story assignments to make room for this." He laughed. "My friend actually wanted that story, so I'm still due a favor. How's that for serendipity?"

"What's serendipity?"

"A fortunate accident."

"An accident that goes your way," I said.

"Yes," he smiled.

We made a plan to talk two days later and said goodbye.

"My great day just got better!" I shouted to Birgard, who congratulated me from a nearby bench where he had sat for some studying.

"I like good news," he said, "even if it isn't mine. If you want, you can tell me about it on our way to the café."

Lana danced with me, mimicking my movements, happy for my happiness. She said to Birgard, "Lin is happy!"

"Yes," he said to Lana, "Lin is very happy."

Lana and I danced and laughed until we fell to the ground, our sides aching.

"I'm going to miss you," I told her when it was time to leave.

"Good," she said.

Birgard and I made our way to the World Café where we were meeting up with a history study circle for lunch and learning.

"Tell me the good news," Birgard said.

I told him about my elaborate plan to cheer father up and to get him to meet the Trias by holophonic projection so he would agree to let me travel with them during Travel School.

"You have a talent for scheming," Birgard told me.

"Thanks," I said.

"You could be a politician."

"I want to be an advocate. It's sort of like being a politician, but more interesting and fewer meetings."

"Your talk on being a lawyer was funny," he said.

"It's a funny profession, turns out. Funny and tragic. I'm definitely not going to be one."

"Tragic?"

"Sometimes you have to defend a person you know is guilty. I think that's tragic, don't you?"

"You could call it tragic, I guess."

"I think I might end up being a counselor," I said.

"A counselor," Birgard said, letting the word linger as if to ponder it.

"Yes. That or a language teacher, but ... I don't know. It's too soon to tell."

"You've got two years to declare your track."

"I know, but my personal goal this year is to decide now."

"Oh, right," he chuckled. "I forgot."

"Elda told me that it really doesn't matter what I choose because I can change my mind later. She said it's the process of exploration that counts. That's where the learning is. In the exploration. Yesterday she tole me that learning is an adventure, and it made me shiver. Somehow I think that can help me get my proficiency scores up, but I haven't figured it out yet."

"Well, I hope you do, and if I can help, I will."

"Thanks, Birgard, you're a good friend."

"You are too, Lin."

"We're all in it together, aren't we?"

"Who do you mean by we?"

"I'm not sure," I said. "The words just came out that way. But when I think about it, I think we is the whole world. Everyone."

"Everyone."

I thought about it and nodded. "Everyone."

## 33  BLAME IT ON KONO

I gave Brister Liggan a good interview. That's exactly how he said it. I was happy for the compliment, but I was even happier that three days later he would be interviewing father in Bree.

Four days later, Aunt Tala called in the early morning.

"Your father's furious," she said.

"What?" I said. "At who?"

"At you."

"*Me?*"

"Yes."

"What did *I* do?"

"Something about conniving a plan to get him to agree to do something that he didn't want to do — what, I don't know." Aunt Tala stopped her pacing long enough to smash a bug on the kitchen counter and flick it in the dregbox. "Your father was rather incoherent about it."

"No, no, no," I begged. "Please tell me this is just a nightmare. You're not real. This is just a dream."

"It's not a dream."

"But how did father find out?"

"So you *are* conniving a plan," she said more than asked.

"Well … not exactly. Father's got it all wrong. And he shouldn't even know anything. Anything at all."

"Does this have to do with Brister Liggan? He's in town, you know. The two were laughing and carrying on all night on your father's boat. Woke me up and half of East Bree."

"I think I'm going to be sick," I said. "This is completely horrible. It's worse than horrible. My whole plan backfired. I shouldn't have told Brister Liggan."

"So you did connive a plan?"

I didn't answer her.

"And what *did* you tell Brister Liggan?" she asked.

"I told him that father needed cheering up."

"And?"

"And?"

"There must be more than that," she said.

"I said father needed cheering up so he would give me permission to go traveling with the Trias during Travel School."

"Is that all?"

"And so he would get the nerve up to be more friendly with the wedding planner."

One side of Aunt Tala's face softened and nearly smiled. "Anything else?"

"That's it. I promise."

"Then he's angry that you're meddling."

"I suppose so," I said. "I was only trying to help."

"I know, I understand that. But sometimes our help isn't wanted, Lin, as well-intentioned as it is. If you want to help other people, it's best to be sure they need it and want it."

"Father definitely needs help," I said. "And I think he wants it, he just doesn't know it yet."

"Yes, but even if that's true, it's not your place to assume."

"How furious is he?"

"Mildly furious with a kono hangover. Brister Liggan brought some fancy imported kono root. It's much stronger than the kono that grows here."

"Well that explains it," I said. "It's kono to blame."

"It's your meddling to blame, and the kono made it worse."

"What do I do, Aunt Tala?"

"I think we all need to wait and let this blow over. It will pass. These upsets always do. But I suggest not calling your father for a few days. We don't want to make a bad situation worse."

"He's never going to say yes. All father cares about is depriving me of joy."

She stopped pacing, looked me right in the eyes, and said quite sternly, "You know you're talking nonsense, don't you? Your father loves you, and he's said yes to far more than either of us expected. I recommend you take some time reflecting on that."

"No, you're right," I said. "But I don't know what to do now. I don't know how to turn this around."

"Do nothing," Aunt Tala said. "Nothing. At this point any effort you make to turn it around will probably end disastrously."

"Do nothing? But what if—"

"Nothing," she said again. "Consider it an exercise in maturity. If you love maturity as much as you say you do, then you'll have no difficulty. And if you want to do something to help your father, I recommend you throw yourself into your studies. Your next proficiencies are two weeks away."

"Right," I said. "That's actually good advice. I'm going to go to as many study circles as I can. Some are early in the morning before school, a few are during lunch, and the rest are after school and at night."

"That's good, Lin. Concentrate on your studies, and this problem with your father will clear up. Trust me."

***

I got a call from Mira the day Brister Liggan's article was published.

"It's his best article yet," she told me.

"Best how?" I asked.

"It's funny, it's poignant—"

"Poignant?"

"Sad," Mira said. "The kind of sadness that makes you feel good."

"Oh, sweet sadness."

"Right."

"What else?"

"I would call it very complimentary. To you and your father."

"It says good things about father?"

"Yes," Mira said. "A lot of good things."

"Have you seen him yet?"

"No, but I saw your aunt in the marketplace and she told me to tell

you that he's overjoyed and the storm has blown over. She said you'd
know what that means."

"I know exactly what that means. She was right. Sometimes you
don't have to do anything. Other things can happen that do all the
doing for you."

"What are you talking about?"

I told Mira the Brister Liggan story, and we laughed about it. I
laughed from relief and Mira laughed from humor.

"A comedy of errors," she said. It was a literary phrase. "By the
way, I talked to Brister Liggan while he was here. He told me all about
the newspaper reporting business."

"He kept his promise," I said.

"So you *did* ask him to talk to me."

"I told him that I've been interviewing professionals about vocations
and how helpful it's been."

"Thanks, Lin. I love you for that. He gave me good advice. And he
told me when the time came to apply for college, he would write a
recommendation for me."

"It will be a good one too. He admires you," I said, "he told me so.
He said no ten-year-old had ever been published in a national
newspaper. None that he'd ever heard about. That makes you a special
person, Mira. An excellent and special person."

"With vast potential," Mira said, "to quote Brister Liggan."

"He's a nice man," I said. "He's a trouble maker, but he never
means to make trouble. And look how much good he's done me and
father and Bree."

"Who would have known, that first day we met him?"

"When he interviewed me, I spoke in Culti. He loved it."

"I know," Mira said. "That's in the article too."

"I can't wait to read it," I said.

"Do they actually sell copies of the paper there?"

"No, I can get it on my Gen 8."

"Oh."

"Hey, my brain-training is working great."

"How can you tell?"

"I feel smarter, and I'm remembering things that I used to forget like math formulas and things that happened in history and grammar rules. It's too bad you have to have a Gen 5 or higher to use brain-training."

"Does it keep you awake?"

"No," I said, "I don't hear it all. And it only works when I'm in a certain sleep state. Don't ask me what that means. And get this, I haven't had a single nightmare since I've been doing it."

"Maybe you discovered a cure for your nightmares."

"Wouldn't that be great?"

"Were you expecting that?" Mira asked. "The no-nightmare thing?"

"No. It's total serendipity."

"Serendipity," Mira said. "I love that word. Fortuitous is good too. They're synonyms."

"Your Culti's getting so much better, Mir."

"We're learning it everyday in school now. Teacher Gwin uses her holophone to project that virtual Culti teacher from the Education Portal."

"The one we learned from on Hodri nights at the Pavillion?" I asked.

"Yep, the same lady."

I smiled at random memories of my life in Bree. They made me happy but wistful too. "We had some good times," I said. "I really miss those days — some parts, anyway — but only when I think about them. There's always so much happening here."

"Some people thought you'd completely forget about us," Mira said. "Some said you'd never come back. But I knew you wouldn't forget. Bree's in your blood."

"Like it or not."

"Looks like we're getting more fake groile for Bree," Mira said. "You won't believe who asked for it."

"Bissa and the Evolutionaries?"

"No, the Mayor. He wants to make sliding down mudflows a punishable offense."

"That's not so bad," I said. "Groile sliding is far superior to mud sliding. And it's cleaner and safer. What are you laughing about?"

"The Mayor's reason for outlawing mudflows."

"What is it?"

"You know that big mudslide near his house? Last week Chib and

Krin went sliding there. His first slide down, Chib tumbled on a stone and careened off the slide. He fell through the flasan roof of the Mayor's terrace and crashed onto the dining table where he was lunching. Chib got in big trouble with his parents and the Mayor. But at school, the boys are treating him like some hero. He's eating up all the attention."

"I can't believe how much Bree's still the same," I said.

"Just because we have fake groile and fake flowers and that sticky stuff on the piers that keeps you from slipping doesn't mean Bree will change. We're going to need a lot more technology than that for real progress to ever happen here."

"If Bree weren't so hopelessly hopeless, I'd come back and devote my life to making Bree a better place. But I think it would be a total tragic waste of my talents. And I don't have the patience for it. It would take way too long. And father would be miserable and we'd be fighting all the time, and after what we just went through, I never want that to happen again."

Mira gazed at me compassionately, her head tilting toward her bent-ear side, which gave the appearance that the pull of gravity — not a genetic flaw — was to blame for the defect. It was a habit she had formed when she first found out her bent ear wasn't ever going to straighten on its own.

"Sad but true," Mira said. "I don't like that it's true, but I'm glad you're being realistic about it. For a long time you actually believed you could change Bree."

"It was the only way I thought I could survive there. But you're right, Bree's not going to change, not enough for me, especially now. I need a bigger life than Bree."

"And you need a crusade or you're not happy."

"I suppose so. So I'm making Egli slaves my crusade. If I could, I would set them all free. And who knows, I might try to some day."

"I wouldn't be surprised," Mira smiled.

"I wonder if I should call father or wait to see if he calls me?"

"Who called who last?"

"I'm not sure," I said. "But with us, I don't think that matters."

"If you want him to call you, then wait."

"I guess I will. Our proficiency tests are in three days, and I think I should concentrate. Wish me luck."

"I won't wish you luck," she said. "Good grades aren't about luck. They're about remembering what you already know. So I wish you ... unforgetfulness."

## 34  GRANGEFISH AND ALL

I gave the news to Aunt Tala who gave the news to father who gave the news to my grandmother who gave the news to Mira.

"I just heard about your scores," Mira breathlessly said in a message she left while I was talking to Aunt Tala. "Sorry I'm running. I'm late for school. I saw your grandmother ... she stopped and gave me the great news. So ... congratulations! Call me when you can, scholar of Bree!"

Aunt Tala kept our call short because Merchant Kam was away disbursing funds and property from his grandfather's will.

"I'm swamped with details," she said. "I'm on my own on this next business trip, not just the planning but all the traveling as well. Anyway, we're very proud of you, Lin. I wish you could have seen your father's smile and genuine pleasure. He said he's going to call you, but don't be sad if he doesn't or if it takes a few days. He's still being inundated with phone calls from admirers who read Brister Liggan's article."

"Is his mood good again?" I asked.

"It's very good," she said. "It's excellent. Brister Liggan's visit did a lot to cheer him up."

"Even though father got really mad at me."

"Yes, well, he's not mad at you now."

"You were right, Aunt Tala."

She smiled and told me, "You'll usually find that I am."

"I hope he calls soon," I said, "while his mood is still good."

Father did call soon, and his mood was good. I was having lunch with my schoolmates on Sunset Peak when the eye film of my Gen 8 displayed father's face and announced his call.

"It's father!" I leapt to my feet and ran up a small hill to Cloud Point.

"Well done," father beamed. "You improved every score."

"And I'm going to improve more on the next proficiencies," I said. "Then even more on our final exams."

"If you keep to your studies," he nodded, "I've no doubt you will."

"I've no doubt I will too. Studying has gotten a lot more interesting."

"That's good," he said.

"Guess where I'm standing? I'm on the tallest place on the whole island. It's called Cloud Point, on the very top of Sunset Peak."

"I see," he said. "And how are ocean conditions today?"

"Not too choppy. The winds are quiet today and there's no rain. Just those funny swirling clouds. I'll show you."

I video-captured a 360-degree panorama of the sky, ocean, and Sunset Peak, narrating the scene. "See how strange the clouds are today? And see the tall silver poles all in a line over there? They hold up these big invisible nets that are rainproof and windproof and make the warmth of the sunlight much warmer. Adibadis and robots worked together to put it up."

"Adibadis and robots?"

"Yes," I said, "working together. I saw them do it myself, right here, this very net. The robots order the adis around because they're smarter. And the adis always obey. They do everything you tell them to do. They're genetically bred that way. You would love having an adi."

"I'm sure I would," father said.

"And there under the net are my friends."

"Which ones?"

"All of them. They're all my friends now. At first I only knew my Team 10 teammates, but now that I've been going to all these study circles, I know almost everyone."

"You're taller, you're changing," father said, studying me curiously. "Your face, it's grown more mature, and your ears, they've grown purple."

"They look good, don't they?"

"It's a good color on you."

I held up my tail. "And here's the trinket I got. It's small and elegant."

"Hold it steady so I can see the shape," he said. I held it steady, and he smiled. "A heart."

"Because there's nothing better than love," I said. "Nothing in the whole world."

Father was silent, silent but smiling.

"I'm sorry I meddled," I said. "I know that you know why I asked Brister Liggan to write the article, and I want you to know that I only meant it for good. To make your life better."

Father wrenched his neck to one side then another, his searing eyes locked on mine. "I knew you meant well," he said. "But yes, you did meddle, and I didn't like it. Where you get this meddling trait, I don't know. Your mother wasn't that way."

"Aunt Tala kind of is."

As I hoped, he smiled, but only a little. "This meddling brings you trouble, Lin, and I worry for you. I worry for those who are left to clean up your messes."

"I don't mean to make trouble," I said. "I only want to do good."

"Well, as you grow older, you'll find better ways to do the good you want to do. In the meantime, I want you to make me a promise."

"What promise?"

"If you want something from me," he said, "*ask* me. Don't go behind my back with some connivance. Just straight out ask me."

"But what if I ask you and you say no?"

"Then accept my answer."

"But what if I don't accept your answer? What if you were in a bad mood when I asked, and I was just unlucky?"

"And how often have you had this bad-mood bad luck?"

"More often than any girl should."

Father's face went cold, and I wished I had said anything but what I'd said.

"I didn't mean that in a blaming way, father. I was trying to be funny, but I wasn't. All your bad moods have been sadness. Sadness about your leg and about mother and about raising me alone and maybe about having to live with Aunt Tala. All those things would make any man sad. I was just trying to make light of a heavy situation, that's all."

"I'm sorry there's been so many misfortunes, Lin. This is not the life I wanted us to live ... life without your mother."

"I hope you don't blame me," I said. "For mother."

"It was an accident, Lin. A lesser man might blame you. But I'm not a lesser man."

"No. You're a great man. You're the Fisherman of Bree. You're world famous now. Everyone here knows you. Everyone. And they all want to meet you ... in person. You'd be a big celebrity if you, you know, if you...." All the right words were stuck in my throat.

"If you have something you want to ask me, Lin, then ask me."

"Well, I really want you to come to Vona in Rasa. You can bring Aunt Tala or someone else, and there's going to be a big storytelling competition that I'm sure you would win."

"As I said before, I'll give that some thought."

"All right," I said. "Also, I want you to meet the Trias. I can project you here through our holophone connection. They really want to meet you, and I want you to meet them."

"Yes, I'd like that too."

"So you will?"

"I will, yes."

"I know you're going to like them. And they already like you, and now they will even more. I'll make arrangements."

"That'd be fine," father said.

"I also want you to call the wedding planner."

"For what purpose?"

"To be friendly and ... to invite her to Vona."

"I don't know her well enough to invite her to Vona."

"All right," I said, "forget about that. Just call her to say hello. I know you like each other, so why not talk once in a while? It'd make both of you happier and less lonely. She's all alone, too, you know. And she's already called you. You'd just be returning the favor."

"I will, Lin, I'll call her."

"I can't believe it," I said. "This really works, asking you straight out. It's easier and quicker."

"Do you see?" he said. "It will increase your chances of success if you aim directly for your objective."

"I'm so happy about my proficiency scores."

"I am too. But be careful. Don't gloat over your win too long or complacency will set in."

"What does that mean?"

"It means keep studying as if your scores hadn't improved at all."

"I will, father. And I actually don't mind studying. Studying can be really fun if you do it with friends in a beautiful place, like here on Sunset Peak."

"You're doing well, Lin. Very well."

"Aren't you glad you agreed to let me study here?"

"As much as I miss you, yes, I'm glad."

"I miss you too, father. I'll talk to the Trias about meeting you. Maybe this Adri morning? That would be early afternoon for you."

"That'd be fine."

The Trias agreed to the date, and early on Adri morning I called father to remind him and to check on his mood. It was better than good, and I made him laugh with some stories from school.

Later in the day, I called father from my soundproof sleepingroom.

"They loved you," I said. "They loved you!"

Father grinned. "They're good people," he said. "Charming and bright and quick to laugh."

"They are, aren't they? They said they couldn't remember when they had laughed more. You're all we talked about at lunch. Mrs. Tria said you're charming, and Mr. Tria said he admires your wit."

"They're a handsome family," father said.

"Handsome like you."

"But more refined."

"They like that you're a tough, rugged man of the sea who did battle bare-handed with a grangefish. That's how I describe you to people sometimes."

"Grangefish and all?"

"The grangefish is the best part."

We smiled together in silence.

"I like it when we get along," I said.

"So do I."

"And I'm glad you like the Trias. And so, will you let me go?"

"Where?"

"Northern Wershonia."

"With the Trias?"

"Yes," I said. "For Travel School."

"No," father softly said. "I want you here."

"But ... I'm not supposed to be there. I'm supposed to be in Travel School. It's required."

Father's whole face tightened, his mouth, his jaw, his eyes. "I said no."

"But you can't say no."

"I'm your father. I *can* say no."

"But these are school rules."

"That you travel for three months with total strangers?"

"They're not total strangers," I said. "You know them now."

"Not well enough."

"Well, what if we come to Bree first, and you can know them in person, and you'll get to see me, and *then* we can go to Northern Wershonia?"

Still father said no, but not softly. He was getting angry. His good mood was gone. Why did he have to be so impossible?

"Never mind, father. I wish I hadn't asked. Look what's happened to us. I'm really sad about it."

"I'm sorry, too, Lin," he told me. "But I'm your father. I'm your protector. And this is how it is."

## 35 THE BAD NEWS AND THE GOOD NEWS

"I know you're busy, Aunt Tala, so I'll keep this quick. Father said no again to Travel School. I promised him I would ask him straight out about things, so I did, and he said no. I don't know what to do now. I'm hoping you and Merchant Kam will talk him into it. I would tell someone at school about it, but I'm too embarrassed and I don't want that to backfire. I can't afford any more backfires with father. Anyway, thanks in advance for doing something about this. I love you, and I hope you're having fun on Merchant Kam's airlift."

I rolled over in bed and cried until it was time to go to school.

At Morning Circles Elda shouted, "Stand tall and strong, there is greatness in you!"

I felt tall and strong, but I didn't feel great. I felt defeated and unlucky and powerless, and I hated it. And to make it all worse, I hated hating. It was so against everything I believed in — goodness and kindness and love.

"Have you talked to father yet?" I asked Aunt Tala when she called me five days later.

"No," she said, "but I will now. Kam's back and getting caught up."

"Thanks, Aunt Tala. You'll talk to him soon? Time's running out, and I've been so patient. I've talked to father twice since I last asked him, and you have no idea how hard it was for me to not bring it up, especially the last time we talked, when he told me the wedding planner was coming to Bree. In three weeks, did he tell you?"

"Yes," she said.

"I asked him if she could visit sooner than that, but he said it was for a wedding on his boat and it was already scheduled. That would have been the perfect time to ask him. You and Merchant Kam and her and father. If you asked him in right front of her, how could he say no?"

"Lin, you're a shameless operator," Aunt Tala said.

"Is that bad?"

She smiled. "It depends on who you ask. And, of course, it depends on the motive."

"My motive is good," I said. "I'm only trying to get him to say yes to something that belongs to me. Travel School is school! I'm not asking for the impossible. I'm not even asking for a favor. I'm asking for the education that I've earned."

"Believe me," she said, "I'm sympathetic to your cause."

"Thanks, Aunt Tala. Will you ask him as soon as possible?"

"We will, and I'll call you as soon as I know anything."

She said we, as in she and Merchant Kam, and that soothed my nerves. Merchant Kam had a way of bringing out the reasonableness in father, and he was a Transition School student himself. He knew all about Travel School.

Three days later, Aunt Tala called with big news.

"I hesitate to tell you this," she said, "but I think, in all fairness, you should know. You're going to know eventually anyway."

"Is it bad?"

"Your father can barely read."

"What?"

"He's almost illiterate," she said. "That's why he didn't read the paperwork he signed."

"I can't believe it."

"It came as a shock to me too."

"You just found out?"

"He confessed it to Kam and I while we were having dinner," she said, "much to my surprise. Your father is so unwilling to admit weakness."

"Why do you think he told you then?"

"He wants to learn to read," she said. "We found a literacy program on the Education Portal."

"I can't believe it."

"I think you and Gilden have been a positive influence on him."

"I can't believe it."

"Don't say a word about this to anyone, Lin. Please. Not Mira, not any of your friends there in Vona, no one."

"Believe me, I won't," I said. "It's too embarrassing and sad."

"It is," she nodded. "It is."

"I still can't believe it."

"So, now that that news has been dispensed," Aunt Tala said, "I have good news for you. Your father said yes."

"To Travel School?"

"Yes. On one condition."

"Great."

"You'll like it, don't worry. He wants you and the Trias to come to Bree at the onset of your travels."

"That's the condition?"

"Yes."

"Oh, Aunt Tala! I'm so happy! He said yes!"

"I'm glad you're happy."

"We're going to see the world's tallest waterfall."

"Yes, you told me."

"Good news and bad news," I said. "I'm glad you told me the bad news first. It should always be done that way. Thanks, Aunt Tala."

"It was Kam's doing. You should call him soon and thank him yourself."

"I will," I said. "I'm giving my final personal goal presentation next week, did I tell you?"

"No."

"I'll video capture it. I think you'll like it and be proud too. I'm tempted to tell you what it's about, but I want it to be a surprise, so I'll wait for you to see it."

"Good," she smiled, "waiting denotes patience."

I was elated as we said goodbye, even though I had just learned the news about father. There was no one to talk to about it but mother, so as I walked alone from the Residences to the airtram station, I told her how awful it must have been for him all these years, not being able to read and doing everything possible to hide it.

I saw Birgard and some schoolmates at the far end of the airtram. He waved me over to join him.

"Hello, scholar of Bree," he said after offering me the window seat next to his.

I laughed and sat and thanked him.

"I heard some good news about you," he told me.

"What could you have heard?" I asked.

"That you won this year's Greatest Improvement Award."

"If that's true, then why don't I know?"

He held up his data sheet. "It was just announced. Five minutes ago."

I studied his face, looking for a sign of trickery.

"It's a big honor," he said with a suspicious grin.

"I don't believe you," I said, turning to watch a sub-orbital slowly descend onto a landing pad on the South Shore.

Birgard chuckled. "It's true," he said. He leaned close and showed me the words on his data sheet.

"The 2296 Greatest Improvement Award: Lin di Ana," he read.

Some nearby schoolmates congratulated me.

"Unbelievable," I said, more stunned than happy. "It's been a day of good news."

"What other good news?" Birgard asked.

"I just got parental permission for Travel School."

"Travel School?"

"The Excursion Months," I said.

"Oh, right, right, I forgot. Travel School. That's actually a good name for it."

"Names are everything," I said. "Sometimes all you have is a name to understand something by. What if someone doesn't know what excursion means?"

He laughed and asked where we were going on our travels.

"First to Bree," I said, "to meet my family and friends. Then we're going all over Northern Wershonia."

"Including Algalon?"

"Yes," I said, "all along the North Coast, and I know for sure that we'll be staying in that big city near your town."

"Why don't you see about visiting my family for a day? I could meet you there in the virtual and show you around."

"I like that idea. I'll ask. I'd love to meet your sister."

"She can't wait to meet you," Birgard said.

"How does she—? Oh, she knows me from the newspaper articles."

"No," he said. "She knows you through me."

"You've told her about me?"

"I've told her about a lot of people. You're one of her favorites. She likes that you're from Bree and that your mother died too — not that that's good, but—"

"I know what you mean," I said. "And I'm glad you told her whatever you told her."

"It was all good," Birgard said.

"How could it not be?" I smiled.

"How could it not?" he agreed.

I felt the silent stares of Birgard's friends and felt a flush of embarrassment.

"You're going to a study circle?" I asked him.

"No, the gadget shop. The new ultra-fidelity earbuds just came in. Then we're going to the beach for a concert."

"Real or virtual?"

"Virtual," he said. "Should be good in ultra-fidelity."

"Do you need parental permissions for these earbuds?"

"I don't think so. You should join us, unless you have other plans."

"I'm on my way to see Oddi and Lana," I said. "I called Hennit, and he said they're both working today."

"Mind some company?"

"No, I don't mind."

Birgard turned to his friends sitting behind. "I'm going with Lin to the tree park. I'll meet you at the pier later."

"Good," said one friend.

"See you there, then," said another.

Then they giggled like girls.

Birgard and I smiled at each other, and I felt a pang of sadness. It was the sadness of knowing I was going to miss him.

## 36 Novi's Idea

I saw Oddi for the last time that day, and Lana only twice after that. I'd wanted to go to the tree park more often than that, but the last month of school was a continuous blur of study circles, tutoring sessions, final proficiency exams, and preparations for my personal goal presentation, which was the last schoolish thing I had to do before the Rasa break when all the parents arrived and the Rasa Competitions began.

It was such a busy month, I only talked to Mira twice. Once was on a Lindri morning. It was a gloomy day of dark clouds and a steady, heavy rain.

"It's raining here too," Mira said. "That sideways rain from high wind. I don't know how many people will be showing up at the Pavillion to talk to you later. On days like this I want one of those weather nets you have."

"A clarkon canopy is great," I said, "but it doesn't help with sideways rain."

"How's school and everything else?" she asked.

"They said school would get harder, and it did. But, it's a lot more interesting. We're doing a lot more learning on our holophones, and I just got some ultra-fidelity earbuds. The sound is so much bigger."

"You mean louder?"

"No, bigger," I said. "There's more of it, and it moves faster and closer and … it's just all around better."

"Faster and closer? What are you talking about?"

"When sound comes at you really fast from far away, and then it moves right through you and then you can hear it behind you, moving away, far away, and then its gone. It can happen in a couple of seconds. It's fun. I asked if these earbuds could work with a Generation One, and they told me no. Sorry about that."

"I don't mind," Mira said. "It doesn't sound that interesting. I'd rather hear about you."

"All I'm doing these days is studying for final exams and writing the big presentation I have to give about my personal goal."

"And what did you decide, vocation-wise?"

"Counseling," I smiled.

She tapped her chin with her kipper-ink pen, squinting and pensive. "Counseling," she said. "You're going to be a counselor."

"Yes, it's perfect, isn't it? I love telling people what to do."

"See," she said, "that's what I was worried about."

"What do you mean, worried?"

"That your father part of you would be doing the counseling, not your mother part of you."

"No, no, no," I said. "I was kidding about telling people what to do. It was a joke, Mir. A joke you took seriously. Counseling is about listening."

Mira tipped her head to one side and squinted. "I'm not sure that's so much better. You've always been a better teller than a listener."

"I listen reasonably well. And I can always learn to listen better. That's a big part of learning to be a counselor. Listening skills."

"Yes, well...," Mira said, her voice trailing off.

"What were you going to say that you didn't say?"

"You don't want to hear it."

"I do want to hear it," I said. "You can't half say something that affects my future and expect me to forget about it. You're my best friend. If you won't tell me, who will?"

"Don't be hurt and don't be mad."

"I won't."

"You're kind of more interested in your own problems than other people's," she said.

"That's it? That's what you weren't going to say?"

"So you agree."

"No, I don't, actually. I care a lot about other people's problems. I'm always trying to help other people. How can you say that?"

"I'll put it this way," Mira said. She was calm and confident, and it made me nervous. "When we talk, we mostly talk about you. I ask you questions about your life, but you don't ask me very much about mine."

"Really?"

"Yes. You can go back and listen to our calls if you don't believe me."

I couldn't shake the feeling that she was right. "Well," I said, "you have to admit, and no offense, but my life has been more interesting than yours. It's a simple fact. You're there and I'm here. But still, that's no excuse. I'll ask you more from now on. I promise."

I asked Mira about her life lately, and I listened. She had a lot to say, and it wasn't any less interesting than my life, just more ordinary and less modern.

"I loved hearing everything you told me," I said. "And it got me thinking, inside we're still the same people. It's our outside life that's different, the Bree and Vona part. And neither's better than the other. They're just different."

"I agree," Mira said.

"Thanks for telling me about my listening problem. I think it's going to make me a better person."

"And a better counselor," she said. "If you be more like your mother and less like your father, you're going to be great at it. I'm happy you finally decided what you're going to do with your life."

"I am too. I'm going to counsel escaped Egli slaves. I'm going to help them adjust to their new life. I'll be working at an embassy, just like you predicted."

"That actually seems kind of perfect for you."

"Thanks," I said. "I was really worried about how to do my final presentation, but Novi gave me a good idea for it, and now, the talk is practically writing itself."

"What was his idea?"

"He told me to tell the story of deciding on my vocational track from beginning to end. He said, 'Don't give away the end until you get there. Keep your choice a mystery.'"

"That sounds like good, basic storytelling," Mira said, unimpressed.

"But it's unusual for a talk because they tell us to state the conclusion at the beginning and then give supportive arguments. I asked Elda if it was all right to disobey that rule, and she said it was. She said they're not sticklers and they'll almost always favor creativity and originality over the rules."

"That's pretty open-minded."

"Isn't it? But the second part of Novi's idea is the better part. He told me that I have wisdom to share, so I should put some wisdom in my talk. So I'm going to. It will probably improve my score, too, maybe by a lot."

Mira nodded. "I'm sure it would. I'd think the better the wisdom, the better the score. Teachers love hearing wisdom from their students. It makes them feel they really got through."

"That sounds right," I said. "So, I've been thinking about it, and I *do* have some wisdom to share. Some of it's about impatience."

"Impatience," she grinned. "What are you going to say about that?"

"That my entire personal goal project was motivated by impatience, and even though nothing bad happened, ordinarily impatience can cause a lot of trouble. It can make us act hastily and stupidly."

There was more I had to say, but I remembered what Mira said about talking about myself so much, so I changed the subject.

"I'm so glad we're coming to Bree," I said, "the Trias and me. Do you think they should stay at Wallun Ranch or Dun Inn?"

"That's hard to say. Wallun Ranch has better views, but Koppi Dun's place is right on the beach. Why don't you ask them which they think they'd like better?"

"Good idea," I said. "I can't wait to see you."

"Me too. How long are you staying?"

"Two weeks."

"That's not bad."

"Is Bissa still president of the Evolutionaries?"

"Yep."

"Do you think she'd mind if Pella and Pia and I came to a meeting while we're there?"

"She'd probably love it," Mira said. "Ever since we got fake flowers and groile, she's gotten interested in improvement projects again. I stopped going to meetings for a while, but now the club is almost as good as it was when you were here. We're working on a petition to get a net for the marketplace."

"That's a good idea. All the merchants would love it."

"They're our biggest supporters."

"I hope Bissa shows up for the call today," I said.

"I'll call her and tell her to be there," said Mira.

Due to a fortuitous shift in the winds, there was a good turn out for our Lindri call. Bissa was there, and I liked saying in front of everyone how proud I was of her excellent leadership of the Evolutionaries Club. I made a point of asking more questions than I was asked, and everyone had a story to tell that was interesting in some way. Some were funny, some were complaining, a few were tragic, and many were happy. Life in Bree had been changing — more than I thought it would — and maybe mostly for the better.

## 37  THE LONG GOODBYE

Saamta Sio was the first to go.

The day after the Cross-Island Races, she and two other girls left on an ultra-speed for the International School of Arts and Sports. I knew all about apprenticeships in fishing and boat-building, but I had never heard of a dance apprenticeship.

"Except for all the traveling, it's not as glamorous as it sounds," she said when I asked her about it the day we said goodbye. "Basically, we do menial labor for the privilege of being around world-class professional dancers."

"What kind of menial labor?" Pella asked.

"Cleaning the stage and sets," Saamta said, "repairing costumes, helping the special effects robots and the stage manager, that sort of thing."

"You'll be their adibadis," I said.

She laughed. "Yes, something like that. Well ... I better go."

I watched as Pella and Nin and Kita hugged her with cheery goodbyes.

"See you, Sio," I said when they were done.

"Thanks for the excellent birthday," she told me. "I'll never forget it."

"We'll celebrate it just the same way next year," I said, "if not better."

"Better sounds good," she said.

We hugged goodbye and let go, the distance between us smaller now. Her eyes traced a trail of tears that had fallen down to my chin, and she smiled.

"I almost forgot," she said. "I have a present for you."

She pulled from her satchel a bundle of tissuecloths. "You're going to need these, I have a feeling."

"Animal University tissues?" I asked.

She nodded.

"How perfect, I'm almost out. They don't last forever, you know."

"No," she softly said.

"Thanks," I told her. "You're a great person with a great future, and I'm so glad I know you."

She dried her face with her own tissue, and I dried my face with mine.

"Hey, Sio," Kita said when Saamta turned to leave. "Don't forget our Team 10 virtual reunion, the first day of each month. I'll call and remind you."

"Good," said Saamta. "See you all then, in the virtual. And see you in the new year, in the real."

"In the real," we said.

She walked alone down the flower-lined path that wended through a field of bright blue and magenta groile.

I turned away, buried my face in my tissuecloth, and let myself cry really hard but completely silent.

"Lin?" Pella asked. "Are you crying?"

"Yes," I said. "But it's all right. Just ignore me. I'm having an emotional moment."

"I guess you take these goodbyes pretty hard," Kita said while the four of us turned to walk to the airtram. We had decided to go to Powder Beach for some afternoon fun. It was a bright, rainless day.

"I'm a crier," I said. "I cry over the smallest thing."

I cried when we went to the tree park and there was no sign of Oddi or Lana or Hennit.

I cried that night at the Residence Commons when I met the parents of Kita and Nin and Novi and they all asked where my father was. "He couldn't make it," was all I said.

I cried when I told Aunt Tala that my Final Scores were the highest of the year and I wouldn't be kicked out of school. "I can tell you this now," she said. "They never had any intention of kicking you out, regardless of your scores. They considered you a special case, and grades were not a significant factor in your performance, not during this first year." I cried when she told me that.

I cried when the father of the boy from Clud was announced the winner of the storytelling competition. His delivery was paltry, he had zero charisma, and his stories were only interesting because they were about the different semi-famous people he had met as a result of owning a national newspaper. My father told better stories in his sleep, and I knew he would have won, if only he had been here. I cried about his lost win, and I cried that he refused to visit.

I cried when he called the next morning to congratulate me for my remarkable achievement and excellent scores.

"I wish I'd had the nerve to come see you," he confessed. "Don't think that I'm not there because I don't love you. I'm just not ready yet for that world. I hope you can understand." I nodded, utterly speechless, so he just kept talking. "I spoke with the Trias, and your aunt has made arrangements for them to stay at Koppi Dun's place. They said they wanted to be as close to the sea as they could be. Pella said she wants to know what it's like to fall asleep to the sound of the waves." He grinned and laughed a little. "They told me you're leaving Vona in five days. I can't tell you how happy I'll be to see you, how much I miss you, how much I love you. You're a good girl, Lin, and you've made me so proud. So, so proud. One last piece of news, and I'll say goodbye. Gilden is going to pay us a visit while you're here."

"The wedding planner? Really?"

"Yes."

"Whose idea was it?" I asked. "Yours or hers?"

"It was a joint decision," he said.

"But who invited who?"

"I invited her."

That was exactly what I wanted to hear, and that made me cry too.

Each day, more schoolmates left, some by ultra-speed, some by sub-orbital, and a few by private aircraft their wealthy parents owned.

Novi left by ultra-speed on a drizzly grayish-pink morning. I ran most of the way from the Residences so I would be there on time to say goodbye.

"Novi!" I hollered when I saw him on the airpad about ready to board. "Novi! Wait!"

He turned and saw me.

"Hey, Lin," he smiled.

"Looks like there aren't many more of us left to see you off," I told him.

"It's all right," he said. "It's better this way. I never wanted some big, crying crowd of friends to be the last thing I see when I leave. It's sappy and depressing."

"Right," I said.

"I'm glad you're here, though. I wanted you to know that you made it a really fun year. A great year. Greater than it would have been."

"Thanks," I said. "You helped me in a lot of ways, especially in the beginning when I needed it most. I'll always be grateful to you for that."

"Time to board," a woman said from inside the ultra-speed.

"Have fun on your travels," Novi said.

"I will. I'll let you know when we're going to be in your town. Maybe you'll meet me there, in the virtual."

"Definitely. And I'll see you at the reunions too."

"Good," I said. "Well ... have fun up there at the North Pole."

"I will."

I wasn't crying, and I was glad. I didn't want Novi to see me cry. I didn't cry until he waved from his window seat as the ultra-speed lifted, hovered, then jetted upward through an opening in the airtraffic zones.

Since I had only two more days left before leaving for Bree, I called Hennit to ask about Oddi and Lana.

"You won't see Oddi before you go," he said. "He suffered a sprain and was airlifted to the mainland."

"Is it serious?" I asked.

"No. Nothing that some physical therapy won't take care of."

"And Lana?"

"She's working today."

"Right now?"

"Yes."

"Then I'm coming right over," I said. "I'd like to see you too. I'm leaving in two days."

"Call me when you arrive," he said. "We'll find a meeting place."

I was there in half an hour.

"Lana!" I shouted when I saw her.

She turned and smiled and dropped her trimming tool. I ran to her, choking back tears, laughing at her total adorableness.

"Lin," she said when I hugged her.

I held her for the longest time, rubbing my cheek along her shoulder and scratching her back in her favorite place.

"I'm going to miss you so much," I said.

Her head tipped to one side. "Much?" she asked.

"I'm going away for Travel School. But I'll be back in the new year."

"Good," she said. It was a bad habit of hers, saying 'good' when she didn't know what else to say because she didn't understand my meaning.

"It's best you don't know I'm leaving," I told her. "I couldn't bear us both being sad."

"Good," she said.

I made a funny face and jumped with a squeal and turned and ran. She ran behind me, laughing. We played until I was exhausted.

"I haven't had any breakfast, and it's almost lunchtime," I said to her as I fell to the ground near a soft-seat bench.

She sat by my side and laughed. "Lunch," she said.

I called the World Café and ordered a fish sandwich for immediate delivery to my present location. Then I called Hennit.

"If you just ordered lunch," he said, "Lana and I will have ours with you."

"Great," I said, "we'll have lunch together, the three of us."

"Yes," he smiled.

I rubbed Lana's feet while we waited for Hennit. A man and a woman sat on the soft-seat bench holding drinks and data sheets. I had seen them here before.

"Look," I heard the woman say, "it's that little girl who plays with the adis."

The man turned and smiled.

Lunch arrived, then Hennit arrived.

"I'm sorry to hear you won't be working with adis," he said when I told him about the change in my vocational aspirations.

"It broke my heart," I said. "And for such a stupid reason."

"Which was?"

"I can't bear to look at animal insides."

"Dissection," he nodded, half-smiling. "I'm not surprised, a kind-hearted girl like you."

I pushed away a memory of the Virtual Dissection Lab and gave Lana a piece of fish.

"Thanks for saying that," I said. "I really liked the Animal University, though. We spent a whole day there."

"Don't know that I've ever heard—"

"I mean Zoo U."

"Oh, yes," he said, his whole face smiling. "I never miss an opportunity to go back."

"You went to school there?"

"Yes, I graduated 30 years ago. We had a reunion a few months back."

"I like reunions," I said. "I've never been to one, but I will the first day of the next three months. All my teammates and I are going to have a virtual reunion."

"That's nice," he said.

"Will you be here next year?"

"Quite sure I will. I've been here 18."

"And Oddi and Lana will still be here?"

"They'll be here," he said. "Vona is their permanent assignment."

Lana had finished her lunch, and I gave her the rest of my fish sandwich. She swallowed it and kissed my face.

"I taught her to kiss," I said.

He smiled and shook his head. "They're going to miss you," he said.

I rested my head on Lana's shoulder, cheered by the thought of that. "Can I call you once in a while for a virtual visit?"

"You can," he said, "but there's something you should know. Adis aren't responsive to holographic projections in the same way we are."

"What do you mean?"

"If I project you here in the presence of Oddi and Lana, they'll recognize you as a moving picture, but they won't interact with you as though you were here."

"Why?"

"They don't understand that a projection of you is actually *you, here,* in a form they can relate to."

"Oh," I said. "So maybe that's not a good idea. Maybe it would only make me sad."

"Perhaps so."

"But can I call you to ask how they are?"

"Of course, Lin. And I can tell them how you are. That will keep their memory of you alive and steady."

"Thanks, Hennit. That would mean a lot to me."

I hugged Lana tight for the longest time before I let her go. Standing close, I took in our last moment together. I stared at her eyes, still amazed how much they looked like my own.

She touched my tears. "Wet," she said.

"Very wet," I said.

Hennit turned away.

I rode home alone on the airtram, staring out the window at nothing and feeling how much I still missed mother. It didn't help that the airtram was empty and the gray skies were nearly black.

"I have bad news," Pella said when I got home.

I fell into her soft-seat chair and moaned.

"We can't go groile sliding today," she said. "There's a bad storm coming. My parents want us to stay in."

"That's it? That's the bad news?"

"Yes," she said. "Sorry."

"Oh, I don't mind," I said. "We can go groile sliding in Bree."

"Good, I'm glad you're all right with it."

"I'm relieved it wasn't something really bad."

"What's bothering you?" she asked. "You're sad again."

"Is it that obvious?"

She nodded.

"I said goodbye to Lana today," I told her, "and I didn't see Oddi at all. I'm going to miss them so much."

"We'll only be gone three months," she said.

"I know."

"Aren't you happy about seeing your family and your friends in Bree?"

"I should be," I said. "I *am* happy about it. Really happy. But with everyone leaving and all these goodbyes, I guess there hasn't been room for the happiness."

"If I were you, all I'd be thinking about is Bree and Northern Wershonia. There's so much ahead of us. An amazing adventure is waiting for you. If you thought more about that, you wouldn't be so sad."

"You're right," I said.

"Want to go somewhere?"

"Anywhere where it's not gray and raining."

We synched up our Gen 8s, put on our latest favorite music, and went to the North Pole to sit on the observation deck and gaze at a pure sky.

The storm passed late the next day and on the morning of our departure, the clouds were fluffy white again.

I woke up queasy, having dreamt that our sub-orbital malfunctioned and kept going higher and higher beyond the clouds and into the black of space and past the Forton satellite and past a bunch of planets. At breakfast Mrs. Tria gave me some medicine to quell my queasiness.

"It's working," I told her when our sub-orbital lifted off two hours later. "It really quelled! I'm not queasy at all!"

Mr. Tria laughed. "Quelled," he said.

"I'm nervous but not queasy," I told Pella. "It's so great."

"*Nervous?*" Pella asked.

"Happy nervous. The good kind."

She nodded and said, "I think I'm happy nervous too."

We stood at the window and watched the island of Vona grow distant beneath us.

"There it is," I said, "our whole life for the last seven months."

"Look, the Assembly Hall," said Pella.

"It's so ... majestic, don't you think?"

"Majestic, it is."

"See over there? That's the Medical Clinic where I went when I broke my arm." I shook my head in disbelief. "That seems like such a long, long time ago."

Pella pointed and said, "Look at the Residences. They're so tiny from here. Can you tell which one is ours?"

"No, I don't think so," I said.

"Me neither."

"I see the groile sliding field."

"And Sunset Peak."

"I already can't wait to come back."

Pella laughed. "I can't either. But I'm glad for where we're going."

"I am too. I'm glad for all of it. I'm so happy to be seeing father and Mira and my aunt and Merchant Kam. You're going to love them."

"I have a feeling I will," Pella said.

We entered a thick cloud layer, and Vona vanished in an instant.

"Oh," I said. "It's gone."

Pella turned away from the window and powered on her Gen 8.

"Want to go somewhere?" she asked.

"Not yet," I said. "I'm going to watch the clouds for a while. Find someplace good, and I'll meet you there."

I looked out at a vast whiteness and thought of everyone back home. I felt no queasiness, just a fullness of joy. I stood tall and strong, and I felt greatness in me.

# CLARKON, AKA GRAPHENE

Though this book is fiction, clarkon is real. Earth scientists call it graphene. They call it the "miracle material". Graphene is made of carbon atoms — nothing more, nothing less — and it looks something like this:

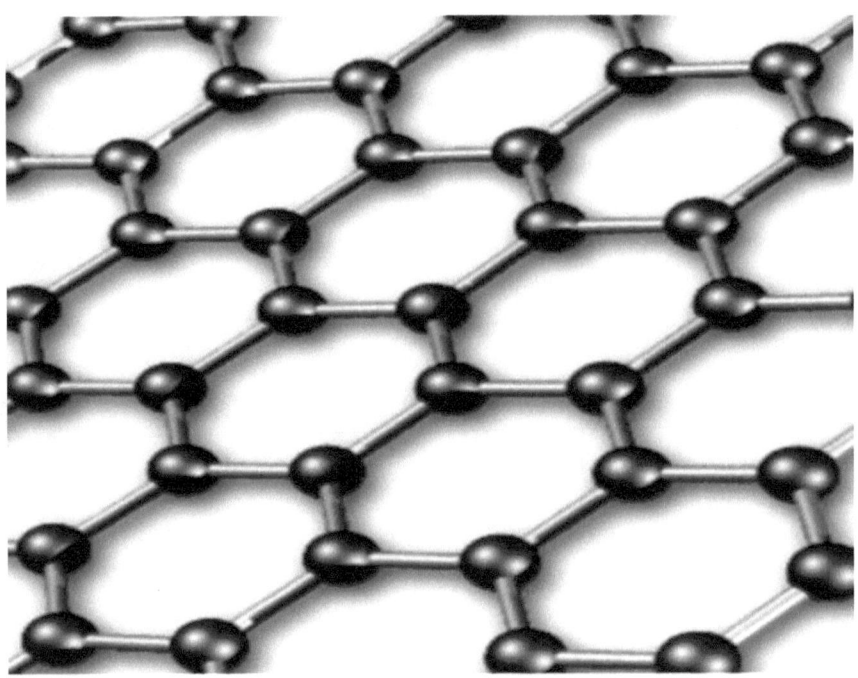

The dots you see are carbon atoms. The lines are the bonds between them. The secret to graphene's miraculousness is in the bonds, which make graphene super-elastic, super-conductive, and the strongest, lightest material yet discovered. There are more amazing properties of graphene, and it is about to radically transform every part of our life on Earth.

Discover graphene at www.luratia.com/graphene.

# THE CONTINENTS OF LURATIA

**The Continent** was once 19 nations, then 11, then seven. It has been a Continental Union for 182 years. The unification of the seven nations came about after half a century of cooperative rebuilding in the aftermath of an asteroid shear that ripped a long gash across the northern half of the continent and set off massive earthquakes in the southern regions. Every country was affected, entire cities were destroyed, and more than two million lives were lost. The tragedy invigorated interest in space exploration and led to the discovery of solar power. Today all of Luratia is powered by solar energy that is harvested in space, sent to the ground, and wirelessly distributed to all parts of the world.

**Wershonia** has six countries and, among them, two languages: Welbi, spoken in the South, and Culti, spoken in the North. Northern Wershonia is modern, having traded with the people of the Continent since the invention of ocean-worthy boats. A treacherous mountain range separates the North from the South, which for centuries cut off the southern countries from any modernizing influence from the North. Parts of Southern Wershonia are among the most primitive places on Luratia.

**Egli,** the smallest continent, is rich in minerals, precious stones, and a crystalline substance once used for fuel. For thousands of years this land has been mined with slave labor. Egli has no countries; it is divided into four sectors that are governed by the majority landowners. Egli is the one place where every Luratian child is grateful not to have been born — if you're born into the rich class, you are despised by the poor and at risk of being kidnapped for ransom; if you're born into the poor class, you are doomed to suffer a life of poverty; and if you're born into the slave class, you're a slave.

**Waturi** is a small continent with a large population, due to its crowded coastal cities and high birth rates. The interior of Waturi is desolate and rich in natural geysers. Its three nations are embroiled in disputes over water rights and other natural resources, but they no longer fight with weapons due to the damage it inflicts on its cities, industries, and ports. Instead they fight with nano warfare — invisible weapons of espionage, poisonings, and strategic system failures.

**Gostin** is so rainy, most of its cities are covered by invisible, self-repairing clarkon nets that shield rain and lightning. Rain falls almost continuously in the northern mountains, which nourishes the growth of medicinal mosses that are exported all over the world. Though they are not as wealthy as Continentals or Wershonians, the people of Gostin enjoy a very high standard of living.

**Deloria** is agricultural and beautiful. Dry crops grow in the southern parts and wet crops grow in the north. Its southern beaches are popular tourist destinations due to the powdery violet sand and occasionally sunny patches of sky. The people here are simple and happy, which some believe is due to their exceptionally good weather.

# WERSHONIA

A wide and steep mountain range separates the North from South, which made land travel between them nearly impossible until the invention of aircraft. Much of the steep, rocky coast north of Bree is uninhabited by people and this further restricted travel between the North and South along the eastern coast.

While much of Southern Wershonia is still steeped in ancient traditions and olden ways, Northern Wershonia has been modernizing for centuries. It ranks second in the world on almost every measurable metric: quality of life, longevity, gender and race equality, technological progress, educational excellence, economic health, and political stability.

Directly south of the port town of Kuli is a man-made island where an embassy of the Continent is located. It was established as a central organizing hub for the many humanitarian service projects it supports throughout this region of the world. It houses medical facilities, a World Holographic Library, and mediation services for conflict resolution. This is one of three Embassy Islands in the world, and each is located nearest the least developed nations, where the humanitarian need is greatest and the ability to travel long distances is most difficult.

# THE CONTINENT OF **W**ERSHONIA

OF THE PLANET **L**URATIA

the
Continent
(Artunne)

ALGALON

ORILON

SIMILON

Tilani Sea

**N**ORTHERN **W**ERSHONIA

STRELLIN

**S**OUTHERN **W**ERSHONIA

○ **Bree**

Waturi
Gostin
Deloria

TOBBS

○ **Kuli**

Strellin Sea

Egli

**Embassy Island** ◯

## Albereo and the
## Phenomenon of Binary Stars

Albereo (spelled Albireo by some) is one of the most beautiful double stars in the visible universe. It is made up of a small blue star and a large golden yellow star. Since they sparkle like brilliant jewels when viewed through a telescope, astronomers refer to their color as sapphire and topaz.

From a distance, a binary star looks like a single star but really it is two stars, paired up for billions and billions of years, locked in a gravitational embrace from which they never waver. The two stars are often of different mass and size, but still they remain joined in perfect equilibrium. You might be amazed to know that most stars in the universe are binary.

Stars grow bigger and hotter as they grow old, and the eventual death of a star is not a quiet passing — some stars expire with a massive supernova explosion. Each star in a binary pair evolves in this way, but they do so at different rates. When one star grows so big that its mass begins to endanger the life of its companion, it transfers its mass to the smaller star. The death-explosion of the larger star is delayed, often for millions or billions of years. By giving part of itself to the other, the larger star lengthens the lives of both. It is a demonstration of a beautiful truth of kindness: *when one shares unselfishly, all will benefit — even eventually the one who gave.*

## About the Author

Melanie Pahlmann is a journalist, editor, love advocate, and ardent optimist. She believes that Earth's best years are ahead of us, despite the dystopian futures that haunt our storytelling. Some may call her views utopian, but she disagrees. Decency, wisdom, and cooperation aren't impossible achievements, not for a person and not for a world.

Melanie is a backyard astronomer and lives in southern Arizona, where the night sky is dark, rarely cloudy, and stunningly starry.

To learn more about Lin's world
and Earth's approaching Nano Age
and to contact the author, please visit

www.luratia.com

# the exoplanetary life of Lin of Luratia